Green Grey Rain

Stevan Treleaven Eldred-Grigg is an award-winning novelist and historian. He was born in the Grey Valley, New Zealand in 1952 and grew up in the small mining town of Blackball and the suburbs of Christchurch. He graduated from the University of Canterbury in 1975 with an MA in history before obtaining a PhD at the Australian National University in Canberra in 1978.

by Stevan Eldred-Grigg

Fiction
Pru Goes Troppo
Bangs
Shanghai Boy
Sheng Xian Qu Ji
Kaput!
Blue Blood
Mum
Gardens of Fire
The Shining City
The Siren Celia
Oracles and Miracles

Memoir
My History, I Think

Non-Fiction
Phoney Wars (with Hugh Eldred-Grigg)
White Ghosts, Yellow Peril (with Zeng Dazheng)
People, People, People
The Great Wrong War
Diggers, Hatters and Whores
Xin Xilan de Wenxue Lucheng
The Rich: a New Zealand History
New Zealand Working People
Pleasures of the Flesh
A New History of Canterbury
A Southern Gentry

Green Grey Rain

STEVAN ELDRED-GRIGG

Published by Piwaiwaka Press
Copyright © Stevan Eldred-Grigg 2021

This book is copyright. Except for the purposes of fair review, no part may be stored or transmitted in any form or by any other means, electronic or mechanical, including recording or storage in any information retrieval system, without permission in writing from the publishers.

Cover photo: Tobias Tullius
Cover design: Helen Innes

ISBN 978-0-473-57151-1 Softcover - POD

ISBN 978-0-473-57152-8 Softcover

ISBN 978-0-473-57153-5 Epub

The deeply welcome support of the 2019 Janet Frame Literary Trust Award allowed me – to paraphrase Janet Frame herself – to keep my computer switched on. Janet Frame is one of the most important writers in my life. I have loved, and been in awe of, her work since the wonderful day in my teenage years when I turned the first page of *A State of Siege*. I can say – again with Janet Frame – that writing saved my life.

Also deeply welcome was the support I got from my own home community. A last draft of my memoir was written in the Brian Wood Cottage, Blackball, while I was staying there as holder of the first Blackball Writer's Residency. Twigs were draped with a lace of white grey lichen. Rain drummed on the roof. Black beeches stood strong. The birds sang. The creeks rang.

for Janet Frame

Their town … was small as the world.

Janet Frame, *Owls do Cry*, 1957

FOREWORD

'What false facsimile have I allowed the past to make me?' asked my first memoir, *My History, I Think*, published in 1994 by Penguin Books (NZ) and republished in 2020 by Piwaiwaka Press. 'I am not yet sure,' that volume went on to say. 'I intend to find an answer.' It turned out to take a lot longer than I anticipated when writing those hopeful words. *Green Grey Rain* is the outcome: a second memoir. A memoir written not because I think my life more remarkable than any other life.

Who in this world has a life more – or less – remarkable than the life of anybody else?

Nor is this new memoir the last word.

Only one more try.

I draw heavily on the words of many people: my grandmothers; my father; one of my grandfathers; some of my aunts; some of my uncles, one of my sisters, two of my brothers; neighbours; a teacher; strangers in the street; unknown authors of folk songs; known writers of school textbooks; Carl Barks, writer and cartoonist of the Duck comics; unknown authors of texts in the children's encyclopaedia *The New Book of Knowledge*, edited by John Hammerton.

A key source are the words of my mother, Valerie Forbes.

Valerie sat down and let me interview her at length while I was researching my novel *Oracles and Miracles*. Audiocassettes and transcripts of those interviews are held by the Macmillan Brown Library, University of Canterbury, archival number MB 857. I have made many changes to the sentences and vocabulary of interview transcripts; one of my reasons is that the transcripts not only contain many incongruities but also a fair few contradictory statements.

Contradictory statements may be simple errors in memory.

Or they may be more complex attempts to grandstand or hide or twist.

Valerie, like most of us, was often an active liar. When the interviews took place in the 1980s she was speaking to her own son – a son with whom she had a fraught relationship – about earlier years. She was speaking with more or less hindsight. Valerie in this memoir, on the other hand, is not to be understood as speaking, or perhaps writing, with anything like hindsight. Her words are meant to be coming straight out of her skull when the things that happen in this book supposedly were happening.

Green Grey Rain keeps some of her contradictory statements. Others have been cleared away.

Also, her son must be understood not to speak with hindsight but as things are happening. He speaks to himself. Often he speaks silently, making sounds and then words. Often he speaks out loud. He speaks out loud when alone with himself. He is usually alone with himself, after the first chapters of this memoir, even though an observer might think him elbowed by many others in this or that house, street, slag heap, creek, court, car, paddock, train, yard, mill, swamp. At the same time, the sounds and words that he uses come wholly from outside himself.

Or they do – until, at a certain point, he begins making up a few new unwritten words.

One of the things I try to do in the book is look at how we mostly use old words while now and then making new words. And how we do it wittingly and unwittingly. And how we tackle our lack of words. And about what it is with words and story anyway. I try to look knowingly. While knowing that I must also do it unknowingly. And – yet one more turn of the screw – while aware that my mother's words will have led me to make unknowing mistakes of a sort I would like not to make unknowingly.

Mistakes about things. Mistakes about moods.

Ordinary mistakes, some readers will think. Obvious mistakes. While working on my last draft of the memoir I heard from a neighbour who knew my family during my early childhood. I'd been saying in my memoir that 18 Brodie Street was our first house in Blackball. The old neighbour told me I was wrong. Our first house, she said, was 22 Brodie Street. Only a few beats of the heart were needed for me to know she was right. It was suddenly obvious that our first home never had been 18 and never could have been anything other than 22 Brodie Street.

Other blues will not be so obvious, so ordinary.

I hope readers will let me know any other mistakes they think I may have made unknowingly.

The chorus of *Green Grey Rain* comes mostly from the lyrics of hundreds of hit songs broadcast over radio airwaves from Greymouth, played on gramophones in the pubs and private homes of Blackball, and sung by the townspeople in kitchens, mine shafts, sawmills, shops and streets from 1952 to 1958.

All these words shaped my life – and this memoir.

WOMB

Chorus

a world of night
into the world of light
in the beginning was the word
at the edge of the alphabet
two inches behind the eyes
a home in this world
a world of words
world words

Valerie

Ow! The baby keeps kicking me in the wall of my womb. I'm
bloody *sore*!

'A guy,' I sing, 'is a guy.'

I've been singing this song since we come into the Alps. It's
the latest hit song by Doris Day. She's blonde and sweet. Too
sweet, really. We're in a second class railway carriage, a red
railway carriage. And the Alps are green, they're green as green.
And it's only my second time through the Alps. We're going over
to Blackball. We went there for a fortnight's holiday the end of
last year. Which was my *first* time through the Alps. We stayed

with my younger sister and her husband. Me and my sister get on good. And me and her husband get on good enough too. And it's a friendly wee township, Blackball. A coal town, like everyone knows. I talked Gil into applying for a job in the mines office there, which he doesn't mind, he says he can push a pen anywhere, so why not Blackball?

'Blackball people seem to have a strong sense of community,' he says.

Which is the sort of thing Gil does say.

Ow!

The bloody baby kicking again.

It's good to be going back through the Alps. I'm too busy trying to keep the kids chained to the seats and not be a nuisance to other passengers, mind you, to look out the window. The kids are just kids. Three little kids. Gil's good at keeping them quiet. He talks to them. He tells them a story. I always feel a bit proud that he's my husband. I mean, I don't want to skite or that. But he's nice looking, Gil. He's clean cut, slim and trim, the sort of chap you might think is the man in the Lichfield shirt advert.

Whereas *me*. Shapeless!

I'm wearing my one good dress. A green dress, with a pleat down the front. And I'm wearing my only good shoes. A pair of ankle boots lined with rabbit fur. I used to work in a footwear factory before I got together with Gil. One of the perks of the work – well, the only perk – was cheap shoes. I miss not having a few pair of good shoes. Anyway, you wouldn't want to put me in an advert unless it was a *before* picture in an advert for something to help women lose weight.

So that's me, a fat young mother whose face looks like a spud, a pasty sort of spud with shiny cheeks. Not that spuds have cheeks. A spud squinting at her kids through two piggy wee green eyes.

The baby's due in a fortnight or so. It's been more or less all right so far, this pregnancy. Although of course now it's got so far

down the track my back's hurting me like buggery.
   'Take me,' I start singing, 'in your arms.'
   Another new hit song by Doris Day.
   A baby.

Chorus

all time
light and darkness
the light of life
the light of a star
stars shining bright
stars in the sky
stars in your eyes
follow your star
the moon
blue moon
how high the moon
the world is waiting for the sunrise
the moon begins to sink
the dawning
the sun is shining
the wheel of fortune
the trail of aching hearts
road of no returning
a lonely road leads nowhere
somewhere there's heaven
the sunset
red sails in the sunset
across the river
peaceful on the other side
the promised land

Valerie

We go through the Otira tunnel. And then there's more Alps and forest and that. And lakes. And then we come to Stillwater. Which is where we get out. Stillwater's just a few houses and a pub and timber yards and two or three yellow railway buildings. And there's bush all round. One railway line goes up the valley to Westport. Another railway line goes down the valley to Greymouth. People bang the doors of our Christchurch train and cross the platform to get onto the Westport train. Other people stay in the carriages because they're on their way to Greymouth.

And a few people, like us, get off for Blackball.

Arthur's there waiting. My brother-in-law. A good looking joker, he's got brown eyes and a head of thick dark glossy black hair and though he's a coalminer and big and tall and strong he's gentle and quite shy.

'G'day,' he says, looking away.

We pack the kids and my big bloody belly into the taxi. The taxi takes us up the valley. The sun's shining. Blue sky. A green, green valley. Funny it's called the *Grey* Valley. Trees, lots of trees. Paddocks, lush with long grass but sort of scruffy. Not like back over the Alps where farms are orderly. We drive a few miles then cross the riverbed of the Grey on an old wooden bridge with railway tracks down the middle, which gives the kids a bit of a scare, and actually to be honest me too.

What'd happen if a train come steaming onto the other end of the bridge?

The wheels of the taxi go thump, thump, rickety rackety, on the worn wooden deck.

'See what Comrade Stalin said the other day?' Arthur asks Gil. 'Says the capitalists are so scared of another slump that's why they're fighting the war in Korea, cause it'll get the factories working, and it'll stop the working class from cottoning on to who's the real enemy.'

'I think he knows as much about capitalism as the baby in Val's womb,' says Gil.

Arthur goes all red in the face.

'You reckon you see things clearer than Comrade Stalin?' he says.

Arthur likes talking politics, like most blokes in Blackball, but gets flustered easy. I mean, he's kind and goodhearted and that, he'd give you the shirt off his back. All he knows, though, is hewing coal and drinking beer and going to union meetings and boraxing the bosses

'No, Arthur. I just think I know a bit about capitalism and I know this country's booming. We've got one of the highest standards of living in the world. The price of the average house has gone up by more than seventy percent in only two years. Our biggest problem isn't making more money but sharing out the money we've already got.'

'You mean nationalising the means of production and distribution of wealth?'

'I mean improving the welfare state so it does its job even better than it's doing its job already.'

Arthur frowns out the window.

'Take everything off the rich buggers, that's what I say.'

'No political party's going to get anywhere in this country with that policy.'

'Take the bloody lot off the bloody capitalists and hand it out good and fair among the working class.'

After the bridge we go past old tailings. Tailings look like big shingly turds squirted out the backside of a dredge. The dredges have all gone these days. The turds are sprouting gorse and blackberry. The gorse is blossoming. Bright and yellow. And then the taxi takes us past some more of that scruffy lush farmland. And then the driver changes gear and we start climbing. The road winds up through big old trees. Huge old trees. Green trees, green bushes, green ferns, all sort of waving and nodding. It's pretty.

Then we come out on a long green flat.

And the first thing you see is the township graveyard.

Grey granite crosses. A red granite urn. A white marble book. You know, the book of fate, carved so it's open on the day of someone's reckoning. Me and Gil walked to the graveyard when we were here on holiday. I like reading what's written on a tombstone. I've always been fond of poking round in a graveyard. All the tombstones in this one are streaky with lichen and the ground between the graves is mounds of bright green moss.

'Dead centre of Blackball,' says the taxi driver, which someone says of course whenever you go past any graveyard.

'Mines are the dead centre of Blackball,' says Arthur. 'The number of good men that've been killed by them.'

After the graveyard you turn onto a long straight road. And you see the smoke of Blackball. It's real smoky, Blackball. Nearly everyone burns coal from the mine when they heat their houses or do their cooking. So when you look out the taxi window you see just about every chimney in sight is flying a flag of smoke.

Smoke flags streaming against the green.

Chorus

on top of old Smokey
all covered with soot
loving's a pleasure
parting is grief
false hearted lovers are worse than a thief
false hearted lovers will lead you to the grave
the grave will decay you
and turn you to dust
not one man in a hundred a poor girl can trust
never place your affections on a green willow tree
the leaves they will wither

the roots they will die
you'll be forsaken
and never know
why?

Valerie

A deep ditch on one side runs with rainwater. And on both sides you can see a row of houses. The houses are mostly what they call miner's cottages. You know, wooden houses with a red iron roof on top. Houses plonked down in tangled green bushy shrubby yards. Yards bursting with bracken and flax and gorse and bamboo and blackberry. And behind the houses you get glimpses of green river gorges. And behind the gorges you can see mountains smothered with dark green forest.

And here on the road there's cheerful looking people standing around yarning, and kids playing.

You go straight for about half a mile before you get to the real township.

A crisscross of little shingled streets, that's the township. A few more rows of miner's cottages. And newer houses, wooden bungalows. And the shopping streets. Hart Street. Hilton Street. Wooden shops painted bright colours, with wide shady verandas. And three wooden pubs. The Dominion. The Blackball. The Club. And a big red wooden building, real ugly, the Miners Hall. And other cheerful women and chaps standing around yarning. And other kids playing. Blackball people like to hang around in the open and pass the time of day.

A lot of the people on the street take a snoop at our taxi, to see who's inside, so we give them a wave and they wave back.

Arthur helps us with the names.

'That's Molly Muir. She lives next door to yous.'

'She looks a good egg,' I says.

'Yeah. And that's Cyril Nixon, that paunchy joker in the fawn cardigan. Him and his sister live next door to us. He's the caretaker for one of the halla. We call him Pansy Nixon.'

'He one of *those*?'

'Yeah.'

'Who's that lady over there?' I ask. 'That tall flash looking lady in the high heels and pink cardigan?'

'Frances Driscoll. She's infant mistress at the school.'

The taxi turns into a side street. And then into another side street. Narrow streets, with verges of tufty grass. Along the streets are lots of empty sections all bushy and tangled and green like everywhere else in the township. And between the empty sections are short rows of wooden bungalows.

We stop outside 22 Brodie Street.

'Here we are, Bob's your uncle,' says Arthur.

The furniture van has just pulled up, so it's worked out quite good. I get myself out of the back seat of the taxi. Which is easier to say than do, what with the baby weighing me down. Oof. I plant my cheap ankle boots on the stones of the street. I look up. I look all around me, at the mountains all around, dark green, climbing up into the bright blue sky.

'It's corker the way it's so *green*!' I say to Gil. 'Not all yellow and withered like Canterbury.'

'Well, dear, the Coast gets a lot of rainfall.'

'Everyone knows *that*!'

'Blackball gets about five inches a year for every inch that falls in Christchurch.'

He likes to labour a point, Gil. I don't mind. He knows a lot. And he doesn't do it to show off or make you feel a fool or anything. He does it in a sort of educational way. The thing is, he's seen a lot more of the world than me.

I haven't hardly seen any of the world.

Once or twice I went on the train as far up north as Kaikoura. Once when I was still working at the footwear factory I went as far south as Green Island, in Otago. I went with a boy I was seeing. He wasn't much of a boy. Green Island turned out not to be an island.

And that's been the extent of *my* travels.

Chorus

flying the ocean in a silver plane
Killarney, Paris, the Rhine
auf wiedersehen
oui, c'est la guerre
Algiers
the Nile
pyramids on the Nile
the Congo
jungle wet with rain
baboon, monkey, chimpanzee
Moonlight Bay, Old Smoky, Kentucky
Missouri
across the wide Missouri
whippoorwills on Mockingbird Hill
tra la la, tweedle dee dee dee
dancing with my darling
the Tennessee waltz
dancing the Tennessee waltz
waltzing together
dreaming a melody
we'll never change partners again
hound dog, bayou, pirogue, river boat, steamboat, state prison
lotus, rickshaw, oriental music, swaying palms, perfumed flowers
Shanghai, Singapore, Mindanao, Malaya, Bali
a thousand isles, tropical skies
Shangri-La

Valerie

Our house is like a kid's drawing of a house. You look at it from the street and see a wooden wall going up to a peak. Gil calls it a *gable*. A door opens smack bang in the middle of the front wall. On one side of the door you see a window shaded by a little iron hood. On the other side of the door you see a veranda on wooden posts. And the walls are painted a nice bright green, with darker green facings.

And the roof is red.

The house belongs to the Department of Mines. Like most of the houses in Blackball.

You go through the front door into a narrow passage. Two bedrooms to the left of the passage. One bedroom and a lounge to the right of the passage. At the other end of the passage, a good big kitchen with a coal range. And right out the back, behind the kitchen, a veranda. And a washhouse with a copper and a wooden tub. The back veranda and washhouse are sort of another little house stuck onto the bungalow. The toilet is down at the end of the backyard. A wooden dunny, with a wooden seat.

And a wooden garage. Though we haven't got a *car* to put in the garage.

The house, like most of the others in the street, has a bit of lawn in the front and out the back.

'Well, not so much lawn as rough pasturage,' Gil says.

I don't care, though, it's a good big yard. And we've got a fowl run, too. A big fowl run with nice chook cages.

'I'd love some fowls,' I says.

'We'll buy a few once we're settled,' says Gil.

I close my eyes and see myself sloping down to the fowl run every morning. Me holding a bowl of feed. And the chooks crowding round me, clucking. And me scattering the feed onto the ground.

And the chooks pecking.

Ikey comes over the next day. Her and Arthur only live a few blocks away. She couldn't come any earlier because she's got a new baby, her first kid. She's skinny and bony, Ikey. Skinny and bony with red hair she can never get to sit flat no matter how hard she bashes at it with a brush. Her and Arthur have named their baby Wendy.

'Wendy's going to drive me up the bloody *wall*,' Ikey says after taking a first slurp of a brew. 'I'll be *climbing* the walls if she won't start sleeping more regular.'

'You just need to get everything into a routine,' I says, taking a slurp myself.

'Tell that to *her*!'

'You'll be right in a while.'

'I bloody feel like I'll never be – I'll never be right again, ever, Darkie. I feel like there's no me to feel *anything* – right or not right – I feel like there's no me, just her her *her*! Buggered if I know how you manage with *three*.'

Darkie's what they call me in our family. As a kid I had a big tangled mop of dark brown hair, so they called me Darkie for a nickname and from then on Darkie was who I always was.

I give a grin.

'Wait till your fourth's playing footy inside your womb.'

Ikey grabs a couple of hanks of flaming red hair in two freckled fists and gives the hanks a tug.

'I'll get the kitchen knife out of the drawer and – I'll stand at the kitchen sink and – I'll cut my bloody womb *out* before you see me having four.'

We laugh so much we start snorting tea out of our noses.

Ikey's canny with money. That's why we call her Ikey. Olga's her real name but we never called her that when we were kids. When we were kids she was so shrewd with a penny we called her Ikey the Jew. Ikey, Kikey. She's handling pounds now. Arthur's a miner and makes good money. They've got a strong union, the miners. A joker who works underground can earn a decent crust.

'Your house is a lot better than ours,' she moans. 'I'm getting sick of our dump – it's too small and it's too hard to keep it warm.'

She lives in one of those old miner's cottages.

'I can't see that,' I says. 'You've always got this big *roaring* fire in your kitchen and your bedroom.'

'It's a nark cleaning out the grates every day.'

'It's more of a nark if your grates never get clagged up because you can't *afford* coal, like when we were kids.'

She lets out a sort of laughing bark.

'Thank christ that's not – thank christ we're not kids any more – kids stuck with bloody Mum!'

Arthur and Ikey get free coal, like every family with a breadwinner on the mine payroll. You can see a mound of free coal in most yards. We've got one, too. Gil's now a mineworker. If you can use the word *worker* for someone on a salary. It's funny. When we first got together, him and me, it seemed to me he was better than me. You know, he comes from a sheepfarming family. A family with lots of land. He grew up looking out at green paddocks and green lawns and green trees. I grew up seeing red rust and black coal dust. And he went to high school, which I didn't. And he went to varsity, which not only I didn't but I hadn't even really *heard* of varsity.

'I see you're a middle class chap,' one bloke said to him last summer when we first come here and were meeting people.

Gil was taken aback.

'I'm a worker,' he said. 'A white collar worker.'

'You won't be someone who'll back Labour, I bet,' the bloke said, not meaning to be rude, I don't think. 'Vote for the Tories, do you?'

'It's a secret ballot,' Gil says.

I actually don't know whether he votes National or Labour. I mean, Griggs are National. They've got money. So of course they vote National. But he doesn't quite see eye to eye with any of the others in his family about the ins and outs of government and parliament and class and things like that.

I mean, he married *me*, didn't he?

Anyway, last summer for a start people were a bit wary of us. After a while it was alright. People here are friendly, like I said already. And they saw straightaway I was just an ordinary tart from an ordinary family of factory workers. And it helped when they knew Ikey was my sister, because people here like Ikey. And they saw how friendly Gil was, and how easygoing.

'He's a very easygoing bloke,' they said to one another. 'He's a nice chap.'

'A very nice chap.'

So that's worked out good, too.

We're going to be happy here in Blackball. Well, we're going to be happy once I've got this bloody *baby* out of my womb.

Chorus

home safely
home sweet home
a little nest, night and day
the loveliest night of the year
the morning side of the mountain
the cool, cool, cool of the evening
some enchanted evening
the tide has turned
days grow short
precious days
dark clouds
thunder and lightning
watch the rain
flame
fire

shadows deepen
leaves will wither
the bitterberry tree
each lonely night
the darkest night
the path below
back home
the grave
dust

LOVE MAMA LOVE

Valerie

I'm dreading giving birth to the baby. I don't mind afterwards, the work after the baby's born, the breastfeeding and the nappy changing and the nappy washing and that. What I hate is going into labour. I just *dread* the labour pains. I spend hours visualising those pains. I think to myself, well, I've forgotten what labour pains are like but I know that as soon as they start I'll know too right!

Anyway, it's a Sunday morning. The baby's overdue by about seven or eight days but I'm not worried because my babies are always overdue by days. Gil gets up to make a brew. He rolls the holland blind open so I can look out our bedroom window at the new day.

Showers are pattering onto the roof, spattering on the street.

'A bit of a southerly,' Gil says.

'Rains a *lot* here, doesn't it? I mean, I knew it was a rainy place when we made our minds up to come to Blackball, but I didn't think it was going to be *this* rainy.'

'Good for growing things.'

'Bad for bloody *drying* things. I'll have a lot of drying when this baby comes out.'

I sit back against the pillows and wait for my brew. Birds are singing. Rain keeps falling. Gil comes in with a cup and puts it down on our cheap bedside chest of drawers. The chest of drawers is badly nicked. It's been knocked about by kids.

'I love you, Val,' he says.

'Ta,' I say

I'm lucky I've got Gil. He's a good husband. He's a good father for the kids. He helps with the housework. He's nothing like my old man. My old man never won any prizes for fathering. He never won any prizes for anything. He drove a lorry. He did the odd bit of labouring in timber yards. He went away cocksfooting round the bays. And he drunk a lot. Well, I grew up with the belief that he drunk a lot. Mum was always saying he liked his drink better than he liked her or us kids or anybody. After work he always went to the Club Hotel in Sydenham. Mum didn't drink. Well, only an occasional shandy. Apart from that, she didn't drink, and she didn't smoke, and in her books the old man was a smoker and he was a pisshead.

'That bastard,' she'd say, 'he's got softening of the *brain* with the booze.'

Anyway, he'd turn up every now and then for a few weeks. He'd get her pregnant. And then he'd slope off again to find work. And in the end he never come back.

I don't remember bugger all about him otherwise.

Chorus

never been kissed
dream the night away
anyone can dream
comes along a love
love at first sight
forget our troubles
a smile
a tear

Valerie

Anyway, it turns out this is the morning I give birth to the baby. It's quite good that it's a Sunday. It's not good that it's giving birth to a baby. Ikey and Arthur hoof it to our place to look after the kids. A taxi rockets me and Gil to Greymouth. Which is only eighteen miles down the valley but my waters break in the taxi and the baby gives me a lot of grief before we get to the Grey Hospital. A gingery sister in a starched white cap comes running out.

'Now just hang on, dear,' she says, looking a bit scared. 'Baby's head has been born already.'

They hurl me into a lift up to the maternity ward. They fling me onto a birthing bed. They pull my dress up.

And out comes the rest of the baby.

Chorus

I found you
I'm yours
someone to care
keep me warm
to have and to hold
I live for love
my one true love
I'm yours
because of you
because you're mine
nobody but you
sweetheart true
cling close
it's you I adore
you're my all

that's *amore*
mystery
ecstasy
trance

Valerie

I come out fast when I was born, too. I shot out onto a lumpy kapok mattress. Mum and the old man slept on it. It was in a rented dump in South Christchurch. Mum was on her own. She didn't have anyone by her side to help. After I was born she tucked me into a drawer in her duchesse because we didn't have a cot. *Dumped* me rather than tucked me. I never heard of her tucking anybody. I never heard of her treating any kid tenderly. She already had five other girls. And six sons.

And after a year or so there was another girl on the way, Ikey.

And after that, there was another boy.

Chorus

my baby
you are my baby
we live and we love
the wonder of you
vows for eternity
love will not die
a slave to you
singing
swinging
I love but you
I love you, too
our love is true

a world of joy
no other lips
kiss me
baccia me
a goodnight kiss
a kiss to build a dream on
a penny a kiss
kiss of fire
hold me, thrill me
our hearts beat together
never let me go
fill my dreams
sweet desire
baby talk
hold you close
rock, roll, all night
no one but you
endless love

Valerie

'You look glowing, dear,' says Gil when he comes to the ward. 'Any thoughts about a name for the baby?'

'Stevan,' I says.

'I was thinking Eldred, after Pop.'

'Stevan,' I says. 'S-t-e-v-a-n.'

'Well if it's your wish, Val. Why such an odd spelling?'

'It's a name in a story. A story I was reading last week. A story about a governess who meets this handsome landowner. He's called Sir Stevan. And him and the governess like each other. But there's misunderstandings. You know, the usual story.'

'Alright, darling. Shall we say Stevan Eldred?'

'If you want.'

'I'll register him after this visit.'

I'm in a cast iron bed inside a square room in the maternity ward of the Grey Hospital. Three other mothers are in the room too. We're all from country districts. One mother is from up the valley, from Ikamatua. One's from Otira. One's from Haast. Which is more than two hundred miles away. She says it's hardly anything but bush down there. Bush and big rivers and wild coast. You can only get out by plane, she says. I'd love to live somewhere like that.

Somewhere far away.

It's quite good being a mother from out of town. We don't get the *visiting* every night. Not like the town mothers. Our husbands can't manage to get to us easy. We sit propped up on pillows, wearing our cotton nightgowns, the four of us. We don't need to worry how we look. Our tits like pumpkins.

We swap thoughts about men and kids and that.

We play cards. Sevens, mostly.

We sing the latest hits.

Nurse aides bring bedpans for the first four days. You know, whenever you need to do a wizz or a poo. On the fifth day a nurse helps me up. She says she'll walk me across to the balcony.

'I've been dying for a breath of air,' I says to her. 'What's the weather been doing?'

'Wet and blowy,' she says.

We get to the balcony. I look out. I see the red roofs and green gardens of Greymouth. The town's squeezed between steep hills on one side and on the other side black lagoons. And a big brown river. And a steep beach being smashed by breakers under a spring shower. You can see bins of black coal being loaded onto green and white ships at the riverport. You can see smokestacks of red brick pumping soot up into the sky. I look away from the smokestacks to the lagoons.

A lot of white birds are diving and ducking.

'Is it true a little boy was drowned in one of those lagoons the morning I had my baby?' I says to the nurse.

'I wouldn't worry about that, dear,' she says, a bit too quick.

'I'm not saying I'm worried. A husband said it to us. The husband of the lady from Otira. He said a boy drowned in a lagoon. The other husbands wouldn't say yea or nay.'

'Well I'm afraid it's true. An eight year old boy. The poor little chap was on his own, fishing for herrings. It was the peak of the spring tide and he was taking a risk. I don't blame his mother or father. You know what boys are like. You mustn't think gloomy thoughts. You've got your own bonny baby boy.'

'I hear his body was found in a waterhole behind the stables at the trotting club.'

'*Don't* think gloomy thoughts, dear,' she says.

'Dying isn't gloomy, it's just dying.' I says back. 'Funny, isn't it – us spinning round on a ball in space, being born and dying.'

The nurse looks at me like I'm a bit mad.

Chorus

don't let the stars get in your eyes
the stars in the sky
stars in my eyes
every star above
a thousand stars
one million stars

Valerie

Mum was a mixed up person. She was very *cold*, Mum. I think – well, I think due to her circumstances she wasn't loving towards us. I just sort of felt that we were with her through accident. And there was nobody loving us. Nobody paying us attention. She never kissed or cuddled us. She never told us she loved us. If anybody ever spoke kindly to me, you know, an aunt or a neighbour or somebody, which they hardly ever did, my eyes would fill up with tears.

Which I *hated* myself for.

I don't think Mum liked girls. Well she didn't like anyone much. But if she liked anyone, it wasn't her daughters. It was her sons. She showed her favour to the boys in regards to everything. The boys did no work around the house. Us girls did the washing. We did the ironing. We did the scrubbing. A girl, by the time she was eight or nine years old, was just a skivvy. One of the big boys, with a bundle of dirty clothes in his fists, would come to our bedroom. He'd stand in the doorway. I'd be lying on my bed doing homework, or reading a love story.

'Here, do *this* Fatty,' he'd say to me.

And he'd throw the bundle all over me. I felt really *angry* when one of the boys did that. But there was nothing I could do about it. Mum always backed up the boys.

'Darkie was lying on bed reading, Mum,' the boy might say.

Mum hated us reading. Reading was lazy.

'Get that book away!' she'd yell.

'But why?' you might try.

'*Don't* give me back chat, miss!' she'd snap. 'You're that fond of work you'd lie down beside it!'

Mum wasn't too fond of work herself, to tell the truth, even though she was always droning on about how she was a martyr to us kids. She did do the baking of a Saturday. But she liked baking. I do too. And she cooked the meals. Apart from that she didn't do a lot of work.

She made up for it by moaning.'Yous *bloody* kids,' she'd say. 'Yous kids, running me ragged and what's the thanks I get for it – bloody *nothing*!'

Chorus

blue moon, blue moon
the moon in splendour
the moon is shining
heaven's door
paths of paradise
outside of heaven
the gate to paradise
the great somewhere
stars have lost their glow
evil star

Valerie

He's a happy baby, Stevan. He was no trouble inside the womb. Well, other than that *kicking*. And he's no trouble outside the womb. He's nice looking, too. He's got big green eyes. His head is nearly bald, which is a bit of a dag. He's got a little crease between his eyebrows as though he's frowning. But, like I say, he's happy. And he feeds good. I never have any trouble breastfeeding a baby. And after he's drunk his fill from my tits and I've slung him over my shoulder and patted his back he always brings up his wind quick.

And best of all is that when you put him down he'll sleep and sleep and *sleep*.

So he slots in easy when the fortnight in hospital comes to an end and me and him get a taxi back to Blackball. It's good getting back. The streets and roofs of the township have all been freshly washed by another one of those warm spring showers. The sun's shining on the red roofing iron and the green leaves of the wild shrubby yards. Lots and lots of puddles are sparkling like little ponds. Kids are running round barefoot, splashing in and out of those puddles and laughing.

Stevan starts to cry when the taxi stops in Brodie Street. I'm cradling him in my arms while Gil settles up with the driver. And I'm climbing out of the backseat. And I'm waddling my way along the path towards the front door. Once we get inside and the other kids come hoofing up the hallway to see their new baby brother I try chucking him on the cheek – fat cheeks he's got – but he still keeps crying.

He can probably sense that I'm starting to tense up a bit, ticking things off in my mind.

See that the kids haven't been wrecking the house, like kids will do.

Check that the coal range is burning good and hot.

Get the kettle filled and on the range.

Put the baby down in the cot.

Sit down and –

Rat tat tat.

A knocking on the back door. A perky, cheeky sort of knocking. I open up and see a smiling girl of thirteen or fourteen wearing a high school uniform. A bright red cardigan. A blue and red tartan skirt. It's the uniform worn by girls who go to St Mary's convent school in Greymouth. So she's a Catholic. I was brought up to look askance at Catholics. The girl's face is pink and plump.

'G'day, Mrs Grigg,' she says. 'I'm Erleen – Erleen from next door – Erleen Muir.'

'G'day Erleen. Sorry about my crying baby.'

'Oh, it's the baby I'm here to ask about, Mrs Grigg. I heard him crying. And you must have hundreds of things to see to now you're back from the maternity ward. And I could give you a hand with him, you know? I could help out with him for half an hour or that while you get settled. I love babies. I'm an only child. I've always wanted a wee baby brother. If you want to give him to me I could take him for a walk and sing to him and that, cheer him up. Or do you think he might want feeding right now?'

She stops to catch her breath.

I always knew my family could talk the handle off a pot and it sounds as though this girl Erleen might be able to keep up with us in that regard. She looks like a nice kid. She's eyeing up Stevan. She's eyeing him up like she wants to eat him up.

'Ta, that would be good,' I says.

She gives a little skip on the back step.

'Corker!' she says. 'I'll treat him with kid gloves Mrs Grigg.'

'You won't need to do that. Babies have soft bones. They don't break easy. They bounce if you drop them.'

She looks at me a bit surprised then starts laughing.

'I'll never drop *him*, Mrs Grigg. I love him too much already.'

Stevan's not crying by now. He seems to be sort of listening. Which he can't be listening, he's too young. I hold him out to the girl. She scoops him up carefully. She feels his weight in her arms. She looks down at him and sighs. She looks back up at me, blissfully.

And then off she heads with him, saying she'll carry him round the block.

Molly, the mother, pops in to make herself known next day.

'Just wanting to say, what with your new baby and that, your other kiddies – anything you want – if you need a hand with anything – just sing out, love.'

She's a bony, active sort of a woman in her forties. A woman with warm, kind, cheerful ways. Her face is as bony as her body. She's got a jaw. Which makes me like her even more. We've got a jaw in my family, too. When I think of Mum I often think of her hatchet jaw. My own jaw would be hatchet if it had half a chance but it's hiding itself under fat right now.

'G'day, I'm Val,' I says. 'Come in – would you like a brew?'

'A brew! Well, if we were two jokers! It's a bit early in the day for us girls to be drinking beer though, isn't it, Val?'

'I don't hardly *ever* drink beer,' I says laughing. 'I mean a cup of tea.'

She gives me a droll goodhearted sort of look.

'Well why not say a cup of tea?'

'We say brew for a cup of tea in my family.'

'Oh. Right. Penny dropping. Well, Val, don't reckon I've ever turned down a cup of tea in my life and certainly don't intend to start now.'

We're soon swapping our stories. Molly sups her brew. She chews one of the caramel biscuits, hot, that I've just baked in my coal range. She tells me she was born and grew up at Moonlight. I love that name. Moonlight. Molly Muir from Moonlight. It's a creek, Moonlight. A creek a few miles up the valley from Blackball. A creek and an old gold township. And a working timber mill township. Molly goes on to tell me she's only left the West Coast twice in her whole life, and that was to go by train to the trots in Christchurch.

'I went with my husband, Jack,' she says. 'He's a fitter at the mine, Jack.'

I'm not quite sure what fitters do. I know they tinker round with gas pipes. Or I think some of them do things with motors and that. I do know they're skilled workers, not just labourers. So they make good money.

'He a Coaster too?' I says, which is better than nothing.

'Coaster through and through. You'll get on good with Jack.'

Molly's motherly in all her ways. She doesn't do any wage work, even though she could. You know, since she's only got the one kid she could work for pay a few hours a day. She says she doesn't want to work for pay. She says she loves looking after the house. And looking after Erleen. And looking after Jack. And their cat and their chooks and that. She even feeds a couple of magpies that are nesting in a scruffy sort of pine tree in their yard.

I've always hated magpies.

Those beady red eyes and those wicked white beaks.

I'll go a *long* way to avoid a magpie.

Molly likes birds, she says. And she likes cooking. She likes sewing. She likes knitting. She likes vege growing. She likes flower growing. And after a few more days she's always popping in with freshly baked scones under a tea towel. Or she's taking my kids under her wing. She gets them over to her place. She cuts them segments of oranges to suck. She makes them mugs of cocoa to sup. She lets them have the freedom to run round the house and yard wherever they want to play.

She *really* likes kids.

But she likes everybody, Molly.

She likes everybody so much, and she's so kind and motherly to me, and she's so kind and grandmotherly with my kids, that it soon sort of feels like we're a family. Jack, too. Jack turns out to be an easygoing sort of chap. He wanders over, wearing a cardigan, rattling a toffee tin for the kids. The kids come scrambling. Molly makes the toffee. Erleen meanwhile keeps running in to scoop up Stevan. And she kisses him. And she cuddles him. And she kisses him some more. And she takes him next door. She likes to prop him up in the sun on their front porch while she sits with him and plays the guitar. Old ballads, she plays. A corker guitar player, Erleen. A very good tap dancer, too.

We're all in and out of one another's houses day in and day out. Which is good. It feels real good. It feels like –

Well, it's like what I'd have loved to have had back home when I was a kid.

'Molly's a bottler, isn't she?' says Ikey.

'A pearler,' I says.

'What a mother should be.'

Funny to think about our own mother stewing her bitter thoughts back over there in Christchurch. Funny to think I've found a sort of foster mother here in Blackball. And that the foster mother is Catholic. I grew up thinking – like I said – we were brought up to believe there was something wrong about Catholics.

'Catholics!' Mum used to say. 'A different *breed*!'

She had such a hatred of Catholics it made me dislike them

too. I disliked them because they were something else. Another sort of people. I didn't know what it was, but they weren't the right sort of people, they were wrong.

When really the wrong one was bloody Mum.

I don't miss Mum. I don't miss anything or anybody. I've got Gil. I've got Ikey. I've got Molly. I've got my kids. I'm happy.

Gil's happy too.

'Blackball is a little idyll, as far as I'm concerned,' he says one night after he's had a few beers with Jack Muir. 'I can see us thriving here for many a long year, darling.'

Chorus

house\
pillows\
home by the fire\
the floor, the door\
the face of the clock\
the dining room table\
the tinkling piano\
the chimney\
the clock\
the wall\
the clock\
this room\
tea, a rose\
windows\
a leaf\
the clock\
the flowers\
leaves on the trees\
smouldering leaves\
falling rain

the clock
just walking in the rain
the clock
this road
soaking wet
counting days
the clock

Stevan

ah ah ah oh oh oh ew ew ew ma ma ma ah ah ah ma ma ma da da da ma ma ma da da da

Valerie

I get myself into a good routine round the house after another week or two. I always need to have a good routine round the house. I'm like my own mother that way. Of a weekday the morning starts with Gil getting up to make me my brew. I sit back against the pillows. I drink it slowly. I look out the window at the forest on the mountains. Green forest. Gil shaves and swallows toast and drinks a cup of tea for himself. He pops in to take my cup and give me a kiss.

'I love you, darling,' he says.

'Oh,' I say.

He's wearing his work suit. Navy. He goes out the front door and walks off to the Mines Department. The office is just a little wooden bungalow. Gil's the paymaster. A woman, working alongside him in the office, she's the typist. The two of them handle all the paperwork for the Blackball State Mine. And all the paperwork for the Paparoa State Mine up the road at Roa. The office has got these big leatherbound ledgers listing all the men on the payroll, and the payments made to them, and that. Gil keeps those books up to date. He writes everything out in copperplate.

The paymaster.

Quite an *important* person by Blackball standards.

The milk float comes to a stop outside our letterbox. Gil puts two billies out at the letterbox before going to bed at night. I hear a clanking sound. It's the milkman with his big steel scoop. He's spooning the milk from a steel urn into the billies. He likes to whistle while he works.

Today he's whistling a song that come out last year, *Paths of Paradise*.

I like that song.

I like nearly all songs.

I get up and wash my face and dress myself. I've got only three dresses. All of them are cotton. Two are *latey* old models. The third one is my good dress. You know, the green pleated one. I keep it in case I have to go to the doctor's. Or to Greymouth. After I've pulled one of the latey dresses over my big shapeless body I slide my big shapeless feet into a pair of worn woollen slippers. I wear these slippers round home. Or a pair of cheap Jap sandshoes.

Anyway, once I'm up and dressed I hit the deck running.

Radio to be switched on. Firebox in the coal range to be heaped up. Pot of porridge to be got going. Stevan to be put to the breast. Kids to be got up. Kids to be got dressed. Porridge to be dished out. Firebox under the copper to be stuffed with wood and got alight. Copper to be filled up with water for boiling. Kids to be given a quick wash with the facecloth. Stevan to be given his morning bath. Wash his bum and teapot. Pat him dry. Powder him between the legs. Pop him into a singlet and jersey and his nappy. Settle him in his cot for a sleep.

Get onto the other kids.

I'm always busy. I'm in my element. I'm happy. I'm sweating inside my kitchen, my washhouse, my breasts full and bursting.

I duck out the back again holding a bowl of kitchen scraps for the fowls. We bought some not long after I got back from the maternity ward with Stevan. A clucky little flock of Leghorns. I open the netting gate into the run. The fowls with a flutter of feathers come scuttling up, crowding round my legs, ogling me with their beady wee eyes, begging me to scatter the scraps. They're good at laying. The eggs come in really handy. Once or twice a week I make an omelette for the whole family.

A magpie swoops down on me sometimes when I'm outside feeding the fowls or pegging out my washing.

I hate magpies.

You're outside in the sunshine just getting on with your job. You hear wings beating. You look up. You see a black bird with white markings. A big bird. Coming straight for you! A sleek spiteful bird with two black beating wings. And two sharp black claws. And two sharp snapping white nibs to its beak. And those two beady read eyes. And a black and white tail fanned out like an assassin holding a poisoned hand of cards.

'It's the nesting season,' Gil always says when I tell him about those bloody magpies. 'They'll be guarding the nest.'

'Well who's going to guard *me*?'

'I've never heard of anybody being hurt by a magpie, darling.'

'I'll remind you of that after it's gone and pecked out my bloody eyes and I'm stumbling down the street tapping the footpath with my white stick!'

The radio relays the hit songs while I clear the kitchen table and send the kids out to play. I stand on the front veranda for a while and watch them scoot off. Older kids are out in the street too. On their way to school. One or two women trot along with string bags. Off to the shops. You can hear rakes of big black wagons being dragged from the mine to the railway.

Rattles. Snorts. Thumps.

Now, back to the kitchen to get stuck into the breakfast dishes and sing along to the radio.

I keep the radio on all day. I listen to two of the Greymouth stations, 3ZA and 3ZR. They both play hit songs. I sing along with Al Martino and Johnny Ace. I dry the dishes and stack them in the cupboard. I sing along with Doris Day and Johnnie Ray. I go down to the rooms and make the beds. I sing along with Jo Stafford and the Fontane Sisters and Patti Page. I go out to the washhouse and dump dirty clothes into the boiling water in the copper.

Perry Como, Guy Lombardo.

I give the clothes a good possing. I go back to the kitchen to start cleaning. Cleaning isn't too big a job. We haven't got many things that want cleaning. We've got a dining suite that we bought new about three years ago. The table is square, rimu. The sideboard is oblong, rimu. The chairs are rimu too, with leatherette seats. The leatherette is cracked bad already. And we've got a rimu bedroom suite that we bought at the same time as we bought the dining suite. We bought both those suites on time payment from Calder Mackay.

The floors are a bit of work. We've got lino on the kitchen floor. Brown lino. I get the wooden mop and the galvanized bucket and mop it down. I go down to the rooms. We've covered the bedroom floors with woollen felt we bought in Greymouth. Green felt. I give those floors a sweep.

I make sure it's a good sweep.

Women like me, women with young kids, they're likely to get a bit slatternly. One or two women in this street are real slatternly. I'm buggered if I'm going to get slatternly.

Nobody's going to point the finger at *me* and say I can't keep on top of my housework.

After sweeping the bedroom floors I go into the lounge. We've got a nice green square of carpet in the lounge. Gil's father gave us a hundred pound to fit the room out. We bought that carpet. And we bought a brand new lounge suite. The three-seater couch and the two matching armchairs are upholstered in a light brown flecked all over with little flowers in green and gold.

That lounge suite is the pride and joy of my life.

I've always wanted *nice* things.

I think it goes back to childhood. We didn't have anything. Only old sticks. Me and my sisters used to dream about how one day we'd live in bungalows. We'd dream about how we'd kit up those bungalows. You know, how we'd kit them up with fridges and frilly curtains and moquette lounge suites and cedar whatnots.

After I've got the house tidy, and got the washing out, I make myself another brew.

I sit down with the brew and my knitting. Or I'll do some darning. Or sewing. I've got a sewing machine, a Wertheim. It's good German workmanship, trustworthy. Only a treadle machine, though. And old. I sew and knit for hours every day. Once a week the lino gets a polish. I like polishing my lino. I swipe an old rag into a tin of polish and smear it onto the lino. And then I get an old woollen jersey. I shine the lino up. Once a week, too, the doorknobs get a polishing. All our doorknobs are brass. I love it, cleaning brass. I go out to the washhouse and get a tin of Brasso. I love a tin of Brasso. You know, that striped pattern on the tin, white and red and blue. I start on the back door and work my way, still singing the hits, right through to the front door. I have all those doorknobs *gleaming*.

Which doesn't last long. Blackball's always smoky. The smoke from the coal here isn't black, it's sort of creamy. So at first you think it won't make things black.

But it does.

Well, that's a nark but the coal costs us nothing. We can burn as much of it as we like. Nobody has to stint. Arthur and the other miners reckon it's one of the best coals in the world.

Ikey likes to drop in of a morning.

'How's bubs?' she'll say.

'Snoozing, snoring, shitting,' I'll say. 'How's Wendy?'

'Shitting, snoring, snoozing,' she'll say.

The kids are back for a feed in the middle of the day. Gil walks home from work. I do a hot cooked dinner. Hogget or sausages or fritters or mince or that, with cooked veges. And then a pudding. After, Gil heads back to work and I slam the kids down for a sleep. I never have any trouble putting down the two boys. John does what he's told. Alan follows John.

Lynne, mind you – Lynne likes to play up.

'Off to bye-byes,' I'll say.

'Make me!' she'll say.

She's soon snoring. I make myself another brew, sit down again with my knitting and listen to more hit songs. The kids are awake again after an hour or so. I send them outside to play. A couple of hours later I hear a voice singing out.

'G'day, Mrs Grigg!'

'G'day, Erleen!'

She comes over as soon as she can once the school bus has brought her back from Greymouth. She bursts into the kitchen. She thumps down the passage to the rooms. She gets Stevan out of his cot. And she thumps back up the passage to the kitchen. And she changes his nappy. She stows the dirty nappy in the washhouse. She tucks Stevan into the pram, an old cane rattletrap we bought secondhand a year or two ago. She wheels the pram to the back door.

'Ta-ta, Mrs Grigg.'

'Ta-ta, Erleen.'

A big grin on her big round face, she sets off. She likes to take him for an outing every day unless it's raining.

After she's gone, I paddle out to the line to bring in the washing. I unpeg the things. I stow them in the cane basket. I paddle back inside. I dump the basket on the kitchen table. I unfold the ironing board. I'm singing along with Georgia Gibbs. I start the ironing. I don't like ironing. I quite like the smell of clean dry clothes under the hot steel. And while I'm doing the ironing, I stop now and then to get the tea started. Kids are calling and laughing out in the street and yards.

I'm singing along to the radio.

Kay Starr. Pee Wee King. The Weavers. The Hilltoppers.

Erleen gets back by around five o'clock. You can hear mothers up and down the street opening kitchen windows or front doors and cooeeing.

'Teatime!' they yell out. 'Tea, yous kids!'

Gil gets home after twenty minutes or so, pecks a kiss on my cheek and changes into flannel trousers and an old polo shirt. The kids are *flying* around the house, noisy and hungry. I dish up the food. Scrambled eggs, fried tomatoes, toast, scones hot from the oven, sort of style. Plates, forks, spoons, pots, pans. Eating, washing, drying.

And then it goes quiet.

The kids get back to their play. Me and Gil sit in the lounge and listen to the radio. He smokes a few fags. I click away with my knitting needles.

The kids, when it comes time for them to go to bed, are always good. Me and Gil take turns getting them into their pyjamas. And we take turns reading to them in bed. We read from an encyclopaedia we've just bought. It's a set of eight books. The books are in red binding. And they're stamped with gold lettering. We got the encyclopaedia through mail order and we're paying if off on the drip feed. The books are mostly about geography and history and art and science and that, for older kids, but one of the books has stories for little kids. Aladdin. Sinbad. Robin Hood. And it has nursery rhymes too. Mary had a little lamb. Ride a cock-horse. Buttercups and daisies.

We *thrash* that encyclopaedia.

For a start, in our early days together, it seemed a bit dilly to me that Gil wanted to buy books and read them to our kids.

'What's the point reading books to a baby when it can't even *talk*?' I said one night.

'I grew up that way,' he said. 'I looked forward to it all day.'

'Well that's just stupid.'

He's right, though. The kids love it. I quite like it too.

After the kids are down we sit listening to the radio. Or once a twice a week we'll play cards with Ikey and Arthur. On their way over they'll drop in at the back door of the Club Hotel. You can always get drink after hours in Blackball. Arthur will pick up a jar of beer for him and Gil to drink their way through steadily. Me and Ikey will have the odd shandy. Me and Ikey will play Chinese patience. Gil and Arthur will play euchre. I don't know how to play euchre, so it sounds sort of sophisticated when they're calling.

'Hearts trumps.'

'No trump.'

Or all four of us will play sevens.

Me and Gil sit down at the kitchen table once a fortnight with his pay envelope. A paymaster's salary isn't too good. It's a battle stretching it to cover the rent, the power and the food. Food for kids who eat like hungry gannets. Anyway, after we get them off to bed and make a brew we sit at the table and open up the envelope. We work out what wants paying. We work out what to put aside for food and that. And we see if there's anything left over to save. There's hardly ever anything left over. Gil keeps back five shillings. That's so he can go to the pub for the odd beer or two and buy a bit of tobacco. He rolls his own smokes, to keep down costs. As often as not he hands a bob or two back to me next payday.

But we can't seem to save anything.

One thing we do save money on is contraceptives. We save money on them by not buying any. We did try french letters for a while. But they're a nark. You've got to go to Greymouth to get them. Or you can phone through to a town chemist, order them, and they'll put them on a bus for you. You buy them in packs of three. And they're not cheap. And I don't like them anyway. I get a rash when we use them. A sort of eczema on my thighs and in my groin and all this sort of thing.

'Take it off,' I'll say to Gil. 'It's dry and raspy.'

'You sure, dear?'

'Yeah. I can't be bothered with it.'

We take a few risks, in other words. I don't particularly want another baby. But it doesn't worry me, really. And it doesn't worry Gil. After a while I miss my period and put on my green pleated dress and go to the township doctor and see what's happening.

'Well, I'll do a test, Mrs Grigg,' he says. 'However, given that you're still breastfeeding you're not likely to be pregnant.'

But I am.

Chorus

sitting at a window watching the rain
a love song is a sad song
hi-lili, hi-lili, hi-lo
cigarette, lipstick, drink, night spots
bank, money, dough, cheques
a dime, a nickel, a cent
rags to riches
millionaire
shotgun
debt
crowd
cabaret, party
dancing, dancing
dance, dance, dance
jiving, rhumba, tango
a jungle wet with rain
black as night
drops of rain that fall

49

hi-lili, hi-lili, hi-lo
oh so far away
lonely nights
the nights
the night

Stevan

ah ah ah oh oh oh ew ew ew oo-ee oo-ee baby oo-ee oo-ee baby titty love mama dada titty love mama hello love ta-ta milk love baby bye-byes ooo-ooo-ooo rain love sun rain sun love rain mama titty happy mama dada oh wo wo wo oh oh love rain rain sun rain love koo-ba koo-ba koo-ba ah-ha-ha ah-ha-ha-ha hey-oh hey-oh over and over dun dun dun dun dun d-d-duh d-d-dun d-d-dah dah dah ratta ta ta too, ooh ooh doo oo oo oo oooouuu huu ouuuouuu huu ouuu uh-huh uh-huh uh-huh ooooooh ooooh-ooooh

Valerie

Stevan's still sleeping in our battered old wooden cot a year after he's born. He won't be there much longer. The new baby's due around Christmas. I'm a bit on edge about it. Not because of having another baby. Well, other than knowing that getting the baby out will bloody *hurt* like always. I'm on edge because of Gil's mother, Ellen. She's a lady. She wrote a letter saying she'll come over and look after the house and the kids when I go into the maternity ward.

'*And* she's bringing her aunt with her, some bag a thousand years old,' I tell Molly. 'She says they'll bring camp stretchers and stay till I come home from the maternity ward.'

'That's jolly nice of them,' says Molly. 'That's a lot of trouble for them to go to for you, Val.'

'It's a lot of trouble for *me* to go to, you mean, Molly.'

'How do you reckon that, Val?'

'Well they're not like you and me and the rest of us. They're not working class.'

'Won't be that bad, will it? Grown women. They'll know about kids.'

'I'll be at my wits' end trying to keep things nice for them.'

Ikey pops in with Wendy. I put the kettle on for a brew. Soon the three of us, me and Ikey and Molly, are sitting at the kitchen table with cups of tea at our elbows and knitting on our needles. My kids are outside somewhere, wandering round the streets, poking sticks into ditches and making up games and that. My kids are great at making up games. Stevan and Wendy are on the floor together rooting around in the pot and pan cupboard. I've opened the cupboard so they can drag the things out. Stevan starts lining all the pots up in a row. He still can't walk. He's crawling backwards and forwards on the lino, adjusting the things. He likes things to be in a row. Wendy's down on the lino too. She can walk already but she thinks it's more fun crawling around down there with her cousin than standing up on her own.

'They're good cobbers aren't they, Steve and Wendy,' says Molly.

'All our kids get on good,' I says.

I'm knitting a wee cardy for the new baby. The wool's green, a grass green. Ikey's knitting a light summer jersey. The wool's bottle green. We like green in our family. Molly's knitting a complicated cable knit jersey for Stevan.

'They're good kids,' she says.

The skein unravelling as she knits is red. And when I say red, I mean *crimson*. Crimson shot through with fawn.

Molly loves red.

'What colour do you reckon Steve's hair will be when it settles down?' she says. 'You reckon it'll be chestnut like yours or black like Gil's?'

Chestnut! I feel quite pleased that she used such a nice word for my rat's nest.

'I hope it's black. I like black hair.'

'You two girls are both lucky you've got handsome husbands with beautiful brown eyes and glossy black hair. Olga, what with your red hair and your Arthur with his black hair, when you two are together you're striking.'

Ikey can't handle compliments. Nobody can, in our family.

'He'll do,' she sort of grunts.

'He's very fair for a Maori, isn't he?' says Molly. 'It's only that gorgeous glossy hair and his big brown eyes that give it away. Gil's got a bit of Maori too, hasn't he? Not just the black hair but the olive skin?'

I let out a hoot of laughter.

'Ellen wouldn't thank you for *that* comment,' I says. 'As far as that tonky madam's concerned her whole family are purebreds. Griggs only ever have dealings with Maoris when a shearing gang comes to snip fleeces off their sheep.'

Molly looks a bit upset to think of the sheep.

'Gil's such a nice chap,' she says.

'He'll do,' I says.

'Is his mother really a tonky madam?'

'Oh, she's alright. Alright for someone with money.'

'Look down at the floor,' says Molly. 'Steve's listening to us talking.'

'What?'

'I've noticed that about Steve. He likes listening to people talking.'

I look down at the floor. You *could* easily think he's been listening to us talking. He's gawping up at me with those green eyes of his. Which are my green eyes. His face is serious. Or is it just that wee crease between his eyebrows?

52

Chorus

beautiful brown eyes
beautiful, beautiful brown eyes
you'll never love blue eyes
no more

Stevan

love love love ah ah ah oo-ee baby titty love Mama dada titty love Mama hello love ta-ta milk love baby bye-byes oh oh oh ew ew ew oo-ee oo-ee baby oo-ee ooo-ooo-ooo rain love sun oo-ee oo-ee baby Mama milk Dada love oo-ee ooo-ooo-ooo milk rain sun love rain Mama milk titty happy Mama Dada oh wo wo wo oh-love oh-rain oh-rain sun rain love Erleen Molly milk love ah ah ah oo-oo-oo koo-ba koo-ba koo-ba ah-ha-ha Mockingbird Hill love love hello love ta-ta milk Mockingbird Hill rain sun Molly ah-ha-ha-ha hey-oh hey-oh John love Dada love Mama dun dun dun duh d-duh d-dah Dada m-mah m-m-mah Mama milk rain love love love love.

MADPIE

Valerie

Noel, that's the name we give to the new baby. We give him that name because he's born on Christmas Eve. He comes out of the womb no trouble. Except that, as usual, getting him out hurts like buggery. He's a nice looking little boy. He takes to the breast good.

And, thank god, he *sleeps* good.

Mind you, the weeks before Christmas have been hard on me because of Ellen staying with us. And not just her, Aunty Sue. They come over the Alps by railway. With them they brought this whole big *swag* of gear. Not only the two camp stretchers but a couple of bales of sheets and pillows and blankets. And they brought four big suitcases crammed full of clothes. Ellen has nice clothes. She wears a lot of mauves and violets and lavenders. Or sometimes dark red. Oxblood. And she always wears fashionable shoes. Her eyes are black. Her hair's black as black. She's got the lovely olive skin that she handed on to Gil. And, as Gil's always telling me, she's got trim ankles.

'Nobody has trim ankles like my mother,' he likes to say.

It's not that she's a snob. She's kind. She works hard to muck in. So we get on good enough, me and Ellen.

Aunty Sue's all right, too, a sweet old thing.

It's just that it was extra work for me with them staying. And always having to make sure the house was ready in case I had to rush off to have the baby. And we had a lot of rain. Warm rain. All day long, *humid*. All day long thick rainclouds hanging low over the Paparoas. The Paparoas are the mountain range behind Blackball. A big high range with heavy bush. It's beautiful, that range. Anyway, Ellen likes windows open, to air the house, which is good. And she likes doors open, too, which isn't so good. She forever kept opening the doors and I forever kept asking her if she'd mind closing the doors.

'It's real muddy out there right now and Stevan crawls out if we leave the doors open,' I'd say.

'Oh no, Val,' she'd say. 'I must have good fresh air.'

'Well after he crawls out into all that mud and it's time for him to come back inside I have to get the mud off him. Which is a job I could do without.'

'A little mud won't hurt him, Val.'

But we weren't talking about a *little* mud. We were talking about a kid who looked like a cow pat. I'd have to go to the kitchen and turn the tap on the tank behind the coal range. I'd have to draw off some water into a tin bucket. I'd have to lug the bucket through to the bathroom. I'd have to pour the water into the bath. I'd have to strip off Stevan. I'd have to wash and soap and rinse him to get all that mud off. I'd have to dry him. I'd have to dress him in clean clothes. I'd have to put him down on the floor to play. I'd have to take the muddy duds out to the washhouse, to soak. I'd have to get back to my sewing or knitting or ironing or cooking.

And then, while my eyes were on my work, *she*'d leave another door open.

And as soon as look at you he'd be outside wallowing in the mud again like a little piglet. And I'd be in the yard again, *dragging* him in from outside, and he'd be crying, all covered with mud.

'Boys will be boys,' Ellen would say.

Moral!

One of her other fads is phrenology. Quack science. She sat herself down with all the kids. She poked and prodded their heads. She dug her thumbs under the backs of their skulls. She worked her fingertips forwards to their foreheads. She did John's head. After him she did Alan's head. And then she did Lynne's head. She didn't have anything new to say because she'd already done them when we were still living in Canterbury. Then she got Stevan on her lap.

'Hmm,' she said. 'Hmmmm.'

Aunty Sue was watching sort of *reverently*.

'What do you make of this young gentleman, Nelly?' she asked.

Ellen looked up, very solemn. She really believes in this stuff. She looked up and spoke low, a sort of mooing.

'He has the bump of knowledge.'

'The bump of knowledge?' echoed Aunty Sue.

'The occipital bone. The bone at the base of the skull. We all have it. Stevan's, though, is striking. It's very strong.'

'How can it be strong?' I cut in. 'He doesn't know *anything* yet.'

'We learn a good deal even when we're in the womb, dear, and keep learning every day of our lives,' she said, not so much mooing now as crooning. 'Stevan appears already to have learnt a good deal.'

A lot of hooey, in other words.

After I come back from the maternity ward with the new baby he started playing up, Stevan. Crying a lot. I don't know why. The day I come home he was so excited to see me he started sort of crowing. Then he crawled across the floor to me, babbling. I suppose he was wanting a cuddle. But my arms were full with Noel. So he started to cry, Stevan.

And then, when I popped out a tit to give the new baby a feed, he kicked up a *real* stink.

Chorus

Jezebel
double-crossed
cold, cold heart
tears begin to fall
vanity
jealousy
jalousie
misty eyes
the heart that cries
love, it fades and dies
I broke my heart in two
dreams that won't come true
teardrops start
hungry heart
lonesome and blue
my heart cries for you
you danced, danced, danced
down the trail of achin' hearts
cruel lips
torture me
pain
I'm blue
I trusted you
my heart is numb
I sing of woe
a sad song
sorrow
sadness
tears
bitter
I pine
cry

Stevan

Mummy bad. Daddy bad. Noel bad. Noel no. Don't. Mummy cuddle. Mummy titty. Mummy milk. Noel. No. No. Noel bad. Mummy bad. Daddy bad. Don't. Don't. Don't!

Valerie

My work's cut out for me now that I'm back home with the new baby. Stevan keeps playing up. And he still hasn't started walking. Most kids are trotting round like Jackie by his age. He just keeps crawling. And now for some reason he's become all *clingy*. So a lot of the time I find I've got two big lumps of kids in my arms, him and Noel. And I'm having to swat him away when I'm breastfeeding Noel.

And the other kids keep me busy, too.

John's a great help. He's a very good kid. He's slim and he's got glossy black hair and olive skin like his father and like his grandmother, Ellen. He's real nice. I've got a sort of *deep* feeling about John. Well, him being my first one. Me and Gil both think there's something a bit special about John.

'He looks a lot like you in your photos of when you were a boy,' I says.

'Poor urchin,' says Gil, but you can tell he's pleased.

'What'll he be when he grows up?'

'I'd like him to go to varsity and get a profession.'

'Oh?'

And I'm pleased, too.

John's a good cobber for Alan. They invent games, and all that sort of thing, without any strife. The pair of them are very *placid* kids. You'd have to use a crowbar to split them up, though to look at the pair of them you wouldn't even think they come from the same family. Alan's pale and stocky. He's got a big round white face like a moon. A moon cratered with lots of gingery freckles. And his hair is sandy. And on summer days he gets sunburnt real easy.

Anyway, both those boys are never any trouble, really. They never get my goat.

Lynne's another story.

The other kids don't call her Lynne. They call her Sissy. She's slim, like John. Her hair's not dark. Her hair's very fair. Straight hair, which I keep cut short, just done in a fringe. She's old enough now to start fussing about how she'd like it long. And how she'd like a ribbon in it. And how she wishes her hair was curly.

'I hate it,' she says. 'I *hate* my straight hair!'

Molly buys a home perm machine on time payment at Calder Mackay. She sits Lynne down one winter day. Lynne's wearing a pair of grey woollen trousers which I made myself. I always put her in trousers in the winter and I always make them myself. And I make her little cotton dresses for summer. Molly, smiling, gets busy with the curlers and the tongs and the chemicals. Lynne sits there, good as gold. Afterwards, when it's all over, Lynne thinks it's *marvellous*.

'I don't want straight hair anymore,' she says. 'I don't want it ever ever again.'

'We'll see,' I says. 'It'll grow out in a few weeks and then we'll see.'

'No!' she yells. 'Never ever!'

'Never ever's a big word.'

'Never ever's *two* words!' she yells.

She knows it's two words because she likes reading a lot, Lynne. She won't be starting school for another year but she can read quite a lot of words already. All my kids like reading.

'Cut your cheek,' I says. 'Nobody needs a know-all.'

So her bottom lip droops and she goes into a sulk. She sulks for days. She's got a real temper, Lynne. She's always been trouble. Like, when she was little she never let me give her a kiss and cuddle. John did. Alan did. Stevan did. Noel does too. Lynne, though – on no. Well she *does* kiss and cuddle with Gil. He's very good with Lynne. She likes him a lot.

I don't think she's ever been too keen on me.

'Now you've got yourself a little lass I bet she'll be spoilt,' everybody said to me when I had her. 'She'll be your pet.'

'I treat all my kids the same,' I told them.

I made up my mind to prove to people that I wasn't spoiling her. If anything, I've been tougher on her than on the boys. I don't want her growing up saucy. I smack her for things I won't smack the boys for. I smack her for giving me backchat. She does that a lot. I'll ask her to do something and what will she say?

'Make me!' she'll say.

And she'll *stomp* out the doorway.

'Don't slam that door!' I'll say.

And she'll slam the door. So I'll run after her, grab her, and give her a bit of a smack. Only on the bum. Or the arm. Or whatever other bit of her happens to be handy. She's full of cheek. I can't stand that. I smack the kids quite a lot, to be honest. It's my temper. I get fierce easy.

I don't know why, but I've always got fierce easy.

One weekday me and Ikey and the kids catch the bus into Greymouth. A big *expedition*. We're going to do some shopping. And we're going to buy lunch in tearooms. And then we're going to do some more shopping. I've been looking forward to the trip for days. At the start it seemed like the shops in Blackball would stock more or less everything we'd be needing but of course they don't really. Hart Street and Hilton Street shops only sell the basics. And those basics are a bit dear, too. The shopkeepers mark everything up. They have to, Gil says, to cover the extra cartage.

I miss department stores.

I mean, it's one thing to slope in your Jap sandshoes through the puddles on Hart Street or Hilton Street and mooch into those wee wooden shops and poke around among the skimpy offerings.

And it's another thing altogether to tug on a pair of nylon stockings and a pair of gloves and *drift* through those big *gleaming* department stores in Christchurch. The bright lights. The glass display cabinets. The mannequins. The hiss of pneumatic tubes when dockets shoot through the showrooms inside brass bullets.

DIC, Beaths, Millers, Hays.

Not that I like nylons and gloves. I *hate* nylons and gloves. But I love department stores.

Anyway, we get off the bus and wander into Woolworths. The aisles are pretty busy. Women and kids. The shop's much bigger and much busier than anything in Blackball. I'm enjoying the bustle. I've got Noel and Stevan crammed inside the pram. Ikey's turning over some toys in a glass display case. Lynne's holding hands with Wendy.

And cracks up.

'I have to go *outside*!' she starts screaming. 'I can't *breathe*!'

I look down at her. I'm furious.

'*Why* can't you breathe?'

'I can't stand crowds! I can't stand crowds! I can't stand crowds!'

Quarter of an hour later we're on the bus heading back to Blackball. The kids are crying. Ikey's biting her tongue to stop herself from saying something catty. And I'm holding Lynne by the wrist. I'm holding on with both my hands. And I'm twisting her wrist. I'm twisting it, giving her Chinese burns. She screams every time I do. None of the other women on the bus can see what I'm doing, so I keep doing it.

'This'll teach you,' I says to her.

At home she takes it out on the boys. She snatches their toys. She pokes out her tongue at them when they cry. She elbows them out of her way. She makes fun of them when they get a word wrong when they're talking or singing. She doesn't mind hurting them, if she's in the mood. They come to me complaining.

'Sissy hit me,' John says. 'It hurts.'

'Sissy bit me,' Alan says.

So what with one thing and another Lynne's ended up a nasty little *madam*.

I don't talk to Gil about the Chinese burns when he comes home from work. He doesn't need to know. He's not very happy when I smack or pinch any of the kids. He's not a smacking or pinching person, Gil. Often, if the kids are playing up during the day, I'll threaten them by saying he'll give them a hiding.

'Wait till your father gets home!' I'll snarl, but it doesn't scare the kids.

'Paddy's coming!' they'll say to one another, giggling.

They mean a paddywhack. Gil, when he does get home from work, will stand quietly and listen to me moaning about what they've been up to. I'll tell him they did this. I'll tell him they did that. I'll tell him to give them a belt. The kids, while I'm dobbing them in, will bury themselves under their bedding. You can see them wriggling and tittering beneath the blankets.

Gil will give a sigh. He'll go into the bedroom where they're pretending to hide. He'll lift his right hand and whack them through the thickness of the blankets.

'Don't – you – ever – do – that – again!' he'll chant in time to each whack.

Which is no bloody use at all, because the kids just keep giggling.

'You need to get out your *belt*!' I says.

He never does. And then one day when he gets home and I come to him moaning, he says it's up to me to discipline the kids while he's at work.

'I'm not going to hit kids for things done when I'm not here,' he says.

Otherwise he sees he does his bit. He washes dishes. He dries dishes. He changes nappies. He's got a vege garden going out in the backyard. He does a *lot* around the house and yard.

He's not like my own old man.

I don't think, when I was little, I ever saw my old man him so much as lift a finger in the house to help Mum. And he was away for weeks at a time, drifting in and drifting out and drifting back in, like I said already. And then by the time I started school he'd cleared out for good. The youngest of us would be about six weeks old when he left. He wound up in Kaikoura.

It's over fourteen years now since I last saw him, that last morning when he cleared out.

So thank god for Gil.

We're both at a bit of a loss, though, when it comes to Stevan. After he starts walking he also starts rocking. You know, rocking himself backwards and forwards. He does it when he's sitting on the floor. He does it when he's sitting in the cot. He never did it before I come home from the maternity ward. Lynne used to do it, too. She did it for a year or so. She'd just sit, not looking at anyone or anything, and she'd be rocking and rocking and rocking. She always did it quite quiet. Stevan does it different from her. He really *swings* himself backwards and forwards.

He sort of sings to himself while he's doing it, too. I can't quite work out what he's singing.

'Ma-ma-ma-pie,' it sounds a bit like.

'What's he trying to say, do you reckon?' I ask Gil.

'Dashed if I know,' he says. 'It's pretty baffling isn't it?'

Molly says she thinks Stevan might miss being breastfed. She says it might make him feel better if I give him lots of kisses and cuddles. I tell her I like giving my kids a cuddle and a kiss when they're newborns but you can't keep it up when they start walking. You don't want your kids growing up to be sooks.

'He'll just have to get over it,' I says.

Molly spoils him rotten anyway.

One day after he's spent hours and hours next door he won't touch his tea and says he wants something. I can't work it out. Neither can Gil. The mental little kid keeps making the same sounds and shaking his head and getting sort of annoyed and restless.

'Eye see shooh goo,' he seems to be saying.

Gil goes next door with a bag of carrots and a bunch of silver beet from his vege garden and comes back with eyes twinkling.

'Molly says she gave him a bit of a treat at midday by pouring a heap of icing sugar onto a saucer and giving it to him. After that, he wouldn't touch anything else so she kept topping it up. She says he was wetting his fingertips and dabbing them in icing sugar all day.'

'That's not a good healthy diet for a little kid,' I says. 'And it's bad for his teeth.'

'Apparently he was happy as larry. Molly means well, darling.'

'Molly's corker. He can't eat only icing sugar, though.'

'He'll eat properly when he needs to, won't he?'

'Oh, I suppose so.'

Erleen still spoils him rotten, too. Mind you, she can't take him off my hands as much as she did at the start. She left school a few weeks after turning fifteen and got herself a job. A good job. Bookkeeping at some outfit in Greymouth. She's quick with numbers, Erleen. She goes in and out by bus every day. Stevan's always hoping she'll come home early from Greymouth. He stands at the picket fence between our yard and their yard. Jack Muir took down a picket to let him through more easy.

'He's so patient,' says Erleen. 'His wee white face at the gap in the pickets is the first thing I see when I get home at the end of my working day.'

'Kids are a dag, aren't they? I says.

'He's my very own little kiddy,' she says.

Funny enough, he wriggles and squirms when she picks him up.

'No *squeeze* tight, Erleen!' he says, or we think that's what he's trying to say.

'I'm just giving you a love, Steve,' she'll say back, looking sort of flustered and happy.

These days, of a night when we've had tea and settled down in front of the radio and Ikey and Arthur come over, there's a lot of singing. Me and Ikey are the ones doing the singing. We beat time on the tabletop with the flat of our hands. Arthur and Gil play cards. Me and my sisters have always been keen on singing. And my brothers. And not just singing. We didn't have the money to learn to play a piano or an oboe or a violin or that, but we played the spoons, or pots and pans, or a comb.

'She's got a good voice, Rosemary Clooney, don't you reckon?' says Ikey one night after we've been singing along to *Half as Much*.

'Yeah.'

'And you have to give it to her for her range, don't you reckon? She'll take on any style just about.'

'She takes on too many styles, I reckon,' says me.

'You reckon she should say no to some of the songs she does?'

'Yeah.'

'Yeah, I reckon you're right. I don't like the way she does *Beautiful Brown Eyes*.'

'I don't like the way she does *Baccia me*.'

'I hate the way she does *Come on-a My House*.'

'Oh?' I says. 'I really like *Come on-a My House*.'

'I like the *song*. It's hip. I just don't think it's right for *her*. She's not hip. Is she?'

'No, she's not hip.'

'Yeah. Her voice isn't hip. It's warm. It's all wrong for that sort of song.'

'Yeah, it is a warm voice.'

'Lovely and warm.'

'So why you don't like her doing *Beautiful Brown Eyes*?'

'She does it too sugary. It's not meant to be sugary. It's not, is it? It's meant to be a folk song, isn't it?'

'Yeah.'

'So it should be sort of dry. I reckon the problem is – the problem's the music studios, don't you reckon? Yanks don't like a style that's – a style that's *dry*. Yanks love – they love *sentimentality*.'

'Yeah, they do.'

So that's quite interesting. We both enjoy that. And soon we're making it a habit to get in a bit of two-handed crack about the hit songs. We feel like we're sort of music critics. We were taught how to listen to music at Phillipstown School. We both had this teacher, Miss Livingstone. She wasn't like other teachers. She was good at teaching. And she was really *passionate* about music. I had her for two years. And then Ikey had her for another two years. Miss Livingstone would put a portable gramophone on her desk and inside the record case there'd be a green velvet cloth. A record would be slid onto the velvet and carried across to the gramophone and slipped onto the turntable. Miss Livingstone would look at us all with her eyes blazing.

'Heads down!' she'd cry.

We'd squeeze our eyes shut and bend our heads over our desks and we'd hear Schumann and Schubert and Brahms, and Liszt and Chopin and Rachmaninov.

'What instrument has just taken up the melody, Valerie Forbes?'

'The flute, Miss Livingstone.'

'Very good.'

Miss Livingstone got so carried away about music that your only way of handling it was by just surrendering.

'Music isn't like words,' she said. 'Music can't tell a story and mustn't try to tell a story, it's the most beautiful and the least meaningful thing we have.'

Which sounded a bit mad, but that was Miss Livingstone.

Anyway, nowadays the highlight of our radio listening is the songs on the Lifebuoy Hit Parade. Me and Ikey have been listening in to that hit parade ever since it started a few years ago. We don't like the joker who does the talking, mind you. Selwyn Toogood. You know, that fat *jovial* chap. He's got a plummy voice. He's got tickets on himself, too. And he's a square. He likes nightclub songs. Or swoony syrupy songs. Mario Lanza. Jimmy Sacca. He's not keen on the new rock'n'roll music.

You know, the Crickets, the Flamingos, the Four Tunes, Bill Haley and the Comets.

'It's got good tunes, that rock'n'roll,' I says to Ikey. 'And I like the beat.'

'Yeah it's music you can sing along to good, but – well, it makes my hackles go up a bit.'

'Oh? Why?'

'Well it's a crowd of boys skiting, don't you reckon?'

'Yeah, it is.'

'Skiting about how good they are at *rooting*.'

Gil, overhearing, raises an eyebrow.

Chorus

rock, rock, rock

good rocking tonight

rock around the clock

gimme gimme gimme gimme

hump-be-ump-bump-bump

shake, rattle, and roll

oww, oww, oww

hubba hubba

please be mine

will you be mine?

go! go! go! go! go!

tweedlee dee

67

tweedlee dee\
alone at night\
hearts of stone\
what did I do?\
memories of you\
boo-boo-boo-boo-boom\
doo-doo-doo-oo-oo-oo-oo\
alang alang alang\
sh-boom, sh-boom\
hey nonny ding dong\
boom ba-doh, ba-doo ba-doodle-ay\
ya-da-da, da-da-da, da-da-da-da\
dee-oody-ooh

Stevan

No. No. No. Noel no. No Noel. Noel bad. Don't. Don't. Don't. Mummy bad. Daddy bad. Mummy cuddle. Mummy titty. Mummy milk. Noel. No. No. Noel bad. Mummy bad. Daddy bad.

Rain.

Good. Rain good. Green. Leaf. Tree. Green. Good. Sun. Sun good. Rain. Rain. Rain. Good. Rainbow. Sun, sky, red, blue, yellow.

Bed. No. No bye-byes.

Wah. Wah. Wah.

Bash. Bash. Bash.

Black.

Mummy bad. Daddy. Daddy. Daddy. Mummy.

Bash. Bash. Bash. Bash. Dark. Black. Bad. Night. No sleep. Bash. Bash. Bash. Black. Red. Smack. Wah. Wah. Wah. Wah. *Wah. Wah*! Cry. Cry. Cry.

Valerie

We've got enough kids now so we're using a diaphragm. Which is a real rigmarole. For a start you have to go to the township doctor and get a prescription. Luckily the state pays. You get free maternity care for a while when you've had a baby. After getting the prescription from the doctor you then have to get your kids tidy and drag them and yourself down to the bus station to catch the bus. The bus takes you to Greymouth. You get the prescription filled out at a chemist's shop.

The chemist hands you a wee box, a square black box.

On the way home I opened the box and took a look at the diaphragm. A rubber thing. An off-white colour. And after that, I had to go back to the doctor so he could show me how to fit it properly.

'Not too difficult an operation, I think you'll find, Mrs Grigg,' he said, popping it up inside my fanny.

It did look easy when he did it. And he made me take it out while he was watching. To see I did it right. And then he made me put it back in again. And take it out again. And next he spelled out what to do, what not to do. A big *palaver*. You have to keep it dusted with french chalk when it's in its box. And before you stick it up yourself you have to smear this cream on it. And you have to make sure it's ready and waiting inside your fanny whenever you think you might be going to get it off. So you have to plan your sex life all ahead.

Which is a nark.

When I got home from the doctor I put the black box in a drawer in our tallboy. The tallboy next to our bed. Me and Gil start using it. It's a real *nark*. But we stick with it. One day I go out the back to bring in my washing. Stevan's squatted on the path, very serious. He's playing with something. I bend down to take a look.

A rubbery thing. A rubbery off-white thing.

He's filled it up with cinders!

Cinders are all over the back path. We spread them whenever we rake out the copper or the open fire or the coal range. Stevan must have found the black box in the tallboy. He must have thought it looked pretty. He's filled that diaphragm with so many fistfuls of cinders it's stretched about a foot long.

It looks like a big grey turd.

I can't help bursting out laughing. And then take it back inside and clean it up.

After a while we turf out the diaphragm because it's such a big to-do using it the right way. You know, dusting the bloody thing with powder. Rubbing it with cream. Getting it up my fanny before having sex. We try french letters again for a while. But they still give me a rash. So we stop using anything. Anyway, we're not having much sex these days. I enjoy sex but I'm quite lazy about it. Some nights I think, yes, it'd be nice to have a good root. I usually have an orgasm when we do get around to rooting. Me and Gil are a bit lucky that way. Our sexual needs are – I mean, we're quite good together. I've heard of people that just don't get it off together.

So –

But then I think, no, I can't be bothered. I'm real tired by the time I get to bed. And I think, well after all the smooching and build-up, it doesn't last long. The root. So why be bothered? I'd like it to last a bit longer, I think. But I'm always too sleepy. And then when we do it there's always that dryness.

The doctor asks the both of us to come to his rooms so he can talk it over with us.

'You're not indulging in marital relations enough,' he says. 'The less frequently a woman has relations with her husband the more she's likely to fall pregnant.'

'I thought it was the opposite,' I says.

'Rabbits, etcetera,' adds Gil.

'It's to do with the sperm count,' the doctor goes on. 'Quite frankly my advice to the two of you is to enjoy yourselves and indulge more frequently.'

'Oh,' I says.

So for a while that's what we do. We have sex about once a week. Gil takes the initiative. He always makes his approaches in the same old boring way. He's so *obvious*.

'Do you want a cup of tea, dear?' he'll say after we've put the kids down.

'Yeah,' I'll say.

He does it all proper. He fills the kettle and sets it on the range. He gives the range a stoke. He warms the teapot. He gets out our two best cups. Which aren't very good, but they're our best. He pours milk into a jug. He makes the tea. He carries the whole shebang through to the lounge on a tray. We each drink a cup.

'Well, I'll put the milk billies out,' he says.

He trots with the clanking billies down to the front gate. Then he winds up the clock. Then he gets into bed. I come into the bedroom when I'm ready. And he's sitting up in bed. I start getting undressed.

'Stop *looking* at me like that!' I say, laughing.

And then when we're lying down, he'll try one of his usual lines.

'Turn around my way and let me put my arm around you, dear,' he says. 'I just want a cuddle, nothing else.'

'Nah,' I say. 'You're not getting it tonight.'

I turn him down a lot. As I say, in regards to sex I'm basically pretty lazy. I just say no. Now and again he jibs.

'I should go out and get myself another woman,' he says.

'Alright,' I says. 'Off you go.'

We both know he'd never go with another woman. He's as loyal as loyal, Gil. He knows and I know it's bullswool when he says he might look for another woman. He'll never really try to manipulate me through sex.

Gil's honest as the day. He's – he's a good chap.

He's *kinder* than what I am.

Sex was sort of a mystery to me when I was a kid. Mum never talked to me when I started my period. She just shoved a rag at me and told to use it. I felt ashamed. I thought I was dirty. At that time I was sleeping with Ikey and my sister Bella in a saggy double bed. Dork, another sister, the oldest of us four, was in the same room but she had a single bed to herself. Her real name was Doris but we always called her Dork. I don't know why. Of a weekend, her and the other older girls had to take turns cleaning for the boys. The boys would shut their bedroom door. We knew the big boys and whichever sister was in the room with them were doing something. Something wrong. One night one of the boys, smelling of beer, came into our room and got into the single bed with Dork. Soon the pair of them were shuffling and whispering.

Me and Bella and Ikey were tittering and sniggering.

Anyway, that was a long time ago.

Thank christ.

Gil's so honest he hasn't worked out that I use sex occasionally to get my way in little things. Like, if I want to go out of a night with Ikey or Molly. Sunday nights, me and Ikey are getting quite fond of going to one of the pubs for a beer or two. And a game of darts. And a couple of smokes. I never used to smoke. You keep getting offered fags at the pubs, though. People at the pubs will offer you a fag. And if you turn them down you feel like you're not being neighbourly.

Anyway, whenever we want to go out to play darts my trick is to use sex. I cast my spell on the afternoon of the Saturday. I let him know I'm going to be kind to him that night. I string him along through tea. And while we're listening to the radio he's all happy and frisky. We get the kids to bed. And then we go to bed ourselves. And we get stuck in. And afterwards he's so grateful he'll agree to just about anything.

'Oh, me and Ikey was thinking of popping out to the pub

tomorrow night,' I'll say. 'You know, we'd like a round or two of darts.'

'Mm?' he'll say, cuddling.

'Can you look after the kids while I'm out?'

'Of course, Val. Anything for you, my sweetheart.'

Next night me and Ikey will be standing together inside the Dominion or the Club. We'll each be holding a beer in one hand. We'll each be holding a dart in the other hand.

'Be kind to your webfooted friends,' Ikey might say, grinning, letting a dart float towards the island on the board.

She's good at floating a dart. I'm more an archer. Well, I'd like to be an archer. I've got the quickness of an archer but not the smoothness. My throwing's more like a bull at a gate.

'For a duck may be somebody's mother,' I says.

And then me and Ikey start singing along to the pub jukebox.

Chorus

Zanzibar, Zion
Constantinople
sunny Italy
Rome
the Black Hills of Dakota
Indian country, Sierra Nevada
Bimbo

Valerie

John and Alan are going to school now. Blackball School, a state primary. A row of yellow wooden classrooms. A good wide green paddock. And all around, lots of green bushes and green rushes. Not like my own schools when I was a kid in Christchurch.

Sydenham School, my first school, looked like a factory.

The main building was this great big block of red brick. Sooty, grimy, terrifying. I knew you had to work. I knew you had to sit at desks. I knew you weren't allowed to talk. I knew that teachers were bossy. I didn't want to go to school.

Well, I wanted to go but I didn't want to go.

'*Wait* till you get to school,' Mum used to say. 'You get to school you'll learn what's what.'

On my first day she didn't say goodbye. She was out the back. She was probably thinking, good riddance, another one off my hands for a few hours a day. I was sulking. My older sisters took me. They *dragged* me. After school me and them weren't allowed to play or talk with other girls. And definitely not boys.

'Yous tarts are to come *straight* home and get stuck into your jobs,' said Mum.

'Straight?' one of the older girls said when she was in a cheeky mood. 'Aren't we allowed to turn corners?'

'Get a cuff over the ear, back chatting me like that!' Mum snapped.

We were always wanting Mum to be standing on the veranda waiting for us when we got home. Waiting to give us a kiss. But of course she wasn't. We'd find her scowling in the kitchen. Or sitting in the sun on the back steps moaning about her sore legs. I never got one kind word from her all the long weeks and weeks, and then the long two or three years, I went to Sydenham School.

We left that school when Mum found us a better house in Phillipstown.

The new house was at the dag end of Moorhouse Avenue. A tarred stump onto Ferry Road. Old dingy houses with corrugated iron fences. Flaking red paint. I still think of our new house as home, sort of. You know, the home we rented from when I was eight years old right through to when I came out of my time in the factory. I'm kidding myself, though, about it being my home.

I never had a home.

Chorus

my chair
the floor
the room
living room
timber, hardwood
house, bungalow, shack
foundation, cellar, door
broken windowpane
this ole house
the shingles
saw, hammer
oil the hinges
the street, the road
doorknob
next door
neighbourhood
around the bend
on the corner of the street
I've lost the way

Valerie

Gil and me and the kids shift to another house when we've been two years in Blackball. We make the shift because a place with an inside flush toilet has come available. It's a wooden bungalow at 3 Harper Street. Harper Street looks a lot like Brodie Street. A narrow strip of shingle. A deep ditch on one side, cut straight down into the ground, streaming with water when it's rainy and slimy when it's sunny. Two rows of wooden bungalows in green grassy yards.

A few empty sections overgrown with green weeds.

Gil can now just step out our door, cross the yard and he's in his office at the Mines Department.

'Handy for popping back home to give you a kiss,' he says.

'Handy for the mine manager to catch you at it,' I says.

The mine manager lives over the road in the biggest house in the township. A tall house with a tower and turret. Not that our family ever has anything to do with him or his family. Our bungalow will do me anyway. The three older boys we put in one of the front bedrooms. Me and Gil sleep in the other front bedroom. Noel sleeps in the cot at the foot of our bed. Lynne sleeps in the back bedroom. She's started sleepwalking. Which is a worry. We don't really know what to do about it.

And we're still having to put up with Stevan and his rocking.

He's rocking so hard he bangs the back of his skull on the headboard of his bed. Banging that bloody *bump of knowledge* on the headboard. Actually he's not so much rocking as bashing. Bashing, bashing. After a while the bashing makes the bed shift sideways. The wooden feet let out little squeaks as they inch across the lino.

And he's still chanting. We've worked out the words, now.

'Mummy a magpie,' he's chanting. 'Mummy a magpie.'

'Well that's bloody nice!' I say to Ikey, laughing.

'He doesn't mean anything by it,' she says.

'He'd better bloody not.'

He bashes all day. He bashes in bed. He bashes at the kitchen table. He bashes when he's out in the yard. He bashes even when he's sitting comfortable on the couch in the lounge. And now it's not just him, it's Wendy. Any time she's with him. And they're together a lot, those two. They sit side by side. And they bash. And they won't stop bashing.

Wendy apes the chant, too.

'Mummy a magpie, a mag-pie, a *mag*-pie.'

The chant's a bit like a hit song. You know, words that don't mean a lot but go with a beat. Hypnotic in some ways. And when the bashing has been going on for an hour or so I find those words have burrowed right inside my brain and I'm having to fight hard myself not to starting chanting.

'A *mag*-pie, a *mag*-pie, a *mag*-pie.'

You're peeling spuds or boiling up the copper and you find somehow you've stopped being dragged down by gravity. You're lifting right up out of your body. Out of your trunk. Out of your skull. You're floating up towards the ceiling, towards the sky – high – higher – up above the coal township – the plateau – the creeks – the bush – the hills – the gorges – the peaks – the rugged high ridges of the Paparoa Range – up and up and away till you seem to see the world spinning in space, spinning and spinning, and the other planets spinning, and the stars –

'A *mag*-pie, a *mag*-pie – '

I can't pay attention to stupid chanting. I can't be bothered with stupid bashing. I've got to get through my housework.

Like I say, it's important to me that people don't think I'm slatternly. I work real hard. I get things done. I cook. I wash. I scrub. I scour. And all those hours and *hours* every day knitting and sewing. I knit and sew nearly everything the kids wear on their backs. I work so hard to get them fitted out because when I was a kid I had to wear hand-me-downs. Threadbare skirts and jumpers my older sisters had already worn for years and years. Shabby old clothes that me and my sisters got given by the school. A teacher would call your name out in front of the class and you had to go up. The teacher would hand over this parcel of clothes. Clothes given to the school by people with a bit of money. Horrible clothes.

Charity.

Humiliating.

Hardly any of those clothes fitted properly. We had to wear them as is. Mum could have had a go at altering them but she never did. She had a sewing machine, a treadle machine. But she didn't know how to work it. And she couldn't knit. But she knew how to sew by hand. Couldn't she have done something to make those things a bit more bearable?

'Think yourself lucky you've *got* bloody clothes,' she'd say if we tried speaking up.

'Oh, but Mum – '

'*Cut* your moaning!'

So that's something my kids won't have to put up with. My kids won't wear old rags.

We're well known in the township, now. We know everyone and everyone knows us. Word gets back to us what people think about our family. And everything we hear is good. Gil's liked by everybody. I get praised for keeping the kids clean and tidy. Frances Driscoll, the infant mistress at the school – she's tall and thin and always walks on stilts – I feel proud when people report back to me that Mrs Driscoll says how well the Grigg children are looked after, how they're *spotless*. That gives me a bit of a boost. She says this to everybody in general, and of course everybody tells me back.

And in the meantime the kids are all wandering round getting under my feet while I'm trying to get through my work.

And trying not to hear the bashing.

'A *mad*-pie, a *mad*-pie – '

Rain bucketing onto the roof, squirting down the spouts. Kids on all sides. Lynne moaning. Noel crying. Kids and kids and kids. The chant. Magpie. Madpie. Mad.

When things get a bit too much I lift my fist and start yelling at Stevan.

'Shut your gob or I'll give you a clip around the bloody ear!'

'Mummy a *mad*-pie, a *mad*-pie, a *mad*-pie.'

'Shut up! Shut up! Shut up! Shut up!'

Bashing and bashing and bashing.

And bloody *bashing*!

Chorus

Bimbo, Bimbo
with a hole in his pants
where's he going to go-e-o?
what's he going to do-e-o?
does his mummy know?

Stevan

Wah. Wah. Wah. Harper Street. Why? Wah. Wah. Wah. Brodie Street no. Alang alang alang. Sh-boom, sh-boom. Molly? Erleen? Wah. Wah. Wah.

Word. Word. Word.

Why?

Mummy bad. Mummy titty no. Mummy milk no. Mummy magpie. Mummy magpie. Mummy magpie.

Daddy bad. Daddy teapot. Daddy cock.

Sh-boom, sh-boom. Boo-boo-boom.

Oww, oww, oww, ow baby.

Tennessee waltz.

Bad. Bad. Black. Dark

Noel bad. Noel.

No. No.

Hey nonny ding dong.

Boom ba-doh, ba-doo ba-doodle-ay.

Ikey good. Wendy good. Arthur cock. Arthur scary.

Molly. Molly. Molly good. Love. Tea. Scone. Orange. Love.

Erleen. Erleen. Erleen. Erleen good. Love. Love. Love.

Green. Grass. Tree. Leaf.

Erleen. Love. Erleen.

Ya-da-da, da-da-da, da-da-da-da.

Rain. Sun. Rainbow. Rainbow. Rain.

Rain love. Rain good. Green. Green. Green. Good. Sun. Good. Rainbow. Green, blue, yellow, red, purple. Bird. Tree. Leaf. Green. Green. Green. Good. Flower. Red. White. Fowl. White. Red. Hen. Red. Magpie. White. Black. Coal. Creek. Good. Water. Good. Tree. Tree. Tree. Good. Good. Good. Green. Green. Red. Rain. Good. Rain. Rain. Rain. Rain. Good. Good. Good. Good.

Hi-lili, hi-lili, hi-lo.

Mummy bad. Green eye. Bad.

Boom ba-doh, ba-doh, ba-doo ba-doodle-ay.

Daddy. Love. Brown eye. Arthur. Cock. Brown eye. Dog eye. Wolf eye. Bad. Cock. Bad. Mummy titty. Red. White. Milk. Cock. Red. Titty. White. Red.

Wah. Wah. Wah. Cry. Cry.

Hi-lili, hi-lili, hi-lo.

No. No. No. No.

Wah. Wah. Bash. Bash. Bash.

Bash. Bash. Bash. Bash. Bash. Wah. Wah.

Mummy magpie. Magpie. Magpie.

Word. Word. Word.

Mad pie

Mad.

Valerie

New Year, the start of 1955, comes round a few weeks after we shift to Harper Street. Me and Gil are going out for a pub crawl. Erleen comes over to mind the kids. I'm wearing a new dress. A dress I made from material bought on time payment in Greymouth. A sea blue material, sort of satiny. It looked good in the shop. I got it home, cut it out, sewed it up. And now when I zipper myself inside it –

Well, it *clings*. A slippery, slithery sort of clinging.

I'm getting real fat.

Anyway, who cares? I'd rather be fat than go hungry like when I was a kid.

Gil wears grey woollen trousers and a polo shirt and woollen sports coat. Ikey turns up in her best dress. Arthur's with her, in a sports coat like Gil. We have a beer or two in the lounge and sing round the piano. We bought the piano not long before leaving Brodie Street. A couple across the road from us split up. So we offered to buy the piano for ten pound. Gil thinks every house needs a piano. He can't play. I can't play. Ikey can pick out tunes by ear. Arthur can't play. Gil thinks our kids need to learn to play. So far we haven't got around to looking for someone to give them lessons.

We sing some of the songs from when we were all single and used to go out dancing.

'You always hurt the one you love,' I sing.

'Swinging on a star,' sings Ikey.

We start our crawl at the Club Hotel. All the pubs lay on free suppers of a New Year. We order our first drink. Arthur and Gil cut a pack of cards and play Hokitika swindle. Me and Ikey sing some of our favourite swing songs. A lot of couples come up to shout us a drink. And then another drink. Blackball people, if they have money, they just spend it, they don't believe in putting it away.

'It's a hard life, coalmining,' Arthur starts moaning.

'You're lucky the mine's nationalised now,' Gil says. 'You're better off working for the state than for a company, aren't you?'

'Well seeing you're a white collar worker,' says Arthur. 'The state exploits you as bad as us manual workers but you see everything from the point of view of the bastards running the show.'

I try to give Gil a hint not to say anything back. But he doesn't catch my eye. Or more likely doesn't want to catch my eye. So the both of them are soon droning on about wages and conditions and the working class. Arthur talks that sort of tripe whenever he's had enough beers. He never has a word to say that's worth hearing. He's basically dumb, Arthur. Miners go down the shaft in parties of four. One of the chaps needs to have a brain, to do the blasting. Two of the chaps, the hewers, don't need a brain. All they need is *brawn*, to hack into the coal. And – I don't know about the fourth chap. Anyway, Arthur's one of the two brawny jokers without a brain who do the hewing.

'You coalminers are among the best paid workers in the country,' Gil's saying. 'Clerks get nothing by your standards.'

Arthur won't let it go. He's like a dog with a bone when he talks coalmining.

'Clerks don't get poisoned by blackdamp when they work. Clerks don't have to watch out for firestink when they work. Clerks don't get coal dust in their lungs when they work. Clerks don't get trapped under middle muck or rock falls when they work. We've got jokers breaking their legs. We've got jokers breaking their spines. The rock falls in the Slant Dip got so bad a few months ago the bosses have stopped work in it for good.

Me and Ikey are singing that new song by Elvis Presley.

'That's alright, Mama,' we sing.

Chorus

money
a penny
my dreams
three coins in the fountain
diamonds and pearls
champagne
sables
satin
tale
king

a jury
fairy tales
chapel bells
a dime and a dollar
the finger of suspicion
a toy or a treasure?
the cuff of my shirt
spinning top
magic
evil
oil
black gold
a prize, a puppet
plaything
string

Stevan

Backyard. Bah-yah, bah-yah, bah-yoom, sh-boom, sh-boom, sh-boom. Word, word, word. Green grass green tree blue sky. Mummy Daddy John Alan Sissy Noel. Daddy no work today. Day dee-ay, dee-oody-oody-ay. Mummy sing. Hey nonny ding dong. Daddy smoke pipe. Mummy green eye. Ugly green eye. Pig eye. Mummy bad. Mummy magpie. Mummy magpie. Mummy magpie.

Ya-da-da, da-da-da, da-da-da-da.

John Alan make hut. Wood hut. John good. Black hair. Love. Good. John brown eye. Beautiful brown eye. Alan good. Freckle. Hold hand. Good.

Goo-dee, goo-dee, dee-oody-ooh.

Sissy read book. Sissy lots freckle. Sissy fierce.

Noel sleep. Noel bad baby. Ugly baby. Poos. Wizz. Bad baby

Lots block on grass. My block. Mine. Green block. Blue

block. Red block. Yellow block. Orange block. This green block Bimbo house. Bimbo bad boy. Hole in pants. Cock. This green block his house. This blue block other house. This yellow block other house. This orange block other house. This red block other house. *This* red block shop. *This* blue block other shop. This street. This other street. Blackball. Good. Lots house lots shop. Lots bush bracken fern tree gorse blackberry. Bimbo love bush bracken fern tree gorse blackberry.

Boom ba-doh, ba-doo, ba-doodle-ay, dee-oody-ooh, dee-ooh, ba-doh.

Bimbo bad. Cock. Hole in pants. Naughty boy. Dirty boy.

This green block Molly house.

Bimbo go Molly house.

Bimbo walk.

Word, word, word, word.

Sh-boom, sh-boom, hey nonny ding dong.

Street. Lots little stone. Puddle. Splash. Splash. Sun in sky. Blue sky. Ditch. Bee in ditch. Bimbo look. Bee buzz. Bimbo in ditch. Splash. Splash. Good.

Bimbo walk.

Bush tree gorse flower. Lots flower. Flower red yellow. Leaf spiky. Bimbo touch flower. Bimbo smell flower. Good. Bimbo see puddle. Splash. Splash. Good.

Bimbo walk.

Molly house far away. Far far away. Away across Congo. Across wide Missouri. A-roll, a-rolling. Aba daba daba daba daba daba dab. Swinging and singing. Muddy road ahead. Crooked road. Lonely road. Around corner. Bitterberry tree. Along footpath behind bush. Looking for Molly. Looking for Valerie. Secret love. Jezebel. Cheating heart.

Bimbo lonely.

Bimbo sing. Sad song.

Mummy magpie. Mummy magpie. Mummy magpie.

Cheating heart. Song love. Sad song. Hi-lili, hi-lili, hi-lo. Hi-lili, hi-lo. On top of old Smokey.

Molly house. Sun in sky. Molly kiss Bimbo. Bimbo smile. Molly love Bimbo. Bimbo love Molly. Erleen at shop. Bimbo sad. Molly make cocoa. Molly cut orange. Icing sugar. Bimbo eat icing sugar. Bimbo eat orange. Bimbo drink cocoa.

Bimbo happy.

Erleen back from shop.

Erleen smile. Erleen laugh. Erleen kiss Bimbo. Erleen squeeze Bimbo. Squeeze tight. Bimbo hurt. Erleen not squeeze tight. Bimbo happy. Erleen love Bimbo. Bimbo love Erleen. Erleen beautiful. Beautiful brown eye. Beautiful beautiful brown eye. Kiss. Kiss. Kiss. Hey nonny ding dong, alang alang alang.

Molly. Erleen. Molly.

Mummy.

Bimbo go home.

Bimbo walk. Street. Lots little stone. Puddle. Splash. Splash. Other street. Sun in sky. Ditch. Other street. Green tree green grass green bush green tree green bush. *Other* street. Other flower. Lots flower. Red yellow. Water in ditch. Splash. Splash. Splash. Good. Dee-oody-ooh.

Bimbo home.

Mummy cook in kitchen. Mummy hot. Mummy fierce. Lino. Stove. Coal. Hot. Fire. Smoke. Knife. Cut. Cut carrot. Cut spud.

Smack.

Cry.

Mummy why?

Cry. Cry. Cry. Cry.

Daddy why? Why Daddy? Mummy bad.

Bash bash bash. Bash bash bash. Bash bash bash bash.

NEW LAMPS FOR OLD

Valerie

My next baby, my sixth, is a boy. I'm in labour with him longer than with any of the others because he sort of stops halfway out. They tell me to bear down. And then they tell me not to bear down. And – and it gets all confusing. He takes quite a long time to come. Nothing's wrong when he does get out. He's strong and healthy.

We call him Ross.

After I come home with him from the maternity ward we get six weeks of rain. John and Alan are at school but the other kids are at home with me still. Lynne keeps giving me cheek. Stevan keeps bashing. Noel's playing up, too. One day I come across him holding a pillow over Ross. I give the rotten little twerp a couple of smart clips across the ear to give him something to cry about. I haven't got time to try to get those kids in line because I'm real busy. I've got Ross at the breast. And the washing's piling up. I seem to spend hours every day sweating over the washing. Bent over the wooden scrubbing board. Trying not to scrape my knuckles. Standing in front of the copper. Boiling clothes. Possing clothes. Mangling clothes.

Winding that bloody mangle.

Gil borrows the official car from the Mines Department. He drives to Greymouth and buys a brand new electric washing machine from Calder Mackay. We pay a pound down. The rest we'll have to pay off in instalments of two pound a fortnight. A van drops it at our gate next morning. It's what they call a Surgmaster. Gil says it's a good machine. It'll do us for years, he says.

And it'll need to. It's going to have to grind out *thousands* of loads.

So that's a help.

The only trouble is Ross has developed a sort of weeping in the joints. A rash of some kind. A rash that spreads all over his body. At the start the doctor thinks it's eczema. After a while he thinks it's not. He says I'll need to wash the baby's things with boiling water. Which means I'll have to go back to using the copper. So for weeks and weeks I have to get a fire going and fill the copper and boil up everything the baby wears every day. And I have to strip him off every morning. And I have to strip him off every midday. And I have to strip him off every night. And every time I strip him off I have to paint him with purple stuff from a squat little brown bottle.

Mercurochrome.

How do you even *say* it?

The label on the bottle starts turning purple too, from me slopping the stuff around. And then the purple blots turn into brown blots. I'm peering at the words on the label one day and notice that the purple stuff's thirty percent alcohol.

I wouldn't mind having a swig, I'm that browned off about housework.

And it doesn't help that we've shifted away from the Muirs. It's not that we're miles away. You just go a few hundred yards down Harper Street. And then you go round a couple of corners. And you're in Brodie Street. Molly and me still see a lot of one another. The kids are still up the road nearly every day being spoiled by her and Erleen. Stevan especially. A lot of days he spends more time at their house than he does in our house. All the same, it's not the way it was. I can't look out my window and see Molly. I really miss that. I miss looking up from my kitchen bench and looking through the glass and catching sight of Molly. Molly singing the latest hit songs while she sweeps out her porch. Molly bending down to give a bowl of milk to their cat. Molly catching sight of me and giving me a cheery wave.

I miss popping in to her kitchen for a brew, or her popping in to my kitchen for a brew.

There are times, if Gil's at the pub and late coming home, that I sit and brood.

He doesn't drink a *lot*. He's good that way. But he does like to take time over a drink. He'll sit sipping his beer. And then he'll sit sipping another beer. And he'll be chatting with the other chaps. At first, when we first come here, he only went to the pub one day a week. He went with the township policeman. The plod, as part of his job, drops in at the mine office of a Friday afternoon to run his eye over the list of men on the mine payroll. He's looking for any jokers who might have had a run-in with the law. After, him and Gil go for a drink. And that's alright. And the other day Gil got elected secretary of the rugby league club. Of a Sunday morning the club holds its committee meeting at one of the pubs. And that's alright too. But lately he's been going to the pub every day. He'll still only have two or three beers. And then he'll drift into the kitchen about seven o'clock, which –

Well, I'll have had the kids under my feet ever since I woke up in the morning.

I throw his tea into the oven, with a plate over it, to keep hot.

'How's my darling?' he'll say. 'Give us a kiss, sweetheart.'

'Get off me!'

He doesn't get drunk. He just gets tipsy. And when he's tipsy he gets merry. And when he's merry he's – he's revolting. He's all friendly. He's all lovey-dovey. He rubs my head, which I hate. And he talks.

He talks and talks.

'A man's a happy man who can come home to his bonny wee wifey and happy wee kiddies frisking and lisping and playing, yes he's a happy man, he's a man who's happy, a man happy with his lovely Val, his Valerie, yes, his Val-de-ri Val-de-ra Val-de-ri Val-de ha ha ha.'

I can't stand even *looking* at him when he's merry.

So when the kids are asleep I sit and brood. I brood about how my life hasn't moved on from when I was a kid myself. My old man at the pub. Mum waiting for him. Mum getting angry. Well, you've got to watch you don't talk yourself into seeing things too black. Gil's not really that bad. I can't say he's neglecting me and the kids. He's always a great help. We always do things together with the kids. But I do resent the drinking. I've had it with the drinking.

One thing that makes up for him being at the pub is Ikey. We're in and out of one another's houses all day.

One morning me and her are having a brew in the kitchen and looking at the coal burning in the range. The radio's on, like always. Patti Page is belting out *I Went to Your Wedding*. Me and Ikey are belting it out too.

And then she stops suddenly, Ikey.

'Have you ever wondered about why – you know – ,' she says. 'Patti Page – she's a woman, and – you know, she's singing about going with *another* woman?'

'She *is* isn't she? And come to think of it, no. I haven't wondered about it. What a dag!'

We listen to Patti.

She's come to a church to watch a wedding. She's in love with the bride. The bride's her sweetheart. And now the bride's going to swap vows with some man. Organ music. The bride comes down the aisle. She's gorgeous, of course, the bride. Patti's crying. The mum and dad are crying too. The bride's mum and dad. The bride's happy. Patti's happy that the bride's happy.

Patti's singing goodbye to her own happiness.

You're supposed to sort of see her as a man. You're meant to think that she's singing the song as a man, not as a woman. The thing is, though, she's *not* a man. She *is* a woman.

'It's not just a dag, it's – it's bloody – sexy.'

We look at one another.

She's right!

We start grinning.

'A lot of them do that,' says Ikey. 'I've noticed – listening to songs by women – I've noticed they do it quite a lot – a woman singing as though she's a man – a woman sexed up about another woman – as though she's like – '

'As though she's like Miss Crump back Phillipstown School,' I says, laughing. 'Her and her big *tweed* fanny.'

We're both laughing and snorting now.

'You won't hear a joker doing it, though,' says Ikey.

'You won't hear a joker doing what?' I says straight back.

'You won't hear a joker – I've noticed, listening to the hit songs – I've noticed he'll never do it – you won't hear a joker singing as though he's a woman sexed up about a joker.'

'Which if he is sexed up about a joker he won't waste time singing *songs*,' I says, laughing again. 'He'll just hoof it down the road and look in on Pansy Nixon.'

'Yeah, it's only women who're mugs enough to sit at home and not go down the road,' says Ikey.

'Yeah, all us mugs of women do is sit at home,' says me.

'Sit at home and sing songs,' says Ikey.

'And after the husband comes home drunk,' says me, 'all he wants is to get his bloody fingers down your pants.'

'Not if he's looked in on Pansy,' says Ikey.

'I don't mean the jokers who look in on Pansy,' I says, sniggering. 'I mean the joker who's come straight from the pub.'

'Oh, yeah,' sniggers back Ikey. 'He wants to get in your pants. Or he gives you a hiding.'

We look at one another.

'One bloody thing I'll say about Gil,' says me, 'he'd never try giving me a hiding.'

'Arthur wouldn't ever lift a hand to me either,' says Ikey.

'Yeah,' I says.

I say it quick, because I think he does, now and again.

Arthur, like. Arthur lifting a hand.

So that's me and Ikey.

And I don't just spend a lot of time chewing the fat with Ikey. I start seeing a bit of my sisters who live in Canterbury.

Bella's the first one to come over to visit us in Blackball. She comes with her kids and her husband Charley. He owns a motor parts business and makes a bit of money. Not a lot. They drive over the hill in a green van, the delivery van for their business. And they bring their two girls and two boys. And they stay for a few days.

'I love the West Coast!' says Bella when we've got the kids paddling in Blackball Creek. 'I love all the *green*!'

'Well seeing you just make a cameo appearance and don't live here,' I says.

Bella's a couple of years older than me. When we were kids she was my best friend in the family. She's skinny like Ikey. She's clever. She's quick with her wits. She's nervy. She talks fast. Well, we all talk fast in our family. But when Bella's excited by something she'll skip half her words. You have to guess what's missing to keep up. Mum's the same, actually. A woman living over the road from us in the old days said that Mum was the only person she knew who could keep three conversations going at the same time, with three different people, and never get a word wrong.

'And every one of those conversations is always scandal,' Bella said to me after our talk with that woman.

Anyway, as kids we got on good, me and Bella. We knocked around together all the time. We played together. We did jobs around the house together. We stuck up for one another. We were in and out of Mum's bad books together. We had the occasional fight. Only words, never serious. And now, when it comes to the end of her stay, I cry when her and Charley have the van packed up ready to head off back to Canterbury. Me and her don't hug. We don't kiss goodbye.

You'd get called *weak* if you did that in our family.

'We're coming back,' she says. 'We'll be coming over every year to this weedy rainy lichened straggle of weatherboards and beeches and coal and kids and hard cases you call Blackball.'

She loves books, Bella. She loves reading.

Her visit gets me thinking. I write to my next oldest sister, Bonk. She writes back saying I should come and stay with her for a week. We get it organised. I buy a ticket for the railcar. And soon I'm sitting on a red leather seat, all by myself, watching the creeks and the swamps and the bush flashing by. Well, all by myself except for Ross, who's plugged on to my tit.

We hit the Alps. We head into the railway tunnel. We burst out the other end.

Canterbury!

Yellow. Tussocky. And then the plains. Straight lines. Flat. Fenced. Tidy. Orderly. Canterbury seems sort of *wrong* after the wet green mess of the West Coast. But then we come to the suburbs. Bungalows. Streets and streets and streets of bungalows. Shops. Rows and rows of shops. And big buildings. Warehouses, wool stores, office blocks. You see wires and cables and masts and smokestacks. You hear traffic pounding. You see planes flying over the rooftops.

I feel like I've come back where I belong.

Bonk's waiting on the platform at the station in Moorhouse Avenue. She's dark and bony, Bonk. She's tall and moves quick. She's got very piercing blue eyes. Eunice is her real name but in our family she's always been Bonk. We get a taxi to Addington. Her and her kids and her husband live in a little dark house of red brick on a narrow street behind red brick shops off Lincoln Road.

As soon as we get out of the taxi and go inside the brick house we make a brew.

Other sisters come and see me while I'm staying with Bonk.

Betty's the first through the door. She's the oldest. She's got more money than any of us because her husband owns a shop. You can't fault Betty. She sews. She knits. She does all sorts of handywork. She wears twin sets. I'd love a twin set. She wears high-heeled shoes. And she's very generous, in a sort of patronising way.

'I feel beholden when I'm with her,' Bonk says.

'Me too,' I says. 'She makes me feel as though I've got nothing.'

We go and see our sister Lil, who lives in a flat on top of an office building in Cathedral Square. Lil's skinny. Her husband's a red-faced squat boozy little joker who's caretaker of the building. I don't enjoy myself much when I'm with those two. He's sort of horrible, I don't know why. And as for Lil, she never has a kind word to say about anybody.

'You going to look in on old Vinegar Tits?' she says.

She means Mum.

'After a brew or two with Dork,' I says.

Dork's harder to get hold of than the other sisters because she works fulltime in a factory. She's married to a labourer who was in the war and since then hasn't been right in the head.

'Dork needs to leave that sullen bastard but she never will,' I says to Bonk. 'And as long as she's cooking for him, and cleaning after him, and making excuses for him, he won't leave her till one of them drops dead.'

'He might string himself up when he's in one of his moods, so she mightn't have to wait too long,' says Bonk.

'She just doesn't have the guts to try anything new, Dork,' I says.

At the end of the week me and Bonk visit Mum. Mum sits at her scrubbed kitchen table with a brew, snarling. She moans about

Lil. She moans about Dork. She moans about how Betty dropped in the other day and offered to take her for a drive and how Mum said she didn't want to go for a drive and how Betty got bossy and told her she needs to get out and not sit at home all day. And how while all this was going on Betty was pacing backwards and forwards on high heels punching holes in the lino. Mum has an *aversion* to high heels.

'Yes, she's a fine lady, grinding those bloody stilettos into my lino!' she says.

Me and Bonk look at one another, then have to look away quick so we won't start giggling.

I don't see anything of my seven brothers, other than the youngest. Bruce is very easygoing. He's a taxi driver and in the killing season does a stint at the freezing works. The trouble with him is he keeps going on about his girlfriend, Shirley. He thinks she's the be all and the end all. He drones away about how she's kind, she's loving, she's good at sports. After listening for a while you start yawning. But he does take the trouble to talk to us, does Bruce.

My older brothers are too busy being rough and drinking.

And then the week is up and I'm climbing into another railcar and settling myself into another red leather seat. Bonk waves me off. I wave back. The railcar zips past warehouses and factories and suburbs and more suburbs and then we're out on the open plains, hedges and paddocks and plantations, sharp and bright. A glaring yellow sun sits high in a hard blue sky. After an hour we climb into the hills, spiky and tussocky. And after another hour, we're in the Alps.

We whoosh into the railway tunnel.

The tunnel's black as night.

I put Ross to the breast and give him a good feed and get him over my shoulder to bring up his wind. We whoosh out of the tunnel and we're in clouds, wet clouds, grey clouds. Rain streaks across the windows, pelts onto the railway tracks. I sit on the red

leather seat, bringing up the baby's wind. I look out at the wet slippery bush. I look out at the rushing steep creeks.
I look out at the swamps.

Chorus

life is but a dream
gypsies
baby clothes
suburban routine
the laundry, the milk
bottles and bibs, a cricket bat
king, queen, golden crown
government
law
deep in debt
boom-boomerang
boom boom boom boomerang
Hernando's Hideaway
olé!
Davy Crockett
pink Cadillac
Rio Grande
yellow rose of Texas
waving grains, grassy plains
barren waste, red as the setting sun
rivers flow to the sea
lonely rivers
the sea
the open sea
the rolling tide
sail the seven seas

Stevan

Bimbo's at home. Ho-ho-home. He's in lounge. Low-ow, ow-ow-ounge. He's lonely. Noel is in lounge. Noel's suck his thumb. Umb-umb-umb. Ross is asleep. Sissy is somewhere. Sissy's not in lounge.

It's raining. Very raining and raining.

Bimbo is lonely.

Lo-lo-lonely.

The adolts are busy.

Dad's at work. He works next door. In office. Bimbo misses Dad.

Mum's at home. But she's cooking. She's cooking meat. The house smells hot meat. Bimbo not like meat smell. He very not like meat. Meat smell is poos smell. And she's cooking spuds. Mum. And she's cooking pumpkin. Mum hates cooking. She's fierce. Mummy's a magpie.

Bimbo misses John. John's handsome. John's at school.

Alan's at school. Alan is strong.

Bimbo is lonely.

Raining, raining. Bimbo not allowed outside. Side-ide-ide. Wet outside. Eyed-eyed-eyed. Raining. Bimbo not allowed to go to Molly. Too wet to go to Molly. Molly-olly, olly-olly. Bimbo misses Molly. Away across Congo. Far away across wide Missouri. Bimbo very misses Molly. Molly's not a mad pie.

Molly's a good pie.

Bimbo explores house. How-how-how-how. Ow-ow-ouse.

Bimbo goes to bathroom. Looks at bath. Dead moth in bath. Bath moth. Moth-oth-oth. Poor moth. Beautiful brown eyes. Bimbo goes out bathroom.

Bimbo goes to Sissy's bedroom. Sissy's on bed. Sissy's got a book. Sissy's reading. Her hair is yellow. Her hair is all sticking up. Her head looks like a brush. She looks fierce.

'Go away!' says Sissy.

'Al*right*!' says Bimbo.

Bimbo, where you going go-e-o? Bimbo, Bimbo, what you going do-e-o?

Bimbo goes to big bedroom. Big bedroom empty. Bimbo goes to window. He sees green lawn. He sees green bush. He sees other green bush. He sees grey sky. He sees jungle wet with rain.

Bimbo loves wet with rain.

Bimbo goes to other bedroom. He looks at bunks. John and Alan sleep in bunks. Bunks shiny. Shiny brown paint. Shiny and brown like chocolate. The bunks are steal. Bimbo looks at word on bunks. Bimbo can't read word. The word is Vono. John says.

'What's Vono?'

'I don't know.'

'Why don't you know?'

'Vono's what the bunks are. Vono bunks.'

Voh-voh-voh-voh-no-no-oh-oh.

'Why?'

Bimbo looks at own bed. Own bed is wood. Own bed is little. Own bed has no word. Own bed lonely. Secret love. Bimbo goes to window. He sees green lawn. He sees green bush. He sees other green bush. He sees next-door house. He sees next-door house flowers. Yellow flowers. Red flowers. Blue flowers. Golden daffodils. Mockingbird Hill.

Bimbo is lonely.

Raining raining raining.

Bimbo goes in passage. Where is he going?

Bimbo goes to lounge. He looks at fireplace. Coal is cold black. Coal is burning bright. Coal is red hot. Red coal. Black coal. Burning smell. Black and red. Red and black. Bimbo feels sick. Bimbo loves coal fire. Bimbo hates coal fire.

Red. Black. Red.

Smoke goes up chimney.

Bimbo looks at side of fireplace. Square things. Tiles. Square tiles. Bimbo looks at top of fireplace. Square tiles. Square tiles what colour? Honey. Honey colour. Bimbo very likes honey. And round tile thing. Round brown tile thing. Round brown cup of cocoa. Bimbo very like cocoa. Molly. Sun. Cocoa sun. Cocoa sun in honey sky. Bimbo touches cocoa tile sun. Smooth. Bimbo touches square tiles. Smooth.

Bimbo very likes smooth.

Fireplace has silver stripes. One two three silver stripes on side. One two three silver stripes along top. Wings. Silver wings. Silver plane. Flying over ocean in silver plane. Silver wings flying over ocean into cocoa sun. Cocoa sun in honey sky.

On top of top is silver thing. Silver shelf. Silver shelf is a man two piece.

Mum says.

Mummy is a mad pie.

Bimbo gets book. Red gold book. He looks at story. Sinbad. Sinbad is baby camel. He's in desert. Desert far away. Far away across wide Missouri. Bimbo looks at other story. Aladdin. Aladdin is boy. Poor boy. He's in China. He's lonely. China far away. Away across Congo. Far away across wide Missouri. Magician is bad. Magician is scary.

'New lamps for old!' says Magician.

Bimbo shuts book.

Bimbo gets comic. Mickey Mouse. Mow-ow-ow. Mickey Mouse has big ears. Big black round ears. Mickey Mouse has black round nose. No-no-no-no-nose. Mickey Mouse wears big yellow shoeses. He lives in house. He has car. He has dog.

Why?

Bimbo gets other comic. Donald Duck. Duh-duh-duh. Donald Duck has a big beak. A big orange beak. Du-du-du-duck, uckety-uck-uck. He wears a blue hat. He wears a red bow. Bow-wow-wow. He wears a black jacket. He has a bare bum. Where's his cock? Donald Duck is naughty. Why? Donald Duck lives in house. He has car. He has no dog.

Why?

Bimbo goes in passage.

Bimbo can hear Mum. Mum's cooking in kitchen. Why? Mummy's a mad pie. Why? Dad's at work. Why? Dad's handsome. Beautiful brown eyes. Hey nonny ding dong. John's at school. Why? John's handsome. Beautiful brown eyes. Hey ding-a-ling long.

Bimbo standing alone.

Why?

Bimbo, Bimbo, where you go go-e-o, what you do do-e-o?

Valerie

Two or three little wooden boxes, scabbed with lichen and topped with wooden crosses, are scattered around Blackball. They're the churches. The Church of the Nativity is on a corner of Town Belt South. It's Anglican. It's got a wee tower with a bell hanging inside. A bell that used to be a ship bell. Or so they say. They say the ship sank years and years ago trying to cross the bar to the Grey. I think of the boy that drowned in the lagoon. You know, when Stevan was born. The little boy that drowned fishing for herrings. The Presbyterians have got a wooden box of their own. And there's another one for the Catholics. A lot of people here are Catholics, not like over the hill in Canterbury.

'It's a nark getting kids christened, what's the point?' says Ikey.

'As a kid I always felt ashamed we weren't christened,' I says. '*Proper* people get their kids christened.'

'Since when are we proper?' she says, laughing. 'Aren't we just half-pai?'

Mum rubbished religion. She said ministers and priests were dirty sneaks. One or two of my sisters and me went behind her back to the Salvation Army. We went a few times. We were sort of wondering what it was like, in a church. That was when we lived in Sydenham. And then when we shifted to Moorhouse Avenue we tried the Congregational chapel around the corner in Ferry Road. After a while I worked out that girls who came from the better off sort of family went to the Anglican church in Nursery Road. I started going. I wanted to get in good with those girls. They always seemed popular, that group. They didn't have brains, but they were popular. And there was a boy in the church choir who I thought was really nice. So I was trying to worm my way in with those girls and that boy.

It didn't work. Why would that boy and those girls want to talk to me anyway? So I stopped going to church.

'I was hoping you'd be their godmother,' I says to Ikey.

'Alright. What church?'

'Anglican. We got the first three done before we come to Blackball.'

Gil was christened Anglican. And he was confirmed Anglican. By a bishop! So it makes sense to christen our kids Anglican. Gil and his family don't call it Anglican. They call it Church of England.

'Oh, I say, toodle-pip,' says Ikey, laughing.

Sunday morning we all turn up at the Church of the Nativity. I've made new white shorts and new white shirts for Stevan and Noel. Ross is wearing a wee white outfit knitted for him by Ikey. It's a cold day. All three of the boys are feeling sick. Stevan and Noel drag their feet on the way. I push Ross in the pram. We get to the church, which is tiny, really tiny. I've just got Ross off to sleep. We go up the wooden steps and inside. Polished brass. Varnished wood. A dozen or so old women in hats and gloves sitting on benches with two or three old men. The vicar up the front talking to Pansy Nixon. The vicar's wearing one of those white frock things. Pansy's belly bulges under a baggy maroon cardigan.

'What's *he* doing here?' growls Arthur.

'He's the organist,' hisses Ikey.

We shuffle into a back bench with the boys. The vicar looks up and gives us a nod. Pansy goes over to the organ. He takes a deep breath, sits down, takes another deep breath, lifts his red mottled worker's hands and goes *bang*!

Ross wakes up and screams.

All the old women and men turn around and purse their lips. Pansy keeps playing. He's getting carried away. You can see his shoulders going up and down as he works.

'He never seems to meet your eye,' I said once in one of the pubs when people were talking about Pansy.

'Dirty sod needs a good belting,' said Arthur.

Arthur's not really the sort who'd belt anybody. The roughest he ever gets is elbowing Pansy. Or tripping him up. Or slapping him on the shoulder, hard. It's always just joking. Pansy knows that and smiles and takes off his glasses and wipes the lenses and keeps smiling.

Anyway, after we've sat for an hour or more with our bums going numb on the benches it's time for the christening. The vicar comes down the back. We stand up. We group ourselves around the font. The vicar starts with Stevan.

'People of God will you welcome this child and uphold him in his new life in Christ?'

'With the help of God, we will,' say the old men and women.

I see little red spots starting to pop up on the boys.

Chickenpox!

'Stevan Eldred Grigg, I baptise you in the name of the Father, and of the Son, and of the Holy Spirit. Amen.'

Stevan's face and hands are spotted all over by the time he's been done and the vicar reaches for Noel. And then Ross. After, Ikey and Arthur come back to our place with us. We have a cup of tea. We wrap our fangs round some goodies that I've rustled up. Ross is crying. Noel's crying. Stevan's crying. They'll be alright. Kids get over chickenpox. The older kids have had them already.

I feel nothing about the christening.

One more thing out of the way.

The house is less of a tornado these days. Lynne's in school at long last. Noel's no trouble, now. Mostly he just sits sucking his thumb. Stevan doesn't bash any more, thank god. He's turned into a quiet sort of kid. He spends hours and hours sitting on the floor of the lounge laying out coloured hankies on the mat. He lays out those blue and pink and green and yellow hankies in rows. He lays them out in squares. He lays them out in triangles. He lays them out in stars.

'I want to die,' he says while he's laying out those hankies, talking to himself.

He says it in this stubborn sort of way. You can tell he doesn't mean it. He's just narked because you've told him he can't have something, or that. Which is a bit of a laugh because of course he's just a little kid. He doesn't know anything about being alive. He doesn't know anything about being dead.

'What does it mean, being dead?' I says to him one day.

He looks up and furrows that little crease between his eyebrows.

'Nothing,' he says. 'Dead means nothing.'

So it's like I say, he doesn't know.

Other times, when he's not laying out the hankies, he's off on his own wandering around the township. And while he wanders he sings songs from the radio. Which can be a dag, too. He gets half the words wrong. One of his favourites is a song from a year or so ago, *Sippin' Soda*. A silly little song by Guy Williams. The song's about a girl sitting in a milk bar. She's sipping a soda. A chap comes up to her. He sings for a while. And then he sips soda with her. Obviously it's about sex but they can't say that on the radio. Anyway, for some reason that song keeps turning round and round like a stuck record inside Stevan's skull. The poor kid can't say the words right.

'Seppensola,' that's what he sings. 'Seppensola.'

Erleen keeps taking up the slack with him, which is a big help.

The both of them go together to the footy every Sunday. They walk, holding hands. Stevan gets the airing and she gets to watch the game and have a good gossip with the other girls. And eye up the boys. Stevan loves being with her so much that every weekday he bolts through his tea before her bus comes in from Greymouth. After he's had his pudding he's off like a shot.

Out the door. Down the road.

'I always know,' Erleen says to me one day, 'that when the bus takes the corner on Hilton Street he'll be standing under the veranda of the Miners Hall and soon as I'm down the steps he'll be flinging himself into my arms.'

'Let's know, won't you, if he's being a pest, Erleen?'

'He's never a pest, Mrs Grigg.'

'Well, we'll see if you're singing from that songbook when you've got kids of your own, Erleen.'

'I can't wait to have kiddies of my own!'

I start laughing out loud, which makes her look a bit hurt, but then she starts laughing too.

'It's good you were able to stay at school till you were fifteen,' I says. 'Thanks to that you've got a decent job and don't have to work in a factory.'

'How old were you when you left school, Mrs Grigg?'

'Thirteen.'

'Gosh. Mum too.'

Phillipstown School was my last school. A big sooty building of red brick with white stone columns. I still didn't have any confidence in myself but by that stage I was doing really good at my lessons. Miss Livingstone took me aside one day and told me I was coming first in her class by a long way. I knew I wasn't dumb. I would've loved to go on to high school. I thought high school could be the beginning of something.

'Why can't I stay at school?' I asked Mum one day, though I knew why.

'I need more money coming in,' she said. 'You've been a

deadweight in the family long enough.'

I felt terrified of going into the workforce. The nightmare of going into a factory. I visualised a factory as big rows of machines, and everybody bossing me. And that's how it turned out.

'Perry's need somebody,' said Dork.

'A girl?' said Mum.

'Yeah, they don't want to pay a boy's wage.'

Thomas Perry and Sons was a shoemaking outfit in FitzGerald Avenue. Dork was working there as a machinist. So next day she brought me along to the factory. Quite a modern factory. And they took me on. They gave me a machine to work. I had to sit at the machine all day. I hated it. All day, eight hours a day. Working this *juddering* machine in a room with about forty or fifty other girls and women.

Men were in the next room, the making room, where they put the shoes onto the lasts and that. There was about two hundred or three hundred of us workers at Perry's.

It really got me down, the factory.

The hard shiny machines.

The hard bright lights.

I was just a kid. I'd sit at my machine and my eyes would fill up with tears. I hated it.

I hated it for weeks and weeks and weeks.

And then I got used to it.

Erleen doesn't know her own luck. She's sitting pretty. She dresses up nice for her office work. She gets her hair permed regular. She can shell out to buy herself the odd bit or bob. And she's saving. She salts more than half her pay away.

A boy will be looming up on the horizon pretty soon. A boy with a glint in his eye. And when he does she won't be wanting to waste her time kissing and cuddling Stevan. She'll be wanting another kind of kissing and cuddling.

Chorus

let me go
lips that lie
let me be free
let me go, lover
free me from your spell
your come-hither glances
I've learnt the blues from you
you who left me standing
why do fools fall in love?
you've cut me deep
and made me weep
I can't sleep
from the first
I've been cursed
lonesome in the cold
my heart beats only for you
it's all my heart wants to do
please, dear, hear my plea
as a river flows forever to the sea
as waves wash forever on the shore
I'll love you forever more
I'll love you forever more
my eternal vow
my longing cry
love me or I'll die

Stevan

Bimbo is exploring. He's in the backyard. He's sitting on the washing basket. The washing basket is upside down. Bimbo's looking at a fly. The fly's head is bright green. The fly's body is orange. The fly's wings are shiny. The fly climbs on the back of a other fly. The other fly's head is bright green and the other fly's body is orange. The flies are friends.

Bimbo's got friends. Molly is his friend. Erleen is his friend.

The flies fly away.

Bimbo looks for a other fly. He sees no fly. He sees a spider. The spider is standing on a leaf on a bush. The spider's head is yellow. The spider's body is white with red speckles. It's pretty. Bimbo looks for a other spider. He sees no other spider. He looks for a other fly. He sees no other fly. Bimbo puts his hand down his pants. He plays with his cock. His cock feels nice. His cock feels warm. His cock feels soft. Bimbo likes it.

'Bimbo,' he sings. 'Bimbo, Bimbo.'

Rap rap rap rap!

Bimbo looks up. He sees Mum. She's in the washhouse. She's looking out the window. The glass is shiny. It's hard to see Mum's eyes because of it's shiny, the glass. I'll never love green eyes again. Mum's banging the glass. She's banging the glass with her knuckles. Why?

Mum stops banging the glass. She opens the window.

'Cut that out!' she yells.

Bimbo takes his hand out of his pants. He's a bad boy. He's naughty. With a hole in his pants. He stands up. He starts walking. He walks to the road. The road to the mine. The road is steep. Bimbo's walking. The sun is shining. The ferns are wet and the bushes are wet and the road is wet and the sky is blue. The jungle is wet with rain. Bimbo looks in the sky. He sees no silver plane. The mine is over there. Across the Congo. Far across the wide Missouri. Bimbo's walking. He comes to the men's huts.

The men's huts are scary.

The men's huts are little. The men in the huts are big. The men in the huts are strong. The men work in the mine. They dig coal. They tease little boys and laugh and swear and drink beer.

Bimbo shuts his eyes.

He walks one and two and three and four steps.

He opens his eyes. No men are looking. He shuts his eyes.

Bimbo's got big green eyes. He walks one and two and three and four steps. He's got a hole in his pants. He's naughty. He's got a bum. He's got a cock. Bimbo's a bad boy. He opens his eyes. No men are looking. He shuts his eyes. One and two and three and four steps.

Bimbo comes to the slag.

The slag is black. The slag is shiny and slippery. The slag is lots of black hills. Take me back to the black hills, the black hills of Dakota. Bimbo climbs up. He climbs up a slag hill. A black hill of Dakota. The slag is very shiny and very slippery. Bimbo nearly falls down. Bimbo climbs more. He sings a song.

'A love song is a sad song. I'm sitting at a window watching the rain, hi-lili, hi-lili, hi-lo.'

Bimbo sings a other song.

'I get that lonesome feeling. I'm miles away from home.'

Bimbo comes to the top. He's on top of the black slag. Bimbo looks down. He sees the men's huts. A man comes out of a hut. A man with ginger hair. The man sits down on a chair. A wooden chair in front of the hut. The man starts smoking. A scary man. Bimbo looks away. Bimbo looks up at the mine chimney. The chimney goes a mile high in the sky. The chimney is pouring out smoke. The chimney is dirty.

Bimbo looks down at the mine bins.

The bins are a big big building. The building is red and rust. The building is very very high. The building has one, two, three, four, five rows of windows. The bins are noisy. Bimbo listens to the bins. He listens to the bins go *boom*. He listens to the bins go *bang*.

Bimbo sings the song.

'I hear the voice of the Mister Mountains.'

Bimbo goes down the slag. He goes down the black hills of Dakota. Bimbo slides and slithers. He slithers and slides. At the bottom is the crawly pond. The crawly pond is a black mirror. A big black mirror. The crawly pond is very still and very deep and lots of crawlies live in the crawly pond. Crawlies are big pink spiders. Crawlies live in the pond. Big boys catch crawlies. They catch crawlies and cook them and eat them. Bimbo doesn't. Crawlies have nippers. The nippers are sharp. Crawlies are scary.

Bimbo looks in the black crawly pond.

Bimbo's lonely and lonely lonely.

He sings a other song.

Very lonely.

'Seppensola, seppensola, seppensola – '

Bimbo puts his hand down his pants. He plays with his cock. It feels nice. It's naughty. Bimbo takes his hand out of his pants. He picks up a slag. A black slag. He throws the black slag. The black slag falls in the crawly pond.

Plop.

Bimbo picks up another slag. He throws it.

Plop.

A bottle is in the pond. The bottle is a beer bottle. The bottle is floating.

The crawly pond is black and the slag is black and the sky is blue and the bottle is brown and you can see through the brown, the bottle is glass. Glass is easy to break. Why? Beer is brown and tea is brown and the slag is black and the crawly pond is black and the sky is blue and crawlies go red when you boil them in a billy like the big boys do and Bimbo is pink, his skin is pink, his skin isn't burning now, and his cock is pink and he's got big green eyes and –

A secret love.

Bimbo climbs up one more slag hill. He comes to the top. He looks down at the men's huts. He looks down at the railway. He sees a train at the station. Bimbo loves the station. He loves trains. Bimbo never went on a train. Bimbo wants to go on a train. He wants to go on a train to Otira and Hokitika and Ikamatua.

Bimbo wants to go far far across the wide Missouri.

Bimbo goes down the slag.

He goes down the black hills of Dakota.

Bimbo crosses the road. He goes to the station. The station is yellow. Yellow paint. The station roof is red. Red paint. And the signal box is red and yellow. The signal box is a little house. A little house with big windows. A little house high up. A house on posts. A man works in the signal box. The man has a black hat. Bimbo loves the signal box. Bimbo looks at the train on the tracks. The train is a engine and a wagon and a other wagon and a other wagon and a other wagon and a guard's van. The van is red. The van is a little house. A little house with wheels. A little house for the guard. The engine is black. Black and sooty. Black and greasy. The engine has got a chimney. A black chimney. The chimney is puffing. The chimney is puffing black smoke. The chimney is puffing white steam.

The engine goes hiss.

The engine goes whoo, whoo.

The wagons go clank and clank and clank.

A man is driving the engine. He's lucky. Bimbo wants to drive a engine when he grows up. Coal is in the engine. At the back. A man digs out the coal. He throws the coal in the engine. The coal man is dirty. The coal man is yelling words at the driving man. They're laughing. They look out two windows. Two round windows. Bimbo loves the two round windows.

He's singing the song.

'Seppensola, seppensola, seppensola through a straw.'

Bimbo goes away from the station. A lot of black coal lying on the ground. A lot of black slag lying on the ground. A lot of green ferns and green bushes and green bracken growing on the ground. A lot of puddles. Water puddles, with oil on top. The puddles are blue and green and purple. Bimbo looks up at the hills. The black hills of Dakota. The green hills of Blackball. High high hills. Green green hills. Trees and trees and trees. Bimbo loves the trees. He loves the green green hills of Blackball.

Bimbo's singing.

A secret love, secret inside his heart.

Bimbo looks down. He looks at the railway tracks. The railway tracks are beautiful. The tracks on the bottom are brown and rusty. The tracks on the top are blue and shiny. And oily.

Bimbo walks back up the road. The road is steep. The jungle is wet with rain. Bimbo comes to the men's huts. The man with ginger hair is sitting. He's talking to a other man. The other man is a dog. A black dog. A big black dog. No, he's not a dog. He's a tall man. A tall handsome man. A tall handsome man with black hair. A tall handsome man with black hair and golden skin and beautiful brown eyes. A tall handsome man holding a crib tin. A tall handsome man holding a shiny black helmet.

The man isn't a black dog he's Uncle Arthur.

'G'day Steve!' the man sings out.

Bimbo looks away. Bimbo feels funny. Uncle Arthur has got a big cock. A very very big cock. It's scary. It's exciting. Uncle Arthur calls it his worm. Why? Bimbo looks back at Uncle Arthur. Bimbo wants to talk to Uncle Arthur. He wants to laugh with Uncle Arthur.

'Hello,' says Bimbo.

Whispering.

Uncle Arthur smacks the other man on the back. The man with the ginger hair. A hard smack. The man with the ginger hair laughs. Uncle Arthur starts walking. He walks quick.

'On my way to the dog watch,' he says to Bimbo.

Bimbo knows about the dog watch. The dog watch is words for mine work. The miners say dog watch. The miners say other words for mine work. They say front shift. They say back shift. Bimbo looks at Uncle Arthur. Bimbo wants Uncle Arthur. Bimbo doesn't want Uncle Arthur. Bimbo wants to see the big worm. Uncle Arthur's big worm. Not one man in a hundred a poor boy can trust. Oh, they'll hug you and kiss you. But they'll tell you more lies than crossties on a railway. Or stars in the sky.

Bimbo shuts his eyes.

He walks one and two and three and four steps.

Bimbo opens his eyes. Uncle Arthur is walking away. Walking to the mine. The ginger hair man is looking. Bimbo shuts his eyes. He walks one and two and three and four steps. He's got a hole in his pants. He's got a bum. He's got a cock. He's got a worm.

Bimbo's naughty.

Valerie

One morning early in the spring I'm mangling a load of washing when I hear a knock on our back door.

'Cooeee, Mrs Grigg! Are you there?'

I open up and see two older women standing on the steps. One's the policeman's wife. A big fat hearty woman. The other one's Lizzie Taylor. Short and dumpy. Viciously black dyed hair. Oodles of makeup. Lizzie Taylor owns the fish and chip shop. And the hamburger bar.

'Oh, hello,' I says, smelling a plot.

'Mind if we come in for a wee chinwag?' says Lizzie Taylor.

A plot, too right. Her and the policeman's wife and a couple of others have just set up the Blackball Marching Association. All town's been talking about it. A team of girls are going to wear white pleated skirts and red tops. And they're going to start drilling. And they're going to go into competitions up and down the Coast. Lizzie Taylor's been elected president. Her and the policeman's wife want me to be secretary.

'Me?' I says. 'Why?'

'Well, Mrs Grigg, we're wanting a lady who's got a bit of a stake in the town,' says Lizzie Taylor, who can be really smarmy when she wants something, which she nearly always does, and then when your back's turned she'll strip it down to the spine with her tongue, 'and since your hubby's paymaster for the mine and that.'

I end up agreeing. Only because otherwise the township will think I've got tickets on myself. I'm not keen really. The women on the committee are mostly older. They take turns holding the meetings in their houses. I sit through the meetings. I take the minutes. Which is easy enough because all you have to do is listen and put everything down in neat handwriting. I get Gil to do the bookkeeping. Lizzie Taylor loves bossing the show. She's a real latey. She's lived in Blackball for years and years and years and if you want to know anything about anybody you just go to Lizzie Taylor. Nellie McGoogan's on the committee, too. She's another old boiler who's been knocking around Blackball for a million and one years. She takes on with other men, and –

Anyway, I get really bored with it. I only go to about half a dozen meetings then I tell them I'm throwing it in.

'Um, I'm sorry but I'm just too busy with my kids and that,' I says.

Lizzie Taylor doesn't try to talk me into staying.

Afterwards I wonder if it's because she thinks I wasn't doing a good job.

Marching girls always seem a bit stupid to me anyway. Tennis is what we like playing, me and Ikey. The township tennis courts are right at the back of our house in Harper Street. Tarseal courts. All cracked, mind you. The courts have gone to rack and ruin. Me and Ikey buy a tube of tennis balls and four tennis racquets on time payment at Calder Mackay.

'Love-love,' I sing out the first time the two of us give it a go.

Stevan and Noel sit watching, and so does Wendy. Ross is in the house sleeping in the cot. I'll hear him if he starts crying.

'Love-fifteen,' I sing out, because I'm not as good at it as Ikey.

Stevan starts singing to himself. He's singing that hit song

Bimbo. It's a joke song. A queer sort of song. A song about a little boy, a toddler, who loves lollies and girls. It's a song that feels a bit off. The words say that that even though the boy's just a toddler he's got a grownup mind. Listening to it, you think that he's wanting to get his fingers, which are sticky from all those lollies, down their pants. The girls' pants.

'Bimbo,' Stevan keeps singing. 'Bimbo, Bimbo.'

Noel's sucking his thumb. Wendy's picking weed flowers and making necklaces. Ross starts crying, but he'll be right for a while.

'Love-thirty.'

'Bimbo, Bimbo, Bimbo.'

All that spring and summer Ikey and me, and Gil and Arthur, spend hours on those weedy old courts banging away at those furry wee balls.

Chorus

see you later, alligator
ooooo wah, oooooo wah
ooooo wah, oooooo wah
castanets, silhouettes
you're a pretty chick
yes, you're a little hottie
umm-hm-hm, um-hm-hm-hm
whop bob be loo mah
be loo mah bam bom
your sloppy shirt
your clean blue jeans
your blonde peroxide hair
rocking hip by the jukebox
you sure ain't no square
razzle dazzle
you drive me crazy

ain't that a shame?
bom-bom-bom-bom
ba-ba-do-do-do
baby, let's play house
let me play house with you
hm-hm-hm-hm, hm-hm-hm-hm, hm-hm-hm-hm
baby, baby baby, b-b-b-b-b-b baby baby, baby
doo-wop, doo-doo-doo, doo-wop
you ain't no square cat
you're a hipster, you
crazy little mama
oh-oh-oh
do the mambo
dig that boogie beat
you always get that swing

Stevan

Molly puts down a brown teapot. The teapot is wearing a little jersey. The little jersey is red and green and brown and orange and a other red and a other green. The little jersey is bumpy. Molly knitted the little jersey. The spout of the teapot pokes out of the little jersey. The spout is smooth and shiny. Molly's wearing a red dress. A red dress with orange flowers. And she's wearing a orange cardy. Her eyes are shiny. She's laughing. The radio's playing. Molly's slapping the tabletop. She's slapping it and singing.

'Come on, Steve!' she says. 'Let's have a dance!'

'I don't know how to dance,' I say to Molly.

'Anyone can dance, Steve!' she says.

'Alright, I'm dancing.'

I wave my hands. I wiggle my bum. Molly's smiling. She bends down. She picks me up. She holds me. The radio is talking about soap. Molly tells the radio to hurry up and play a other song. The radio starts to play a other song. Molly says this is a good one for dancing. Molly starts singing. Molly starts dancing.

'Tapping down a street with rhythm in my shoes,' she sings, 'tapping away my blues, Mrs Tap Toe.'

Molly and me are dancing. Molly's big bosoms are warm. Molly's big bosoms are soft. Molly's face is happy. I see the brown teapot in its little jersey. I see the toffee tin on a shelf. Molly makes toffee. Toffee is sweet and brown and shiny. I'm happy. Molly is my darling. I'm dancing with my darling. Hand in hand we'll find love's promised land. She belongs to me. We're waltzing together to a dreamy melody. We're dancing the Tennessee waltz. Oh my darling we'll never change partners again. The sun peeps over the hill. Tra la la, tweedle dee dee dee. Bimbo, does your mummy know?

'Dance, Molly!' I say. 'Dance!'

Molly dances.

'Tap tap tap,' she sings, 'tapping away my blues, Mrs Tap Toe.'

Valerie

You need a car to get out and about on the Coast. We told Charley and Bella when they come over on their last visit that we really could do with one. Charley said he'd keep an eye out. One day he rings up the mine office and says he's found a Model A Ford selling for a hundred pound. He says he's looked it over and it's a good buy.

'What do you think, dear?' says Gil. 'Sounds like a bit of a bomb.'

'Charlie knows about cars, doesn't he?' I says.

'It's well over twenty years old.'

Gil grew up in a family where they always drove new cars. I

grew up in a family where nobody drove any kind of car, new or old. Anyway, we agree to buy the Ford. We arrange to pay Charley off in dribs and drabs by sending him ten pound every month from the family benefit, which is this state allowance you get if you're a mother. You get ten shillings a week for each kid. Gil goes to Christchurch by railcar to pick up the Ford. He takes John and Alan too. And then the three of them drive the car back over the Lewis Pass.

Gil's got this big grin on his face when him and the two boys swing around the corner from Hilton Street. The wheels make crunching sounds on the stones in Harper Street. We all come running out. The car's painted bottle green. And though it's old the chrome is shiny.

The kids are excited. I'm excited.

A car of our *own*!

Gil wants to take the kids out the next Saturday afternoon for a drive, but I've always made that my day to bake. The kids are running around, getting ready. Gil comes into the kitchen where I'm starting to sprinkle flour on the bench so I can roll out some dough.

'Are you really not coming with us for an outing?' he says.

'No, I've got to get on with my baking,' I says.

'Well you can stay here and bake if you like, but I'm taking the kids for a drive.'

Which makes me think again how I'm turning into Mum. Mum had all these *days* for doing things. One day for scrubbing. One day for baking. One day for stewing. One day for throwing her mats over the line and giving them a good beating.

I don't want to turn into Mum.

'Hold on, just give me time to put this dough away and cut us a few sandwiches.'

We drive down to the river flats. We turn onto the road to Moonlight. We go past old gold tailings. We cross a creek. We climb up again through black beech. We go past some more gold tailings. We go past green paddocks. We cross a creek. We go past a green swamp. We go past tall trees. Trees that are tall and straight. Dark green, nearly black. Trees sticking up from swamps. Quite a few of the trees look battered and wonky. Gil says farmers here on the Coast try to clear this sort of tree away to make new paddocks.

One of the tall trees has lost every branch on one side and nearly every branch on the other side. All that's left is a sort of tuft of branches at the top.

'It's a toothbrush tree!' Stevan says, all excited, I don't know why.

Gil says that you call these trees white pine even though they're not really pines. He says they belong to another tree family. I wouldn't know. And he says that they like growing in marshy land. So it's no wonder there's so many of them on the Coast.

'A *toothbrush* tree!' Stevan keeps saying.

We get to the turnoff for Moonlight.

Moonlight.

It's where Molly comes from. The valley is all lovely green forest and tea-coloured creeks. We park the car on river stones. We kick off our shoes. We light a fire in our tin camp stove. We put the billy on for a brew. And birds are singing. And the kids are stripping off and swimming. And I lie back on the smooth stones which sort of nudge me and make me feel good. The sun shoots rays through the trees. The kids are laughing and splashing.

'Beats baking, doesn't it?' says Gil.

'Hmf,' I says. 'You'd sing another song if I was the sort of housewife whose biscuit tins were always empty.'

After we've had the car for three or four months I decide I want to learn to drive. Gil's only free to drive of a weekend. And I've always got the kids. I want to be able to take them for the odd outing after school. And I want to be able to get myself easy in to the shops in Greymouth. Because it's such a nark to get a bus into

Greymouth and that.

'I'll be your driving teacher,' says Gil.

'Ta.'

The first lesson we drive up Hilton Street.

'Stop at that lamppost,' he says.

'Oh?' I says, because he showed me how to stop before we started, but I'm having trouble remembering.

He gets a bit toey.

'Throw out your anchor and stop!'

I take my feet off the clutch and the accelerator. And we're not going very fast anyway. So the car slows down and sort of coasts to a stop. The bumper bar hits the lamppost. Not very hard. A wee bit of a thump.

'If that lamppost had been a person you'd be in court on a charge of manslaughter,' says Gil.

'Well, it's not a person it's a bloody post and I why do they put the stupid things on the street when they could put them at the back of the footpaths?' I says.

Gil talks to me quietly. Which he's good at doing. And he gets me to back away from the post. And then we're off again down Hilton Street. I manage the bend where Hilton Street turns into Hart Street. And a right hand turn, though I forget the hand signal, when he tells me to swing into Stafford Street. We trundle along for a few hundred yards. We pass Ikey's house. We trundle along for another hundred yards.

'Now, do a U turn,' Gil says.

I break into a sweat. I start to swing the steering wheel. I don't swing it quick enough. The car rolls right off the road into a big clump of blackberry. I manage to stop. But the ground's sloping down towards a ditch. I've got to put on the hand brake.

Gil's laughing. I'm not laughing.

'Alright, now back out, darling,' he says.

'I can't bloody back out with the hand brake on.'

'Admittedly it's a bit of a trick, but just – '

'I can't do it,' I says.

'You can do it,' he says.

'I can't do it!'

'Just take it slowly and patiently.'

'*You* bloody drive the bloody car *yourself.*'

I lunge for the door handle. I throw the door open. I fling myself out. I shove my way through the blackberry. My arms and legs get scratched bad. I stump off towards Harper Street. Gil drives past me down Stafford Street. He waves as he goes by.

He's setting the table for tea by the time I get home.

The kids wonder why my arms and legs are bleeding. The radio's playing *Summertime in Heidelberg*. Mario Lanza. I can't stand Mario pansy Lanza. He sounds like treacle mixed with glue. And bullswool. Gil doesn't say anything about the ditch. He doesn't say anything about the blackberry. He's good, Gil. I tell the kids I'm bleeding because I was picking berries with Ikey. I get busy with the tea.

Gil gives me another driving lesson in the weekend.

And then more lessons.

And after a few weeks I'm taking the Ford out on my own. Soon, before you know it, I'm zooming backwards and forwards with a carload of kids between Blackball and Greymouth.

Chorus

bum bum bum bum bum bum bum bum
oh, yes, ahh ahh, ahh ahh, wop wop, wop wop wop
ahh, ahh, ahh ahh, wop wop, wop wop wop
hey, why not swing with me?
me-eee waa-ooh
aah ooh waa-ooh
ooh-ooh-ooh-ooh
woo-woo-woo-woo

rock-a-beatin' boogie
you make me rock to the rhythm
you make me shake to the rhythm
you make me jump!
you make me jive!
be alive!
roll, roll, roll
roll, roll, roll
rock, rock, rock
rock, rock, rock

Stevan

'Arithmetic just makes me sick,' says Dad. 'The figures never act the same, they're always so contrary.'

It's bedtime. We're in our bedroom. Dad and John and Alan and me and Noel. Noel's little so he's sleeping. John and Alan and me are awake. We're sitting on the bottom bunk. And Dad's sitting on the bottom bunk. The shiny brown steal bunk. The Vono bunk. Dad's reading us a story. A story in the red and gold book. Dad's in a dressing gown. The dressing gown is tartan. Red and brown tartan. John and Alan and me are in our pyjamas. John's pyjamas are yellow with brown cowboys. Alan's pyjamas are blue with red and green cars and trucks. My pyjamas are blue with brown bunny rabbits.

'What does contrary mean, Dad?' says John.

John always asks what contrary means, and Dad always tells him.

'Contrary means that a thing means one thing sometimes and other times means another thing. Or someone says one thing and means another thing. A good man isn't contrary.'

'Can a good boy be contrary?'

'Sometimes,' says Dad.

'Why?' I say.

Dad looks at me. He smells of beer. John and Alan and me smell of toothpaste. Our toothbrush is green, like the Toothbrush Tree on the way to Moonlight. We keep our toothbrush in a white cup in the bathroom. Mum brushes my teeth and she brushes Alan's teeth and she brushes Sissy's teeth and Noel's teeth. John's a big boy. He brushes his own teeth.

'A boy's learning and makes mistakes,' Dad says.

'Why?'

Dad pats my cheek. His hand is warm. His hand is big.

'Let's go back to the book,' he says, and starts reading, and then more reading and then more reading. 'The first is zero as you see, and then right down the line are one, two, three and four, five, six, then seven, eight and nine.'

I don't know what means a lot of the story. I don't know arithmetic. John knows arithmetic. Alan knows arithmetic. Arithmetic is at school. Dad knows lots and lots and lots of arithmetic. One time John asked him to count to a hundred. And he did. One and two and three and four and – and a hundred. And he knows lots and lots and lots of words. Mum doesn't know lots and lots and lots of words. Mum talks a lot. Dad doesn't talk a lot. Mum sings a lot. Dad can't sing.

'I can't hold a tune to save myself,' he said one day.

I don't know what that means.

'You're tone deaf, too right,' said Mum.

I don't know what that means.

'Did I tell you when I was at high school and the music master got to choosing the boys for the choir he picked me out and put me in the front row?' Dad said. 'I asked him why he'd chosen me and he explained that he wanted me in the front row because of my good looks and that I was under orders to mouth the songs but never actually sing.'

I don't know what hardly any of that means. I don't know what's a music master. I don't know what's a choir. I know Dad's good looking. I know he's got brown eyes. He's got beautiful, beautiful brown eyes. And John too. John's good looking. He's got beautiful, beautiful brown eyes. And Uncle Arthur too. Uncle Arthur's good looking. He's got beautiful, beautiful brown eyes. Mum doesn't. Mum's not good looking. Mum's ugly. Mummy's a mad pie. I'll never love green eyes again. Mad pie, mad pie, mad pie. Mad mad mad mad mad.

Dad's coming to the end of the story.

'And eight minus two make six, dear me, how fast the figures run!' he says. 'And now, just look, they've formed again and nine minus eight make one.'

Which I don't know what any of that means.

Dad tucks me into bed. My bed is warm and cosy. My pillow is fluffy. My blanket is scratchy. Dad tucks Alan into the top bunk of the Vono. He tucks John into the bottom bunk of the Vono.

'Nighty night, boys,' he says. 'See you in the morning.'

We won't see him in the morning. He works.

'Nighty night, Dad,' we say.

Adolts have to work. Why? I shut my eyes. I hear words. Lots and lots and lots of words. Aladdin. Erleen. You belong to me. Fly the ocean. Pyramids on the Nile. Sinbad. Across the wide Missouri. A silver plane. A jungle wet with rain. Donald Duck. Dancing with my darling. Waltzing together. Tennessee waltz. Molly. We won't change partners again. Dad. A love song sings of woe, ask me why I know. Red and gold book. I'm sitting at a window watching the rain, hi-lili, hi-lili, hi-lo. The sun peeps over the hill. Sunny Italy. Arthur. A false hearted lover will lead you to the grave. The grave will decay you, and turn you to dust. Ikey. Tra la la, tweedle dee dee dee. Whippoorwills on Mockingbird Hill. Mum. Mad pie. Blue moon. Blue moon. Blue moon. Where you going go-e-o? What you going do-e-o? Does your mummy know? Blackball. A secret love inside his heart. Moonlight.

A QUINCE IS A COUSIN

Valerie

It's a nark about our house in Harper Street that it doesn't have a veranda out the front or a porch out the back like the house in Brodie Street. I could do with at least a small porch because when it rains I have to hang my washing up on a clothes horse in front of the fireplace in the lounge. And of course it rains most days. And what with the kids getting their clothes muddy all the time you need to put at least two loads through the washing machine every day. So the clothes horse is sitting there permanent. And if the kids are in the lounge playing, they keep knocking it over.

'Get outside and play, yous kids!' I tell them, unless it's absolutely pouring.

Which is what they like doing anyway.

Getting outside to play.

Our yard isn't much of an attraction. It's just tufty coarse grass out the front, with a drainage ditch between the grass and the shingle street. And out the back it's more tufty coarse grass. We don't keep fowls in Harper Street. Nobody ever went to the trouble to build a fowl run here. Not like in Brodie Street. So we sold our chooks. Gil says it's not worth the cost and work to build a fowl run from scratch. He's not bothering with a vege garden anymore, either, even though in the other house he did his best trying to grow cabbage and carrots and peas and that. The soil's real poor in Blackball, he says. He says it's stony. And he says the rain leaches out the goodness. And he says there's lots of slugs. He says there's so many slugs because the weather's so wet. The slugs here are so bad they just eat everything you try to grow.

So there's no point, really, he says.

Sometimes I think it's because he wants to spend more time at the pub.

Anyway, even though our yard isn't anything to write home about – not that I do write home – the kids like getting out onto the grass. They like it even when they've got their nose in a book. They like to take their books outside and swap them with one another. The older kids can read now. And the younger kids look at the pictures and guess what the words are saying. And then they'll chuck the books down and start playing a game together. Or they'll go off and start wandering.

John calls it exploring.

A lot of the time I don't know where they go. I think they like hanging round the single men's huts. After mooching round the huts and pestering the single men my kids will slope off to the slag heaps. Apparently there's a pond between the heaps. Gil says rainwater must pool in the slag because it won't have any way of running out to the creeks. Crawfish, which the kids call crawlies, live in the pond. So everyone calls the slag pond the crawly pond. Our kids spend hours playing in the slag heaps. They slide on the slag. They throw chunks of slag into the pond. They race round the pond. The slide some more on the slag.

Well, they have a lot of fun but when they get home they're filthy.

So that's more washing and scrubbing for me to do. I stand each one of them in turn in the washhouse tub. I get out the scrubbing brush. I scour their knees.

'Oh, that hurts Mum,' they whinge.

'It'll hurt more if you don't bloody stand still.'

The smoke's getting me down too. I mean, I grew up under stink and smuts from the factory smokestacks and the gas works in South Christchurch. But at least you get a lot of sunshine in Canterbury. Here it's rain, rain, rain and smoke, smoke, smoke. The coal you get free from the mine comes so easy you end up burning it all year round. You burn coal for cooking. You burn coal to heat water for a bath. You burn coal to dry the washing. You burn coal just because you *can* burn coal without thinking about the cost.

And when you burn coal from the mines here it pours out this whitish yellowish sulphurous smoke.

'Goodness gracious me,' Gil says. 'When I was a boy back home in Canterbury we drove up I don't know how many avenues of oak trees leading to country homesteads while here we drive up and down avenues of smoke trees.'

I've never driven up an avenue of oak trees.

Am I ever going to see the world?

Chorus

a DC plane
flying in a TWA
the wayward wind
two different worlds
Sherwood Forest
French cuisine
boulevard
Italy
arrivederci Roma
non posso più contare
como dolce è questa serenata

Stevan

Tea today is sausages and mashed spuds and cabbage. I like cabbage. Mum cooks it in a big pot and when it turns soft and yellow she tips it into the colander and chops it up into little strings and then she mixes up the strings with white pepper and lots of butter. That's how she always does cabbage. So that's alright. But the mashed spuds are horrible and lumpy. It's because Mum doesn't like mashing spuds. She just mashes them for a little while and then she gets sick of it and she gives up. And the spuds have black bits in them too. Mum calls them the eyes. They don't look like eyes. They look like mouse poos. I know what mouse poos looks like because mice got into the flour bin one day. Mum had to throw all the flour away.

'Good money I'm turfing out because of those mice,' she said. 'Good bloody money.'

'Is there any such thing as bad bloody money?' Lynne said.

'Cut your cheek,' Mum said.

'Give me a bloody knife and I'll cut it.'

'*And* you bloody stop your bloody swearing.'

Anyway, the cabbage is alright but the spuds are horrible and the sausages are horrible too. Inside the sausages there's lots of chewy blobs. John says the blobs are called gristle. And there's not only those chewy blobs inside the sausages there's lot of little bits of hard sharp stuff. I think they're bits of bone. They look like the little bits left behind when a cup falls onto the floor and smashes and Mum sweeps it away but she doesn't sweep everything away and there's these wee tiny sharp bits of white broken cup, like tiny teeth, on the lino. Mouse teeth must look like those wee tiny sharp bits. But I don't know. I haven't looked inside a mouse's mouth. Mice run away too quick.

After the alright cabbage and the horrible spuds and the horrible sausages we have pudding. Which today is jelly. Lime jelly and custard. Lime jelly's alright but the best jelly is blackberry. Custard is alright. But tonight it's lumpy like the mashed spuds. It's lumpy because Mum can't be bothered stirring the custard on the stove till it's all smooth. She stirs it for a while, and then she starts doing something else at the bench or the sink.

Mum's always in a hurry when she's cooking. She doesn't like cooking, that's why.

'It's near enough,' she says.

After finishing my pudding I get down from the table and run out the door because I need to get to the dairy. I run into Harper Street. I get to the corner of Hilton Street. I start running down Hilton Street. It's a hot day. My bare feet feel nice and warm from the tarseal. Black blobs of melted tar start sticking to my feet. I like the feeling of the hot tar sticking to my feet. Away, far away, across the Congo, across the wide Missouri, you can see hills. The hills are sort of soft and blue and green with bush. Which is beautiful. And after the hills, even further away, you can see the tops of the Alps. Which are beautiful. The Alps are purple like blackberry jelly. Scoops of snow are sort of tucked into the Alps, too, but not many scoops because it's summer now.

I get to the dairy. I stop.

The street's quiet. All the shops are closed, except for the dairy. I can hear men laughing in a pub.

The bus will come in a while. I wish I could read clocks. I can't read clocks. A bird is singing. I can't see where it is. I look back up at the scoops of snow on the Alps. How long till the bus comes? I start hopping up and down on one foot. The bus is taking *ages*. I stop hopping.

I start counting.

'One and two and three and four and – seven – and – '

I stop counting. I start hopping up and down on the other foot. Hop, hop, hop, hop.

I kneel down on the ground to see if there's any insects. The ground is really dry. I can see tiny ants. I love ants. Ants build cities and the cities have tunnels and streets. I can see a quite big beetle. The beetle's sort of shiny dark green. It's walking across some moss. I stroke the moss. It's pretty, the moss. I like moss. Today it isn't soft and gentle like usually. It's dried out. It feels like flannels feel after Mum's pegged them out on the washing line and they go dry. And it's not the usual moss colour. It's that colour the adolts call fawn. Which is a sort of light brown like a baby deer. Or it's the colour of rust on an iron roof. Moss is usually the colour of lime jelly. But it isn't anything like lime jelly, moss, so why is it usually the *colour* of lime jelly?

I like jelly but I like moss a lot better than I like jelly.

A lady in a flowery green and yellow dress comes out of the dairy. She's smoking a cigarette. Her hair's twisted up in plastic rollers. The rollers are blue and red and purple. Her hair's the colour you call tow. She's holding a red string bag. You can see a packet of wine biscuits in the string bag. Aulsebrooks. I know that word. The packet is blue and red. And you can see a packet of tea in the string bag. Choysa. I know that word, too. The packet is red and yellow.

'G'day, Steve,' she says. 'You here waiting for Erleen?'

I don't know the lady's name but I've seen her lots of times. I've seen lots of ladies and men in the township with names I don't know.

'Yes,' I say.

'She knew you'd be waiting for her. She left a message at the dairy. She said to tell you today she's staying late in Greymouth. She's getting a lift home with her chap. She said to tell you not to wait for her here at the bus shed.'

'Oh.'

'Alright?'

'Yes.'

'And what do you say?'

'What?'

'You say thank you, that's what you say.'

'Oh. Thank you.'

The lady walks away in her flowery green and yellow dress. She's swinging her red string bag. She's sucking her cigarette. She didn't even ask me if I wanted a wine biscuit. She's a greedy guts, that lady. I feel bad. I don't feel bad because I want a wine biscuit. I don't really like wine biscuits. They're too sweet and they're too soft and they stick to the top of your mouth, inside. I feel bad because – I feel bad because I don't know why. And I feel stupid. I feel stupid because of the lady telling me to say thank you. I feel stupid because the people in the dairy knew why I was waiting.

I hate the people in the dairy. I hate the lady in the flowery dress with the cigarette and the red string bag.

I hate Erleen.

I turn away from the bus shed and I start walking along Hilton Street. I stop for a while to kneel down and look at some flowers. The flowers are on long green stalks. They grow out of green spiky leaves. The flowers are orange. A really *bright* orange. And inside they're yellow. Dad says the flowers are called something starting with mon but I don't know the word. Mon bree something. You see them all over the place right now. They die before the winter, Dad says. And then they come back to life again in the spring.

I wish I could die before the winter.

And I wish I didn't come back to life again in the spring.

Mashed spuds are horrible and mouse poos are horrible but mice are alright. Mice are interesting. And sausages with bits of broken bone and gristle are horrible. And Erleen's horrible and the lady in the flowery dress with the cigarette and the red string bag's horrible and Mum's horrible and Dad's horrible and – and –

I hear someone singing out.

'Hooray, Stevan!'

A lady singing out. I look up. I see our car going along the street. Mum's driving. She's the singing out lady. She's wearing a blue hat. Her head is big and red. Kids are in the car. John and Alan and Sissy. John's sitting in the front next to Mum. Alan and

Sissy are sitting in the back. Sissy sticks her head out of the window. She pokes out her tongue at me. Why? She hates me, that's why. I hate her. She's a bully, Sissy.

The car's gone now. It's gone round the bend in Hilton Street. Where's it going? Why aren't I in the car?

Why isn't Mum driving *me* somewhere?

I feel lonely. I feel bad.

I get home.

Dad's in the kitchen washing the tea dishes. He's wearing khaki shorts. I think he wore them in the war. I can see his long hairy legs. The hairs on his legs are black. Black and shiny. The skin on his legs is nice. It's the colour of wine biscuits, the skin on his legs. The hairs on his legs are *quite* nice. But they're sort of scary, too, the hairs. Dad doesn't say anything. He's too busy. He washes dishes different from how Mum washes dishes. Mum slams and bangs the dishes around. Dad's slow and careful. And after Dad's done the dishes there's no sticky food left on them. Not like when Mum does the dishes.

Noel and Ross are on the lino playing with the wooden blocks. Noel's stacking up some yellow blocks. Ross is sliding a blue block in and out between his lips.

'Dad?' I say,

He doesn't turn round to look at me, because of the dishes and being busy.

'Yes, Steve?' he says.

Dad always calls me Steve. Mum calls me Stevan.

'Where's Mum going in the car? You know, in the car with John and that?'

'They're on their way to Greymouth, Steve. They're going to see *The Man from Laramie*. Your mother was looking in the paper and saw in the adverts that they're showing *The Man from Laramie*. She suddenly made up her mind to go and see it, and take the older ones. So she rounded them up and slipped on a pair of gloves and popped a hat on her head and was off, pell-mell.

You know your mother.'

'Oh.'

He turns away from the sink. He looks down at me. His eyes are quiet and kind. Brown eyes. Beautiful beautiful brown eyes.

'Would you've liked to go yourself, Steve?'

'No.'

I go over to Noel. I look at his stupid stack of blocks. Why doesn't he make something interesting like a house or a city? All he does is stack one block on top of another block. And then another block on top of that block. One block and two blocks and three blocks and four blocks and five blocks and – too many blocks. Noel's stupid. Mum's stupid. Erleen's stupid.

I kick the stack with my bare foot. The blocks fall into a heap on the lino. A lot of yellow blocks. Noel doesn't cry. He starts sucking his thumb.

Stupid stupid bloody blocks.

Stupid stupid *stupid* bloody horrible horrible *horrible* world.

Valerie

'Val, come here and give us a love. We'll only be a couple of hours up the road, so it won't make hardly any difference between me and you. It's a bit further than Ikamatua but it's nowhere near as far as Inangahua. We'll be popping in on one another every fortnight or two, mark my word.'

I'm blubbing.

Molly gives me a hug. She's weeping, too.

The both of us are having a quick wee goodbye in private, in her kitchen. The others are out the front with the van. I don't want the kids and the neighbours to see me howling. Molly's making herself give me a crooked sort of smile. The crowsfeet crinkle round her eyes.

'I know,' I says. 'It's no distance now we've got the Ford.'

Muirs have bought a bit of a farm on the outskirts of Reefton. All their things have been cleared out of their house in Brodie Street. Now they're saying their goodbyes. Me and Molly take one last good look at one another. And then we wipe our eyes. And we head out to the street. A crowd of neighbours are standing around ready to wave them away. Erleen's running from group to group. She's crying and laughing. She stoops down to cuddle Stevan.

'Who's my special wee one?' she says.

He shakes her off.

'Don't *squeeze* me so tight, Erleen,' he says.

'Oh, sorry Steve,' she says. 'I'm going to miss you so much!'

I was worried he'd throw a paddy. But he seems alright. He didn't cry at all when he heard the news. I think the first he knew about it was when he was listening to me and Molly talking about it a few days ago. He didn't say anything. He didn't even look sad. Not surprising, really. Muirs haven't been seeing as much of him lately as they used to. You know, what with having to organise the shifting. Erleen has found herself that chap, too. She's been so busy with him the last few months that she hasn't had time to ooh and aah over some clingy boy always wanting to hang onto her skirts.

Well, he'll be turning four this spring. He'll be alright.

'Ta-ta, Mrs Grigg!' sings out Erleen.

'Ta-ta, Erleen.'

I fight to stop myself from blubbing again.

'Only a couple of hours up the road!' yells Molly. 'Don't forget, Val!'

'Keep the kettle filled and ready on the range, Molly!' I yell back. 'You'll be getting that sick of us dropping in on you at the farm you'll be wishing you shifted to Invercargill!'

And off they go.

And we walk back to Harper Street.

And the days go by. Kids. Cooking. Sweeping. Washing.

I really miss Molly. I feel like I'm sort of an orphan, now.

Molly was my second mother. A good mother, too. Loving. Not some cold cow. Not some shrivelled bitch inside a dark kitchen inside a dark rented dump on some poor street back in Christchurch. An old bitch who never even sends me letters, let alone coming over here to visit me and my kids.

I miss Erleen, too. With her gone we won't have anybody to babysit our kids. You know, of a night if somebody in the township throws a party. Or if you feel like popping out to the pub. Gil and me talk it over one day. We're shelling peas for tea. We're wondering whether to go out later to a do at the Miners Hall.

'Well, let's leave John in charge,' I says. 'He's old enough now to look after the other kids.'

'Do you think?' says Gil. 'He's not even eight yet.'

'The other kids always do what he says.'

And even if something did go wrong it wouldn't matter. The neighbours would soon know. And they'd sort it out. Or they'd get word to us. Or one of the kids could run and find us. A good thing about Blackball is you can get away from your kids for an hour or two without needing to worry. Nowhere's very far away.

'He's certainly very mature for his age,' Gil says. 'Perhaps a bit more mature than is healthy.'

'No, he's alright. He likes looking after things.'

Which he does. He's *always* been great with the kids. The little ones look up to him like he's a sort of prince. The older ones know he'll keep an eye out for them no matter what. Alan and him are bosom cobbers. They go off together a lot, John and Alan. They're usually knocking round with another boy, Patrick Molony. The kids call him Tiptruck. His father's an electrician working in the mine. One of the things John and Alan and Tiptruck like to do is follow the township water race up the hillside behind Harper Street. It's a wooden flue. Alongside it there's a rough track. It's quite a climb. I kit the boys out with sandwiches wrapped in newspaper and a bottle of coffee and chicory. The three of them scramble up the track. They make a beeline for what they seem to think is this special spot.

'It's great, Mum,' John says. 'It's green grass and toetoe – lots of green green grass, and lots and lots of toetoe.'

'What's so great about grass and toetoe?' I says.

'It's beautiful, Mum.'

'As beautiful as me?' I says, batting my piggy little eyelashes and grinning.

He laughs.

'I call it Shangri-La,' he says.

Which sort of makes me shiver like a goose has walked over my grave. I really loved that film *The Lost Horizon of Shangri-La*. I saw it when I was about John's age. And those two words. Shangri-La. Those two words spoken by a growing boy. A boy who's my son, my firstborn. Somehow it makes me feel old. And getting older. And getting nowhere slow. Which is what we used to say about our family. The Forbes family. When I was a kid. A family getting nowhere slow. I see myself here in my kitchen. I'm fat. I'm frowsy. I'm wearing one of my faded cotton dresses. I'm wearing sandshoes with splitting soles.

And somehow I see myself up there, too. You know, up on the hillside behind Harper Street. I see myself treading my way through the green green grass up there. I'm feeling tufts of toetoe brushing against my legs. My legs that are thick and red like ham hocks.

'Well now you're back see you don't get bits of toetoe all over my mats,' I says, because the boys like to cut and collect toetoe stalks to make into bows and arrows.

'Alright, Mum.'

'And see if you can't get Lynne to tag along with you one day.'

She spends far too much time under my feet, Lynne. Under my feet with her nose in a book. She seems to read every single sentence in the red and gold encyclopaedia. She goes right through from A to Z. She's still sleepwalking, too. It'll be night. Me and Gil will be having a last brew before going to bed. We'll hear bare feet pattering on the lino. We'll look up and see Lynne. She'll be in her cotton nighty. She'll have her eyes open but she won't be seeing us. She'll be wringing her hands. And she'll be talking in her sleep.

'Where's my tartan skirt I want to wear to school tomorrow?' she'll say. 'Where's my doll – what's happened to my doll?'

And she'll keep wringing her hands.

If you try talking to her, she doesn't hear. She doesn't know you're there. So one of us will get up. Gil, usually. He'll steer her back towards bed. She never remembers anything about it next morning. It doesn't seem to hurt her, the sleepwalking. So we've given up worrying about it. And about why.

A bigger nark is Stevan.

He's gone back to his bashing.

He sits on the couch in the lounge singing pop songs. And he rocks backwards and forwards. He rocks and rocks the way he did last year. And the year before last. And he bashes his head on the back of the padding. The padding covered with light brown cloth flecked all over with little flowers in green and gold. Which is getting worn and stringy, the padding. Worn and stringy with being thrashed by the kids. He gets on my nerves, Stevan. He rocks and he rocks. He bashes and he bashes. He sings and he sings.

And, now and then, he'll bloody blow his top.

He'll be rocking. Or he'll be looking at a book. Or he'll be peering close at plants or insects or that. Which he likes doing when he's not rocking. And then something will go wrong and –

A big paddy!

'I hate you!' he'll yell and shout at anybody who comes anywhere near. 'I *hate* you!'

And he'll biff toys around. Or he'll get a stick and smash down the plants he's just been admiring. And he'll glare at you like he'd like to kill you. He looks real fierce. Which is a bit of a dag. You can't help laughing. He doesn't know what a dope he looks when he's throwing a paddy. He takes himself so bloody serious when he's in one of those moods.

Chorus

Bimbo, Bimbo
does his mummy know?
where's he going to go-e-o?
what's he you going to do-e-o?

Stevan

Bimbo's bashing. He's on the couch in the lounge. He hates the couch in the lounge. The couch is stupid. The couch is ugly. The stupid ugly couch has pictures of ugly and stupid flowers on it. Bimbo hates flowers. Flowers are stupid and ugly. Erleen's stupid and ugly. Erleen's a mad pie. Molly's stupid and ugly. Molly's a mad pie. Mummy's a mad pie. Daddy's a mad pie. Daddy's mad. Mummy's mad. Molly's mad. Erleen's mad and ugly and stupid and stupid and ugly and mad.

Bimbo starts singing.

Once he had a secret love inside his heart. He told a glistening star, the way a dreamer will often do, how wondrous she was, how his dream had come true. If they'd love him half as much as he loves them, they wouldn't worry him half as much as they do. They're only good to him when there's no one else around.

Ugly stupid songs.

Bimbo, with a hole in his pants. He's only a little boy but he's got a grownup mind. Bimbo, Bimbo, what you going do-e-o?

Bimbo goes next door to say hello to the Wadsworths. The

Wadsworths are a nice family. The Wadsworths are friendly. The two big girls are in the kitchen. They're pretty. One of the big girls has a green ribbon tied round her ponytail. The other big girl wears a bright pink bow. They say hello to Bimbo. Mr Wadsworth isn't there. Bimbo thinks he's at work. Mrs Wadsworth isn't there. Bimbo thinks she's at the shops. On the table the two big girls have got a big flowery plate. The flowers on the plate are green and pink and blue. And on a big wooden board the two big girls have got lots and lots of pieces of sponge. Bimbo likes wood. Wood is warm and strong. Bimbo likes sponge. Sponge is soft and sweet . And on the table the two big girls have got one, two, three, four bowls. One bowl has brown stuff in it. One bowl has pink stuff in it. One, two bowls have in them tiny little pieces of coconut, like lots and lots of little maggots, which is called shredded coconut.

'What are you doing?' says Bimbo.

'We're making lamingtons. Want to help?'

'Alright.'

The big girl with the green ribbon helps Bimbo wash his hands. The big girl with the pink bow waits. She's smiling. And then the two big girls and Bimbo make the lamingtons. Bimbo picks up a piece of sponge and puts it in the bowl of brown stuff.

'That's chocolate,' says the big girl with the green ribbon. 'We made it with cocoa and sugar and water.'

'Oh.'

Bimbo turns his piece of sponge on one side, and on another side, and on another side, and on another side, and on another side. Now it's brown on all sides. Brown and sticky. He puts it in one of the bowls of coconut. He turns it on one side, and on another side, and on another side, and on another side, and on another side. Now it looks like a hedgehog.

Bimbo puts the hedgehog in the middle of the big flowery plate.

'Good work,' says the big girl with the green ribbon.

Bimbo feels happy.

'Can I do a pink one now?' he says.

'You can do a pink one and a green one and a purple one with polka dots, if you want,' says the big girl wearing the bright pink bow.

Bimbo knows he can't make a green one and a purple one with polka dots. The two big girls are laughing. Are they laughing at Bimbo? Bimbo feels bad. The big girl with the green ribbon sees that he feels bad. She stops laughing. She picks up a piece of sponge and gives it to Bimbo.

'Here, dip it in the cochineal paste,' she says.

'What's cochineal made of?' says Bimbo.

The big girl looks surprised.

'Blowed if I know,' she says. 'Pink powder you buy in a packet!'

The two big girls are laughing again. Bimbo feels bad again. Bimbo doesn't care. He puts his piece of sponge in the bowl of pink stuff. He turns the piece on one side, and on another side, and on another side, and on another side, and on another side. Now it's pink on all sides. Pink and sticky. He puts it in a bowl of coconut. He turns it on one side, and on another side, and on another side, and on another side, and on another side. Now it looks like a – like a – he doesn't know what it looks like a.

Bimbo puts it on the big flowery plate.

All the pieces of sponge are soon hedgehogs and he doesn't know what, and are on the big flowery plate. One of the big girls puts the big flowery plate in the fridge. And then the two big girls together take the bowls and the wooden board to the bench and they wash them in the sink. And they dry them. They're talking. They talk about songs. They talk about dances. Bimbo's just standing around. He's lonely. He likes being with the big girls. The big girls are nice girls.

They look at him sometimes, and then they look away.

One of the big girls goes outside. She comes back soon with a lettuce and some tomatoes. Mr Wadsworth grows lettuce and tomatoes and beans and peas and carrots in the backyard. The other big girl takes some cold meat from the fridge and puts it on the wooden board and starts to slice it.

'Mum and Dad will be home for tea soon,' she says. 'Your mum will be giving you your tea soon, won't she?'

'I don't know,' says Bimbo.

The two big girls look at each other. They start giggling.

Bimbo feels bad. Bimbo, with a hole in his pants.

'Cooee, girls!' sings out a lady. 'I'm back!'

The lady is Mrs Wadsworth. She's wearing a sun dress. She looks happy. She smiles at the girls. She smiles at Bimbo. She puts a brown paper bag on the bench. She takes a loaf of bread out of the bag. And she takes a pound of butter out of the bag. And she takes other things out of the bag. One of the big girls is making a lettuce salad. The other big girl has finished slicing the cold meat. She gets a tin of condensed milk from a cupboard. She gets a packet of mustard from the cupboard. She gets a bottle of vinegar from the cupboard.

Bimbo knows what she's doing. She's making salad dressing.

'Can I help you make the dressing?' says Bimbo.

The big girl opens her mouth to say something. Mrs Wadsworth says something instead. She's smiling.

'That's very nice of you,' she says. 'We'll manage by ourselves, though, thank you, Stevan.'

'He's been a great help with the lamingtons, Mum,' says one of the big girls.

They start giggling again.

'Alright, that's enough you two,' says Mrs Wadsworth. 'Get on with the salad and the dressing and I'll see to setting the table.'

Bimbo stands watching them making the salad and making the dressing and setting the table. He doesn't say anything to the big girls. He doesn't say anything to Mrs Wadsworth. They don't say anything to him. Bimbo feels bad. He sees a man in grey trousers and a brown jacket. Mr Wadsworth, that's who it is, he's standing in the back door and he throws his hat onto a wooden peg. And he grins. And the big girls kiss him. And Mrs Wadsworth kisses him. And he sees Bimbo. Bimbo's standing by a chair by the table.

Mr Wadsworth winks at Bimbo.

'Well, Mother,' he says, 'a man's hungry enough to eat a pit pony.'

Bimbo doesn't know what's a pit pony. He's too shy to ask.

'Well you'll be getting a green salad with your cold slices of pit pony,' says Mrs Wadsworth, laughing. 'A man needs roughage so he'll keep regular.'

Which is another thing Bimbo doesn't know what it means.

The two big girls carry the meat and the bread and the salad to the table. The table has one, two, three, four chairs. Mr Wadsworth sits on one chair. Mrs Wadsworth sits on one chair. The big girl with the green ribbon sits on one chair. The big girl wearing the bright pink bow goes to the safe to get a plate of butter. She puts the butter on the table. She goes to the last chair. Bimbo's standing by the chair. She lifts the chair up a bit. She shifts it so she can sit. She puts the pointy legs of the chair down on the floor. One of the pointy legs pokes into the end of Bimbo's foot. The big girl doesn't know. She sits down. The pointy leg digs harder into Bimbo's foot.

It's alright. Bimbo doesn't mind. He's wearing shoes. He has a hole in his pants. The leg of the chair doesn't hurt really.

Well, it hurts only a little bit.

Mrs Wadsworth starts to serve out the slices of meat and the bread and the salad. Bimbo's standing and watching. All the Wadsworths are quite quiet. They pick up their knives. They pick up their forks. Nobody looks at Bimbo. The big girl with the bright pink bow pushes her chair back a little bit. The pointy leg digs even harder into Bimbo's foot.

'Ow,' says Bimbo.

He only says it in a whisper but the big girl with the bright pink bow turns round to look at him. She looks worried. And then she looks down at his foot. She jumps up.

'Gosh, you should've said!' she says. 'Was it hurting you?'

'No, it was nice,' says Bimbo.

And when he says it he knows that it *was* nice. It was nice that it was hurting. It's nice to be with the Wadsworths. It's nice to be in a nice house with a nice family. But they don't believe it was nice, the Wadsworths. They all jump up. Mrs Wadsworth makes him take off his shoe. Mr Wadsworth kneels on the floor next to Bimbo. He looks at Bimbo's foot. He touches Bimbo's toes. He squeezes the toes. He does it gently.

'No pain when I do that, young soldier?' he says. 'No grief?'

'No,' says Bimbo.

Mrs Wadsworth puts a hand on Bimbo's shoulder. He looks at the hand. It has a gold ring. It's a red hand. It's a fat hand. It's a nice hand.

'I think I heard your mum calling you to your own tea, just now,' she says.

'I didn't hear nothing,' says Bimbo.

'Well, I'm sure she must be just about dishing it up,' says Mrs Wadsworth. 'You'd better nip off home now, quicksticks.'

'Oh.'

Bimbo doesn't want to go. He goes. Where's he going to go-e-o? Bimbo, with a hole in his pants. He walks across the Wadsworth backyard. He walks across our backyard. A false hearted lover will lead you to the grave and the grave will decay you and turn you to dust. Bimbo walks into the house. Mum doesn't look at him. She doesn't say anything to him. She's stirring a stew. It smells horrible. Meat and onions. Bimbo goes into the lounge. Sissy's there, reading one of the red and gold books. Noel's there, sucking his thumb. Bimbo sits down on the couch. He looks at the tiles on the side of the fire and on the top of the fire. The tiles aren't the colour of honey. They're the colour of meat and onion stew. Bimbo looks at the silver stripes. The silver stripes aren't silver wings, they aren't a silver plane flying into a cocoa sun. The silver stripes are streets. One and two and three silver streets go one way. One and two and three silver streets go another way.

A silver street crossing the wide Missouri?

A silver street to Reefton?

Bimbo starts bashing.

He hates the silver streets. He hates the stew. He hates lettuce salad and he hates slices of cold pit pony and he hates cochineal lamingtons and he hates chocolate lamingtons. He hates his stupid ugly family. He hates the ugly stupid Wadsworths. Mrs Wadsworth is a mad pie. Mr Wadsworth is a mad pie. The big girl with the green ribbon is a mad pie. The big girl with the bright pink bow is a mad pie. The Wadsworths are mad. Erleen's mad. Molly's mad. Mummy's mad. Daddy's mad.

Bash. Bash. Bash.

Bimbo starts singing.

A silver plane flying the ocean wet with rain. My loved one dancing the night of the Tennessee waltz. Bash. Bash. Bash. No arms will ease the ache within this heart. No lips will stop the tears that start. Bash. Bash. Bash. *Bash.* I'd never be blue if you'd only love me half as much as I've loved you. Bad. Bad. Bad. Bad. Bad. Blue moon, I'm standing alone with no love in my heart. You know who I'm here for. You hear me saying a prayer for someone I really could care for. Blue moon, blue moon, blue moon. Bash. Bash. Bash. *Bash. Bash. Bash.*

Valerie

'Things aren't looking too flash for coalmining,' says Ikey. 'The government isn't helping.'

'Oh?' I says.

'The government won't bring – you know – they say they

won't bring back the coal subsidy.'

'What coal subsidy?'

'The state coal subsidy – you know, the state used to pay a subsidy to keep the mines busy – and the union's been asking and asking for the government to bring it back.'

'Well the government was Labour those days, wasn't it? And now – '

'Yeah, now it's National – now it's a gang of bloody Tory – '

'Are they worried, the union?'

'Yeah. There's more and more idle days.'

Idle days mean the miners don't get full pay.

'Oh?'

'The mines are more than a million tons of coal down since five years or so ago.'

'Well, you'll be right. *You* won't go short.'

Arthur's still one of the best hewers in Blackball. And who cares about the bloody mines anyway? Gil can transfer easy from the Mines Department to some other state department. If things really do go wrong with coalmining. And it might be a good thing. I mean, how many more years are we going to stay over here on the Coast?

How have I ended up here, anyway?

And what about that dream of mine when me and my sisters were younger? You know, that dream about how one day I'd be living in a bungalow. A nice bungalow. A nice bungalow with a fridge and frilly curtains. In a nice suburb of Christchurch. That bungalow was something I was still dreaming about when I started work at Perry and Sons. I told myself I'd stick it out at the factory till I found some nice chap. And then he'd marry me. He'd marry me in a pretty old stone church. And we'd buy a nice lounge suite. And a nice dining suite. And a nice bedroom suite. And we'd live in that bungalow. And I'd stop working.

And I'd polish the suites.

And I'd be happy.

Well, I did my time as a shoe machinist. Which took three years. I got some girlfriends at the factory. Rose and Peggy. They were just working class, like me. We'd sit side by side at work. We'd sling off at one another over the thud and thump of the machines. We'd sing along to the hit songs. The songs playing on the squawking squealing loudspeakers slung from girders over our workshop. Factory bosses play the hits because they think it makes the workers happy. Which it does. And they think it keeps up the speed of work. Which workers do their best not to let it do.

Rose and Peggy and me learnt how to go slow.

Or we'd go quick and get our quota done for the day and then just sit playing cards.

The bosses didn't like it but they couldn't sack you because we had a strong union. And because it was the war. The war meant the bosses and the state set up this system they called manpowering. Which was a way to sort of lock us poor working sods into essential and semi-essential industry. Footwear was classed as semi-essential. So the bosses couldn't sack you. But you weren't allowed to swap your factory for another factory. You know, a factory where you might get better pay. You were tied to the factory like slaves were tied to the plantations in *Gone with the Wind*.

'Oh well, so what,' said Peggy. 'We'll be out of here like a shot when we find a man to marry.'

Anyway, we sang all day. And we talked about boys. And we talked about the latest pictures at the Savoy and at the Plaza and at the Crystal Palace. And we talked about the band rotunda on the banks of the Avon. We went to the rotunda of a Sunday night. We didn't go to listen to the band. We went to eye up the boys. And we talked about dancing. Jive. Jitterbug. Me and Rose and Peggy danced a lot. We danced at the Latimer and the Rendezvous and the Cally. We went to a dance every Saturday night. And sometimes we went of a Friday night. And usually we went one night during the week. The bands played numbers by Tommy

Dorsey and Glenn Miller and the Andrews Sisters.

Boogie Woogie. Blues in My Heart.

I went out with a lot of boys.

You'd meet them at a dance and they'd walk you home and stand outside at the gate with you. And then, if you liked them, you were hoping they'd ask you out again. But a lot of them didn't. And they used to lie, anyway. A lot of jokers were in the air force or the army or the navy. They'd give a go at kidding you. You know, doing their darnedest to talk up their rank.

'Oh, I'm a lieutenant in the army,' they'd say.

But you'd have to be a dope not to be able to read the markings on their uniforms. Anyway, me and my girlfriends would count ourselves lucky even to get a chap as high up as a sergeant. And right then I wasn't looking for rank. I was looking for sex. I was really keen to have sex. But I was a goof about it. I sort of knew what sex was. And I sort of didn't know.

'Let's walk through Hagley Park,' boys would say.

'Alright,' I'd say, but nothing ever happened to me in Hagley Park.

Or we'd go to Lancaster Park. Or the banks of the Avon. I was sitting by the river one night with a chap. He pointed to some people under the next tree who were having sex. But he didn't try anything on with me. I didn't know what to do. I wished I knew how to get chaps worked up. But I didn't. Actually when men first started cuddling and kissing me, I didn't respond very well. I just wasn't used to it. I didn't know how to handle it when some chap put his arm around me. I used to stiffen.

I felt as though I could do it to them. But I didn't want *them* doing it to *me*.

Norm, a boy I went out with for quite a while, was nice looking. He was a drinker, mind you. I did everything to seduce him. But it didn't work. So things sort of drifted. Ray, the next chap I saw a lot of, was an apprentice electrician. Which is a good trade. And he was nice looking too. He liked me a lot. I don't know why. If we went to a dance, he'd buy me flowers. And if we went to the pictures, he'd pay for two of the best seats. But he was so soppy.

'Your mother never need worry about me, Valerie,' he said one day. 'I'm an illegitimate child and I'd never do anything before marriage.'

I *wanted* to do something before marriage, like I say. So that was no good. And after a while I got a gutsful of him because he worshipped the ground I walked on. The next joker I went with was called Tony. He was in the army. He wasn't much to look at. I went home with him one night. I did it to spite Mum. Me and her, only the weekend before, we'd had a row. I'd got home from some party about four o'clock. And she was sitting up, waiting. She tore strips off me with her tongue, of course. And then for the whole of that week she wouldn't speak to me. She just looked my way now and then, glaring.

Anyway, after me and Tony come home from the pictures I sneaked him inside. And we sat on the ratty old couch we had in the kitchen. And he started groping. At first it was his fingers. And then it was something more. I was sort of making myself not think about it. I was just thinking about Mum. I was thinking about how I was showing Mum what was what.

He must have broken my hymen because all of a sudden I felt this excruciating pain.

'That's it!' I thought. 'I've done it!'

One of my other sisters come in, just then. So me and Tony didn't talk about what had happened. And after, when I went to bed, I was thinking, right, so I've tried sex and it's nothing.

I was quite mixed up about love and that.

Mixed up, like Mum.

'How's bubs?' says Ikey.

'She's good. Taking to the breast good.'

We're inside a square room in the maternity ward of the Grey Hospital. I'm in a cast iron bed. The new baby's sleeping in the nursery. Well, I suppose she's sleeping. The main thing is she's not bothering me right now. She's my seventh kid and we're calling her Jan. Gil wanted to call her Jan because his mother's middle name is Jane. You can't call a kid Jane in this day and age because it'd make her sound like some old spinster with cats. So she's Jan. Outside it's raining. It's raining because it's the Coast. It's raining even though this is summer. Me and Gil sent the four oldest kids over to Canterbury. They went over by train and they're staying with Eldred and Ellen. Ikey's looking after the other two kids.

'Heard from your in-laws?' Ikey says.

'Eldred rang Gil up the other day. He says the kids are good. He says they've been helping with the haymaking.'

'Corker.'

'I would've liked being a farmer's wife.'

'Yeah, but it'd be bloody *boring* – wouldn't it? Stuck on a farm – nobody to talk to – nobody except your *husband*!'

'I'd have loved it. I'd have loved living on a slap-up country place in Canterbury. Sheep and plantations and paddocks and that. And I'd have been good at it, I reckon. Gil's sisters-in-law are nice enough. Always very neat. You know, neatly dressed. And – but, well, you could stick them in a crowd and you'd forget about them. I reckon I'd have made a splash if I'd married a sheepfarmer.'

'Back to real life, have you still got the hump with Gil? I've still got the hump with Arthur.'

'I'm keeping him on edge. And just easing up on him in wee stages.'

Arthur and Gil gave us the hump only the other day. The day my pains started with the baby. We'd all had a morning swim in the creek at Moonlight. After the swim we had a brew and egg and tomato sandwiches at Harper Street. And I started to have a few pains. I reckoned there was plenty of time to go to the maternity ward later in the day. I told the others we didn't need to hurry.

Arthur and Gil wandered off down Hilton Street to have a beer at one of the pubs.

And five hours later they still weren't home, and the baby was pushing.

'We've got to get Gil so he can drive me to the Grey,' I told Ikey. 'I've got to go *now*.'

So poor old Ikey had to go down to the pub to get him out. And I mean – that's one thing she hates the idea of doing. And that's one thing I hate the idea of doing. To have to go and get a man out of the boozer. She was furious with Arthur. I was furious with Gil. And then off I went to the Grey.

'I better get going or I'll miss the bus back,' says Ikey.

'Alright. Ta-ta.'

'Ta-ta.'

After my fortnight in the maternity ward is up I get home with the new baby. I give her a feed. And when she's finished feeding I see that she's got this mark. A mark on her forehead. I look closer. It's a wee blister. I keep my eye on it over the next day or two. The blister gets bigger and grows into a sort of red ring. I take her down to the township doctor.

'Oh, she's got ringworm,' he says. 'She must have picked it up in the hospital.'

'Ew,' I says. 'A worm?'

'Actually in spite of the name it's not a worm, it's a fungus.'

He gives me an ointment. Which soon clears it up. But somehow that ringworm gets me down. I keep wondering what I'm doing here in bloody Blackball. I'm still in a bad mood with Gil. The bad mood goes on for another fortnight or so. It goes on right up to the afternoon of the running race between the miners here in Blackball and the miners up in Roa. It's a race they do every year. The runners kit themselves out in sandshoes and shorts. They meet in Roa. They scull a beer or two at the pub. Then they run down the valley to Blackball. It's a big event. Crowds of people come from all over the district to cheer the runners and to shop in Hilton Street.

'I'll do my morning shift, dear,' Gil says over breakfast. 'And then we can go out together as a family to welcome the runners and the kids can enjoy themselves with toffee apples and the lolly scramble.'

Well that sounds fair enough. I get my morning work done. I get myself tidy. I get the kids tidy. Ikey's here with her two girls.

We wait.

Gil doesn't turn up.

'We'll have to go without the bloody bastard,' I says to Ikey.

She's got her baby in a pram. I've got my baby in a pram. The pram wheels rattle on the shingle. Our other kids trail along with us. We stop outside the post office, which is a good spot to watch the running.

The runners come hoofing it along Hilton Street. We're watching. We're clapping.

And then, across the road, I catch sight of Gil. Him and three other chaps. They're standing at a pub window. They're carrying on and joking. They're laughing. They're boozed up to their eyebrows.

Gil looks across at me and Ikey.

He sees us but looks away.

I'm so angry.

'Right – I've *had* it!' I says to Ikey. 'I'm going to leave that prick.'

Chorus

shark
jack knife
millionaires
a trace of red
will I be rich?

the great pretender
the line forms on the right
my blue suede shoes
que será, será
cement bag
bop it!
rip it up!
cash
chain gang
go, cat, go!
do you dig it?
that groovy beat
a frantic little bopper
a jumping jukebox song
getting me hooked
buy now, pay later
work like a slave
working at a mill
bop till I pop
the cats go crazy
I dig that crazy beat
the beat, it sends me
strut your stuff
tear it up
the ooby-dooby
I'm hip to your jive
slippin' and a slidin'
boppin' the blues
hot-rod
go ape!
be cool, man
the rent comes due
lipstick and rubbersole shoes
that rock'n'roll feeling

jump, jive an' wail
a trip into space
bluejean bop
let's rock it!
let's bop!
diamonds
party doll
gold

Stevan

Dad drives us to Stillwater. He's going to buy us tickets for the night train. We're *going* on the night train. Me and John and Alan and Sissy. Me and Sissy have got one suitcase. John and Alan have got one suitcase. Inside the suitcases is everything. Pyjamas and shorts and undies and socks and everything. Exciting! I've never been on the night train. I've never been on a train. We're going to Canterbury. I can't wait. I've never been to Canterbury. Mum's made us egg sandwiches. And she's chopped up chives to mix in with the egg. I love egg and chive sandwiches. And she's made us tomato sandwiches, with butter and white pepper. I love tomato sandwiches with butter and white pepper.

Mum wrapped the sandwiches in old newspapers and then she put them in an old biscuit tin. They fit in the tin tight. The biscuit tin is red, and big. On the outside it's got words and pictures of lots of different sorts of biscuits. One of the words is Aulsebrooks.

'What do all the words on the tin say?' I asked John.

'Aulsebrooks Ritz assorted biscuits 14 packets,' he said.

'Oh,' I said. 'What does Ritz mean and what does assorted mean?'

'I don't know but when we get to Stillwater we can ask Dad. He'll know.'

John always helps me. He knows a lot. Dad knows even more.

Dad knows nearly everything. Mum doesn't. Mum's ugly and stupid. She's a mad pie. She makes good sandwiches.

It's nice driving to Stillwater. It's nighttime. I can't see anything only lights from other cars and I can see lights from farms and I can see lights from sawmills. I can't see stars because it's raining. The jungle's wet with rain. We're not going on a silver plane. We're going on a *train*! Raindrops are blowing on the car windows. Our wheels make splashes in rain puddles. Splish splish splash. I love the sound of splashes in rain puddles. I love rain. The car feels cosy. I like being in the car with the other big kids. I don't know if I like being in the car with Dad.

Dad's alright, he knows a lot and he's not a mad pie, but –

I don't want to think about Dad. So I think about other things. The train. The *night* train. Sandwiches. Ritz assorted biscuits. Splashing through the puddles. The exciting night. On our way to the train. The jungle wet with rain. The train! The night train to *Canterbury*!

I can't hardly breathe when we get to Stillwater.

The station is yellow and red like the station in Blackball. Only it's bigger. And it's all lights shining. Lights shining in the black rainy night. And lots of people. People standing on the platform under the lights. People with suitcases. People with coats. People with boxes and bags. People talking. People looking up at a big clock. People laughing.

Crowds of people.

Exciting!

'Travellers come down on the Westport train and change here for Christchurch,' says Dad.

Which I don't know what it means, but I can't ask. Dad's gone. He's gone to buy the tickets. John didn't ask Dad about assorted and about Ritz. He forgot probably. Anyway I don't really want to know. I still can't hardly breathe. John and us stand on the platform waiting. I look down at the railway tracks. The tracks on the bottom are brown and rusty, like in Blackball. The tracks on the top are blue and shiny, like in Blackball. But there's lots of tracks in Stillwater. Dad comes back with the tickets. He talks to John. He tells him to keep a good eye on us. John's nodding. Him and Dad talk for ages. Ages and ages.

Where's the train? When is the train *coming*?

And then it's coming.

A huge black engine and smoke pouring from its chimney and sparks flying into the black rainy sky. And big pink lights. And big blue lights. And then all the carriages. Red carriages. One carriage and two carriages and three carriages and four carriages and five carriages and – and inside the carriages, lots and lots of lights, yellow lights, and people looking out of the windows, the windows all streaky with rain, and the sound of the train, da-dack da-dack da-dack, and steam hissing, and wheels spinning, all oily and greasy and black, and the train going slower, and going slower, and going so slow it starts to stop. And then it's stopped. And steam's still hissing and hissing.

And doors in the carriages start banging open, and people are coming and people are going.

Dad walks over to one of the red carriages.

'Come on, kids,' he says. 'We'll pop you into this one.'

On the side of the red carriage is a big black circle. The circle is steal, I think. On the outside of the circle there's two yellow lines. And in the middle of the circle are yellow letters and numbers. I don't know what they say. And on the outside of the carriage is another big black circle. Which I think is steal too. And in the middle of that circle is just one number.

Two.

Other carriages have the same circle and the same number. Only one carriage has the same circle but a different number.

One.

'Dad, what's that two and that one for?' I say.

He doesn't answer me. He's busy. He's carrying our suitcases. John's holding the sandwich tin. Alan's holding nothing. Sissy's holding one of the red and gold books. I'm holding another one of the red and gold books. I know the red and gold books are called a long word that sounds like *in cycle pee dear* but I can't say the word because it's too hard, so I just say red and gold books.

'Dad?' I say again.

'Mm?' he says. 'Oh, that's the class of the carriage. You're in second class. That one up there is first class.'

Which I don't know what that means.

'Why?' I say.

Dad doesn't say anything. He's very too busy. He goes inside the carriage. John follows him, and then Alan, and then me, and then Sissy. The carriage inside is beautiful! All shiny varnished wood. And red seats. And a white roof. A curved white roof. A curved white roof with a row of all shining yellow lights. And brown nets hanging down where you put your bags and things. We get to the middle of the carriage. Dad tells us to sit on two of the red seats. He gets John to sit at the end of one seat by the window. He gets Alan to sit at the end of the other seat by the window. Sissy sits next to John. I sit next to Alan. Dad puts our suitcases in the brown nets. He stands between John and Alan and tells them about the window.

'Now, these brass catches are tricky,' he says. 'If you want to lift the window, or drop the window, you have to pinch each of the two catches together at the same time and if you don't keep your wits about you the window will slam down with its own weight, and mark my words that can be bad news for any stray fingers.'

John looks a bit scared.

'Can we just keep the window closed, Dad?' he says.

'I'd advise you to keep it open a trifle,' says Dad. 'Railway carriages get stuffy and it's wise to let in a little fresh air even if a bit of soot comes in from the smokestack.'

'Oh, alright,' says John.

'Tell you what, just leave it in this position and don't touch it anymore.'

'Alright.'

'The four of you will be bound to sleep most of the way, I dare say.'

Which I know I won't. I won't sleep *any* of the way. There's too much to look at inside the carriage. And there's too much to look at out the windows. And there's too much to listen to. The wheels. The engine. The tracks. I won't sleep until we get off the train in Canterbury.

Dad pats John on his shoulder. He doesn't pat Alan. He doesn't pat me. He does pat Sissy.

'Enjoy your holiday, kiddies,' he says.

'We will, Dad,' we all say.

Dad goes out of the carriage. He goes onto the platform. He stands under the lights. We hear a whistle. We hear the noise of the engine get noisier. And then it gets even noisier. And the train is moving! Dad slides away. He's not walking, he's still standing under the lights, and waving, but he slides away! And there's the sound of the wheels on the tracks, daaaaaaaaaa-dack, daaaaaa-dack, daaaa-dack, and lights going by, and houses, and sawmills, and bush, and we're on our way on the night train to Canterbury!

'Stupid train,' says Sissy.

We open the tin and we eat all the sandwiches. The conductor comes to clip our tickets. Alan starts snoring. Sissy starts snoring. *She*'s stupid, not the train. John starts snoring. I'm not snoring. I'm not sleeping. I'm staying awake all the way. I'm seeing everything. I'm hearing everything.

I wake up and it's day, well nearly day.

I look out the window.

I've never seen anything like what I see out the window. Flat paddocks. Flat paddocks and flat paddocks and flat paddocks. Miles and miles and miles of flat paddocks. And the paddocks are wrong. They're not green. They're fawn. And they're dry. And they're full of sheep. Thousands and thousands and thousands of sheep. Where's the green grass to feed all those thousands and thousands and thousands of sheep? And there aren't hardly any trees. Only trees in rows. Narrow rows, long and straight. They look like our playing blocks. Oblong blocks. Oblong wooden blocks. It looks like somebody's put oblong wooden blocks on the flat fawn paddocks and then painted the blocks dark green. The green's so dark it's nearly black.

So this is Canterbury.

Black blocks on flat fawn paddocks.

And sky. A big sky. A sky that's too big. A big dry empty sky. And the sun, a glary sun, slowly coming up over all those black blocks and flat fawn paddocks.

'It's ugly, Canterbury,' I say.

Only it looks sort of *rich*, too. The houses are bright and shiny. And the cars on the roads are bright and shiny. And there's no weeds in the paddocks. And there's no swamps. And there's no creeks. And there's no rushes. And there's no fern and no flax and no bracken and no blackberry. All you can see is cars and paddocks and sheep and those dark green trees in long straight rows.

'We better get ready,' says John. 'We're nearly at Rolleston.'

'What's so special about Rolleston?' says Sissy.

'It's where we get off the train,' says John.

'Why?' says Sissy.

John doesn't say anything. He climbs up on his seat and gets down one of the suitcases. Alan climbs up on the other seat and gets down the other suitcase. I'm starting to feel shy. I'm starting to feel scared. Pop and Nana are picking us up in Rolleston. Dad says we already know Pop and Nana. I don't know Pop and Nana. Mum says they're big cheeses, Pop and Nana.

I don't think they really are cheeses. I think they're old people with lots of money.

Rolleston turns out to be just a railway station in the middle of more of those flat fawn paddocks. A few people are standing on the platform. John points to a man wearing a dark grey hat and a dark grey suit. And he points to a lady wearing a dark red hat and a dark red jacket.

Dark red like dried blood.

'That's Pop and that's Nana,' says John.

'They look old and stupid and *old*,' says Sissy.

The train's clanking and the train's hissing. John and Alan and me and Sissy get down to the platform. The sun's beating down on us. Already it's hot, the sun's really hot. The man in the dark grey suit walks towards us. He's smiling. The lady in the dark red hat and dark red jacket sort of skips towards us. She's holding out her arms. And she's bending down towards us. And she's laughing. She's little and old and she's got brown eyes like Dad. Beautiful beautiful brown eyes.

I love her.

She's kissing Sissy. She's kissing John. She's kissing Alan. And she's coming towards me. Her face is all soft with powder . Her mouth's all red with lipstick, and – I feel frightened – and –

Smack smack.

She's kissing me.

And she's holding me tight.

Nobody ever kisses me. Nobody ever holds me tight. The only ones who ever hold me tight and kiss me are Erleen and Molly. And they don't hold me tight or kiss me anymore because they've gone across the Congo, they've gone far away across the wide Missouri. I don't know what to do. I want to laugh. I want to cry. I want to live forever with Nana. She takes my hand. Her hand feels warm and soft. She's wearing gloves. She takes Sissy by her other hand. She walks us over to Pop.

'All aboard for Ashburton?' he says.

We go round to a shiny car. A big shiny car. They *have* got lots of money. We get in the car. The seats smell like leather and cigarettes and flowers. Pop takes hold of the wheel. He's wearing gloves. He starts driving. He drives onto a long straight road. He starts speeding down the road. There's lots and lots of other cars on the road. So *many* cars! And they're all speeding. It's scary.

Pop tells us the name of a place we pass through.

'Burnham,' he says.

And then there's more paddocks. Flat paddocks and flat paddocks and flat paddocks. And then we pass through other places.

'Norwood.'

'Selwyn.'

'Dunsandel.'

'Bankside.'

We get to a long long straight bridge over a great big wide river. It's wider even than the Grey. It's a river nearly as wide as the sea, probably.

'Now we're entering the County,' says Nana.

I wish she was holding my hand again. Her voice is soft and lovely.

I know about the County. Dad's told us about the County. It's where he comes from. The County of Ashburton. Flat paddocks and flat paddocks and flat paddocks. Pop tells us the names of more places we pass through.

'Overdale,' he says.

And then comes Chertsey.

And after that comes Dromore.

'And now here comes the Borough,' says Nana. 'I'm sure you're more than ready for breakfast.'

I know about the Borough. It's a town in the middle of the County. I think it must be a bigger town even than Greymouth. It doesn't look like Greymouth. Greymouth's wet and sooty. And rusty. The Borough's clean and dry. And it's flat as flat. And the streets are straight as straight and as long as anything. And everything looks clean and bright. I think the town's got lots of money. Only the sun's too hot. We get to Nana's and Pop's house. It's a house that's *brand new*. It's in the middle of a lawn that's all smooth and flat. And the house is red brick. And it's got big shiny windows. And it's got a big white terrace, which is nearly half a circle.

And after the car's been parked you get onto the big white terrace by climbing big white steps.

And inside the house there's thick carpets on the floors. And the carpets are all smooth and flat too. And the couches and armchairs and bookshelves and chess set and tables and beds and silver and plates and pictures on the walls and – everything must have cost lots and lots and *lots* of money.

Nana says she's going to give us a picnic breakfast. She opens up two glass doors. And she runs outside onto the lawn. She's laughing. And she grabs hold of her dark red hat. And she spins the hat onto the grass. The way you see big boys spinning flat bits of slag into the crawly pond. And she grabs hold of her dark red jacket. And she throws the jacket onto the grass. She throws it the way toddlers chuck things. Toddlers don't think about where things will land. They just chuck. And so does Nana!

She's really happy.

'Jolly satisfying to slip that harness!' she says.

Which I don't know what it means. I feel good though. I feel so good it makes me shy. I look down at the grass. At her dark red jacket on the grass. The jacket lying all red and dark and crumpled on top of the soft neat green green grass. The jacket looks like dead skin. Like the skin of a dead dog. A dark red skin sort of yanked off a dead dog. Yanked off and gone all horrible and soft.

Gone all soft in the rain. Gone all wrinkly.

Uncle Arthur.

Nana scoots inside the house and when she comes back outside she's holding a big rug or blanket thing. And it's all green and red criss crosses. The rug. Or blanket. Anyway, you call it tartan. The criss crosses. Nana drops the rug on the grass. She spreads the rug out. And soon we're all spread out on the rug too. And we're all smiling. And there's lots of lovely food. And we're eating scrambled eggs and bacon and toast. And on our toast we're eating butter and honey. And we're eating butter and marmalade. And we're eating butter and rhubarb jam. And we're eating butter and blackcurrant jam.

And we're allowed as much as we want.

We spend the whole morning playing on the grass, and going for a walk to a big park. A beautiful park with big trees and lakes and that. We play in the park. And then we go back to the red brick house. And we have sandwiches and scones and glasses of milk. And then we run out through the glass doors onto the lawn. The dark red jacket isn't lying on the grass anymore. It's not lying there crumpled and dark and red on the green grass looking like the skin of a dead dog. Good. And us kids play some more on the grass. We play for hours. And then we have a lovely tea that Nana calls dinner. We have roast lamb. And we have cream poured on top of strawberries for pudding.

And then that night we all go to the pictures and we see a cartoon film called *Lady and the Tramp*.

'The story's not unlike Gilbert's,' I hear Pop whispering to Nana. 'Bitch and dog vice versa, needless to say.'

'Don't be naughty,' Nana whispers. 'She's far from a tramp.'

'Salt of the earth,' says Pop.

Which I don't know what it means, but I think it might be about Sissy. Sissy's being very good, though, with Nana and Pop. She doesn't give them any cheek. And she stands close to them a lot. I do too. I like Pop. He's got a big gold watch and it's on a big gold chain on his waistcoat. And I love Nana so much I can't hardly talk when she says anything to me. She doesn't mind if I don't talk. She smiles at me. She strokes my hair. She kisses me just for no reason. She tucks me into bed at night. I fall asleep wishing *she* was my mother, not Mum.

Mum's a mad pie.

'Pop's so famous there's a picture of him in the encyclopaedia,' says Sissy.

'I know,' I say.

'No you don't,' she says.

'Yes I do.'

'You show me where then. You show me his picture in the book.'

I take the red and gold book, the one she brought from Blackball. I start turning the pages. The red and gold books are big. They've got lots and lots of pictures. I see pictures of jewels and crowns. I see pictures of Boy Scout badges. I see a big map. You can fold it out. And then you can fold it up again. Sissy says it's a map of Canada. I see pictures of butterflies in the sunshine and comets in the sky at night. I see lots of pictures of China. I really like one of an old Chinese gentleman in a blue jacket and a purple skirt and a little blue hat. It's the sort of hat Mum calls a pillbox hat. The old gentleman's got a white moustache and he's wearing glasses and he's sitting on a wooden chair and he's reading.

The old gentleman looks like someone who knows a lot.

And he looks like someone who thinks a lot.

I like looking at him, but he's not Pop.

At last I find a picture in the red and gold book of an old man in a black suit standing in a garden. A brick wall is behind him. And he's got a gold chain on his waistcoat. And there's a lawn and flowers and that.

'There!' I say.

'It took you long enough,' says Sissy.

The next day we drive past flat paddocks and flat paddocks and flat paddocks to visit one of the family farms which is called Flatrock. It belongs to our Uncle Colan. He's handsome. He's Dad's brother. Pop says he's called Colan because that's the name of a village where our family used to live a hundred years ago. It's a village in England. Uncle Colan's married to our Aunty Rita. She's nice. And we meet our cousins, two girls and a boy. The boy is called Eldred. He's handsome. He's got beautiful beautiful brown eyes. We go to the woolshed. Uncle Colan gets us to stand against a wall. He measures us against the wall. He makes pencil marks on the wall. There's lots of other marks there, too, for our cousins.

It's good to have my mark on the wall with my cousins' marks.

And then we all play. And we eat lots of lovely food and drink lots of lovely soft drinks.

And the next day we drive past flat paddocks and flat paddocks and flat paddocks and visit another one of the family farms which is called I don't know what. It belongs to our Aunty Audrey. She's Dad's sister. She's nice but talks very posh and is a bit scary. Her house is big and new and red brick. Aunty Audrey's married to our Uncle Wilbur. He's nice and gentle and kind. And he takes me for a ride on a *tractor*. Which is exciting and scary. A tractor's nearly as good as a train.

A hawk flies above us in the sky.

We stay with Uncle Wilbur and Aunty Audrey for a few days.

And then another day we drive past flat paddocks and flat paddocks and flat paddocks and visit another one of the family farms, which is the special family farm, which is called Trevillick. Pop and Nana lived there till not long ago. Dad grew up at Trevillick. It's where everyone in his family grew up. The house is called a homestead. It's old and dark and around it there's a great big huge green lawn and around the lawn are great big huge *huge* trees.

We stay at the homestead for a few days.

Outside at the back of the homestead is a little house made of wood. It's like the single men's huts in Blackball. It's for men who work on Trevillick. One day when nobody's there I creep inside with Sissy. Sissy's giggling. I can smell dog. I can smell cock. I think about a black dog. A black dog with sharp white teeth and scary white and black eyes and he's covered all with black fur, with a black pelt, covered all over everywhere with black pelt, stiff black glossy pelt. Uncle Arthur. I look at the walls where there's lots of pictures of ladies wearing nothing. They've got big huge bosoms. Sissy asks me if I want to see her bosoms. I don't want to see her bosoms. I've seen her bosoms lots of times. They don't look like these ladies' bosoms.

'Who'd like to help with the haymaking?' says our uncle when we go back inside the homestead.

'Me!' says Sissy.

'Me!' I say.

We end up in a hot dusty paddock. A big machine is roaring away. It's painted shiny red. Men are working. It's exciting. I like the strong men in singlets and the hot dusty paddock and the big red roaring machine and I like the County. It's good, the County. Our uncle's not a mad pie he's a good pie. Pop's not a mad pie he's a good pie. Nana's a good pie. Nana's a lovely pie.

Hand in hand we'll find love's promised land.

But why is it so *dry*?

After days and days and days we're back on the platform at Rolleston.

'Now, chin up everyone, we mustn't cry,' says Nana.

She's already crying, though, and so's John and so's Alan and so's me and so's Sissy. Pop isn't crying. He's just standing there in a dark blue suit and he's smiling. I look out at the flat fawn paddocks. Canterbury's ugly. I wish there was bush and swamp. I wish there was rushes. I wish there was flax. I wish there was creeks. I wish there was bracken and blackberry. I wish there was *rain*. And I wish – but –

I don't know.

I don't want to go.

I want to be with Nana.

And now the train's coming already. It's hot on the platform. A huge black engine comes roaring into the station with smoke pouring from its chimney. And then all the red carriages, da-dack da-dack da-dack. And steam hissing. And wheels spinning. And – daaaa-dack, daaaaaa-dack, daaaaaaaaaa-dack. The train stops.

Doors bang open in the carriages. People come and people go. Nana bends down to kiss Sissy.

'Ew,' says Sissy, but crying.

Nana kisses John. She kisses Alan. She kisses me.

She's here before me, the only one my arms will ever hold. My heart's filling with gladness. I hear the birds in the treetops. Tra la la, tweedle dee dee dee. I feel such a thrill. I feel peace and goodwill. She's welcome as the flowers. I'm no longer alone without a dream in my heart, without a love of my own. John and Alan and me and Sissy go inside a carriage. John sits at the end of one seat by the window. Alan sits at the end of the other seat by the window. Sissy sits next to Alan. I sit next to John. We hear a whistle.

We hear the noise of the engine get noisier.

And then it gets noisier.

I look at the beautiful inside of the carriage. I look at the shiny varnished wood. I look at the red seats. I look at the curved white roof. I love being back on a train.

And now the train is moving!

Exciting!

Chorus

why do fools fall in love?
just walking in the rain
I'm lonely
alone and blue
in a world of my own
ooh-wah, ooh-wah
ooh-wah, ooh-wah
ooh-wah, ooh-wah
make believe
grieve

Valerie

I want to kill bloody Gil. I'm full of rage. I don't think I've ever felt so angry. He's my husband and he's stuck me with another baby and all he wants to do is get pissed and won't even stay at home and lend me a hand with his kids.

My mind keeps going back to our first night.

It was a summer night. The first summer after the end of the war. I'd just turned seventeen. Me and Peggy from the factory had gone to dance at the Argonaut. We'd been there for a while. We were hot and sweaty. Our makeup was streaking. Supper was over already. The band was playing. Piano and drums and sax. Couples were dancing. And then two men came in.

Peggy turned to me.

'See that chap over there, that tall dark chap?' she said. 'I'd love him to come and ask me for a dance.'

I looked at him. His hair was beautiful and black. He was wearing a sports coat. A tweedy one. And sports trousers. Peggy ogled him a bit. He started walking towards us.

'I knew if I gave him the go ahead he'd come over,' Peggy said.

But it was me, not her, he spoke to.

'Could I have this dance, please?'

I didn't say anything. I just stood up. We started to foxtrot. He talked about this and that. The dance. The band. The crowd. He turned out to be nice. Very polite. Very well spoken.

'I'm Gilbert,' he said. 'Gilbert Grigg.'

'Oh,' I said.

My brain was whirring.

'I'm Valerie Forbes,' I said. 'I'm a machinist in a factory.'

'Oh? I'm a clerk in a government department. Audit Department. I go to lectures at varsity in the evenings, studying accountancy.'

Which was double dutch to me. But I was feeling quite good

about him already. And he walked me home that night. He talked a lot while we were walking. He talked about all sorts of things. Not just rubbish like most chaps. He told me he came from a farming family. Which scared me a bit. I'd already nutted out that he wasn't working class. Now I had this sudden picture in my head of a big house in the country.

A snooty family.

Toffs!

'In the lambing season my mother brings the motherless lambs inside the house,' he said. 'She keeps them warm by the kitchen range.'

Which made me feel all sort of glowing and warm myself.

He asked me could he see me again later that day, Sunday.

'Alright,' I said.

And he came that afternoon. And we went for a walk. And soon we were seeing one other every second or third day. We went out walking. We went out dancing. We went to the pictures together of a Wednesday. And again of a Friday. He'd always pay. And he told me that he was happy to see me even if it meant he was missing classes at university.

'Accountancy is pretty straightforward,' he'd say. 'I can catch up for missed lectures by working from my textbooks.'

'All right,' I said, because to me it was still double dutch.

He seemed very loving. He held doors open for me. He pulled out the chair when we sat down at a table. He walked on the right side of the footpath as though I was a lady. He held my hand at the pictures. He hugged me. He kissed me softly. He said nice things. One night we were on our way to a dance at the Winter Gardens. We were with some others. We all got a taxi together. And the taxi was so full I had to sit on his lap.

'You look absolutely beautiful tonight,' he said. 'Do you realise I've fallen in love with you?'

Urgh, I thought. He was lying. I wasn't beautiful. I was just ordinary. I was fat.

'What are you after?' I said. 'What do you *want*?'

'Your love,' he said.

One other night, we'd been out at the Crystal Palace, and we were standing at the back door talking.

'I've got to tell you this,' he said. 'I've got to tell you because – because you probably won't want to see me again after I tell you.'

I felt sort of sick.

He's going to walk out on me, I thought. He's the first nice chap I've ever met and now he's going to walk out on me.

'Oh?' I said.

'I'm married.'

'Oh.'

'Well, separated. She started playing around with another man. I left her as soon as I found out but we're still legally married. I've filed for a divorce. The solicitor warned me that the red tape won't be snipped in a hurry. Are you still willing to keep seeing me?'

'Yeah.'

I think it made him seem even more glamorous. A married man. A married man filing for divorce. We started having sex not long after that. Our first time was on the scrappy old back lawn at the latest dump Mum was renting. We did it late one night. And it was good. I really enjoyed it. I didn't know what being in love meant. But I thought probably I was, with him.

'I'm very sorry about this, Val,' he said afterwards. 'This is never going to happen again until I get everything cleared up legally.'

But it did happen again, of course. And soon it was happening nearly every night we met. We went out together all through that year. And all the next year too. I found out I was pregnant. Gil said he was sorry. And he said he was very excited about it. I was sort of excited. And I was sort of scared. We decided we'd rent a flat. We'd live in together in that flat. And we'd have the baby.

And then, when his divorce come through, we'd organise a wedding.

Gil rung up his family to tell them the news.

Eldred hit the roof but soon cooled down and said we'd better come to stay with them for a weekend. You know, so I could meet everybody.

'Trevillick, our place is called,' said Gil. 'It's named after a property our ancestors used to own in England.'

Oh my god, I was thinking. It's a whole different world.

We went down by bus. And by the time we got out at Methven I was absolutely shaking with fright. Eldred met us in his car. He was wearing a suit. The car was big. I could hardly speak more than one or two strangled words. And then I *flung* myself inside the back seat. Eldred seemed so high above me, and –

And it was the same with Ellen.

'Welcome to Trevillick, dear,' she said, very small and upright, pecking the air near my cheek.

The house wasn't the mansion I'd been expecting. Only a villa. But everything was good. Good carpets. Good cabinets. Good china. Outside, a croquet turf for summer. And a skating pond for winter. And big trees. Trees so big they seemed monstrous. And everyone was really courteous. They talked about cousins. They talked about cricket. They talked about horses. They talked about wool prices. They talked some more about cricket. Amongst themselves they were very affectionate. Which I couldn't understand. Ellen kept kissing Gil. She called him sweetheart. She called him darling.

Words you wouldn't think they could hardly speak, let alone swallow.

Words that seemed to me to come too easy off their tongues.

That's false, them talking like that, I thought. They're just putting it on. People don't really behave like that.

I understood by then they weren't toffs.

'I know you've heard the Griggs are rich and have the royal

family to stay,' Gil said, 'but we're only distant cousins and don't mix socially.'

'Oh?'

'They belong to the first fifteen of the County. We're also-rans.'

'You went to high school, though, and you're going to varsity. That sounds like a toff.'

He was smiling.

'I went to Methven District High School. Not quite Christs College. High schools are like horses. Christs College is an Arab stallion. Methven District High is a farm hack.'

Which I didn't understand, of course.

'Well even if you're not a toff you're well off compared with us working serfs clocking in and out of a factory.'

It didn't worry me that he wasn't what I first thought he was. Actually it was a relief in lots of ways. It made everything more believable. It made me think me and him really did stand a good chance of being happy. I saw it all opening out ahead of us. He'd work as a clerk for a few more years. And then he'd be an accountant. And he'd earn money. Good money. He'd buy me my bungalow. He'd buy me good carpets, good cabinets, good china.

He'd drag me up out of the gutter and he'd set me down nice and comfy in the middle class.

And what's happening really? Why's he pigging it here in bloody Blackball?

He's dragging himself down into the *working* class!

Chorus

cry bitterly
it worries me
just walking in the rain
I want you, I need you, I love you

I shake my head in sorrow
my heart remembers you
you no longer love me
whatever will be, will be
just walking in the rain

Stevan

Mum's busy with the new baby. Rain's pouring down outside. The radio's playing. The new baby's crying. I'm in the lounge. I'm playing with the wooden blocks and some kindling wood. The rain's going splish splash splosh outside the lounge window.

Splish splash splosh trickle dribble gurgle.

I'm making the County.

Kindling wood is the fences. The fences for the flat fawn paddocks. Sheep are in the paddocks. Sheep made from shredded coconut and spit. I'm rolling the spit and coconut into little balls and I'm putting the little balls in the paddocks. I flogged the shredded coconut from a cupboard in the kitchen. The green blocks are for tree rows. You know, those funny rows of trees over there that *look* like blocks. I haven't got enough green blocks so I'm using all the black blocks too. The red blocks are for the red brick houses. One big block is for the homestead at Trevillick. Other blocks are for the men's hut and the woolshed and that.

Oh, yes I'm just a pretender, pretending I'm doing alright. I need you so much I pretend we'll touch –

The rain sounds lovely.

Gurgle dribble trickle –

The rain starts stopping. The rain stops.

'Get outside and play in the fresh air, yous kids!' sings out Mum.

I pack all the blocks into their bag, which is a brown string bag. I hold onto the string bag tight. I run into the front yard. The sun's started shining. The yard is all wet. I run over the grass in my bare feet. It feels lovely. Wet and green and lovely. And then I run down to the front ditch. I love playing in the ditch. The walls of the ditch are all soft and green and mossy. A lot of different greens. Apple green and pea green and green like blackberry leaves and – and I don't know the names of all the greens. And the walls aren't just mossy. You can see little plants that look like stars. Green stars. And plants that look like tiny tussocks. Green tussocks. And other things. And water's running along the bottom of the ditch where there's soft brown mud and lots of little stones and the stones are orange and green and grey and purple and rust. And everything's going drip drip drip drop, plip plip plip plop.

I kneel down and I tip all the blocks out of the string bag and onto the wet grass.

'The ditch is Blackball Creek,' I say.

I put blocks in a row on the grass a little bit back from the edge of the ditch.

'These are the shops on Hilton Street,' I say.

I put more blocks in another row, which is the houses on Stafford Street. I put more blocks in another row, which is the houses on Brodie Street. I make more rows of blocks for other streets. I stand up and survey all my kingdom. After that, I put one block on the other side of the ditch. That block's where Molly lives, across the Congo, far away across the wide Missouri.

I start singing.

'Away across the Congo sang a happy chimpanzee.'

I go back inside to get some toy soldiers. The soldiers are blue plastic. They're tiny. There's hundreds and hundreds. They belong to John. I go outside again to the ditch. I put one of the toy soldiers next to one of the wooden blocks. That block is the Mines Department. The soldier is Dad. I put another soldier next to one of the other blocks. That's Mum inside our house. I put one more soldier next to one of the other blocks. That's John at school. I put other soldiers on the streets between the rows of blocks. That's ladies going to the shops, and shopkeepers, and men in the pubs, and lots of other people.

The sun after rainfall shines over the hill. I feel such a thrill. I feel peace and goodwill.

I go around to the wooden block on the other side of the ditch. I put down three plastic soldiers. One of the soldiers is Molly, who's baking scones. And one of the soldiers is Erleen, who's squeezing me tight. And the other soldier is Jack, who's holding a toffee tin and shaking it. And they're far away, across the Congo, far across the wide Missouri.

I stand up again. I survey all my kingdom while everything's still.

Tra la la, tweedle dee dee dee.

I love the wooden blocks.

I feel such a thrill.

Valerie

The rot started to set in not long after Gil and me we first shacked up together. Which was in a dirty dump near New Brighton. Mum did a war dance when the both of us faced up to her and told her I was pregnant.

'How many *other* people know?' was the first thing she said.

'Nobody, Mum,' I said, sort of sulky.

'Well *get* down to the registry office quicksticks! And you needn't look at *me* to pay your bloody marriage fee!'

Gil explained about how he was already married.

'Well that's a *fine* kettle of fish!' said Mum.

After getting our ears bent back a bit longer while she ranted and raved, me and Gil looked for a flat. The trouble was, there was a bad shortage of housing. We ended up renting just a room. We had to share the kitchen and toilet and that. And when we asked where the bathroom was we found out that the bath was filled up with coal. The house belonged to a real rough family with five kids. The husband was big and beery. He used to beat up the oldest girl. I think the wife had that girl to another man before getting married. The wife yelled and screamed and swore and cursed. She slapped the kids. She was a proper fishwife. I felt horrible for those kids. And I felt horrible for myself. And I felt horrible for our baby. Gil was away at work all day, and of a night he had his lectures, so I just sat in our room and knitted.

I cried, too. I cried a lot.

Bonk got us out of that dive when she told us we could come and stay with her and her husband in a house they rented in St Albans. Roy's a wiry, ratty, hardworking chap. He was on a night shift in a rubber factory. Me and Bonk got on good. She had a little boy, and a little baby girl.

Our baby was born in the middle of that spring.

John, we called him, like I say. When the nurse first brought him in to put him to the breast I thought, what an *ugly* thing I've produced! His skin was sort of yellowy. And he had *masses* of black hair. Gil was quite hurt when I said the baby was ugly.

'Oh!' he said. 'He's beautiful!'

I got used to the baby after a few more days. Breastfeeding was easy. Lying around in bed being looked after by nurses was easy too. John started to look more like a human being. Three weeks after I went into the nursing home he didn't look ugly, he was nice looking.

'This baby, he's a handsome little Kiwi,' a nurse said. 'He'll make the birds sit up in their nests.'

I just looked at her and didn't say anything.

Bonk was good with John. Her own little boy was a mongol. She must have felt bad about that. She never said. And her baby girl was a lot of trouble, crying and crying. The poor kid had really bad eczema. So I think John, to Bonk, was the perfect baby. She even took the trouble of dressing him up and putting him in baby shows. The first time she did that was at a fair at Linwood

Park, on Labour Day. John won a little silver mug.

But then, somewhere along the way, things went sour.

Roy started saying snaky things. Bonk started flying into rages. She'd go white with fury. She'd storm through the rooms. She'd swear. She'd get so beside herself that I never knew what she was saying half the time. I didn't know why things were going wrong.

'It's not *you*,' she said to Gil one day. 'It's *her*.'

So it was time to go.

Gil and me found a room in Phillipstown. The house was old and rickety. The room next to ours was rented by a woman with black hair cut short and a clip shoved in the side. She had a baby. Her name was Mrs Olley. Well, she *called* herself Mrs Olley. No sign of a Mr Olley. The room opposite us was rented by some people we never saw. And out in the backyard was an old railway carriage. A chap lived in that by himself. He was about fifty and drunk a lot.

We dreaded it when John woke up in the night and started crying because Mrs Olley would bang on the wall.

'Stop that kid crying!' she'd yell out.

Nasty bloody bitch she was, that so-called Mrs Olley.

The divorce come through when I was pregnant again. Gil wanted us to sort out a wedding. I was lukewarm about it. Mainly because I knew I'd have to go and buy myself something to *wear*. Which I couldn't be bothered doing. And we'd have to do paperwork. And we'd have to go and hang around for an hour or more in a registry office. And the whole to-do would cost us *quids*.

'I can't be bothered,' I said. 'I can't be bothered with things like that.'

'My family would like it,' Gil said. 'They'd like you to become another Mrs Grigg.'

'Well bully for them.'

Anyway, in the end me and Gil caught the tram to the registry office in Hereford Street. I wore my best. A bluey-green linen suit that I got on time payment from Hays. Gil was wearing a pinstriped navy blue suit. We got off the tram opposite the post office. We walked up a big marble staircase. We stood in front of the registrar. A clerk at the registry was our witness.

'Do you, Valerie Rita Forbes, take this man, Gilbert Eldred Grigg,' the registrar said, 'to love, honour and obey.'

I said I did but secretly I was jibbing at that word *obey*.

I wasn't going to *obey* anybody.

The new baby was well on the way when we shifted from Phillipstown to Brooklands. We weren't keen on living all the way out there, twelve miles from town. But we saw an ad for a bach. And we decided to take it on because otherwise we couldn't get anything. The bach was bitsy. A bloke had knocked it together out of fibrolite and corrugated iron. And it was just plonked down in a sort of wilderness of sand. A few pine trees poked up into the sky. You could hear the sea when there was an easterly. You could hear lots of birds, too. Magpies and oystercatchers and gulls and that.

Cows let out the odd moo from a paddock.

And that was Brooklands.

Gil had to get up real early on weekdays to bike all the way into town, to work. He'd come home knocked out. All he wanted to do after tea was play with John. So he stopped going to varsity. Which didn't bother me because I didn't really know why he'd been going anyway. I cooked and cleaned and looked after John.

And it wasn't long before I had the new baby, Alan.

And then Alan was a year old and I was pregnant with Lynne.

And then I had her, and then she was a year old and I was pregnant with Stevan.

And now here I am trapped with seven bloody kids inside a rented bloody mines house on a puddly dirt bloody road in smoky sooty seedy shiftless hopeless boring weedy muddy bloody Blackball!

Chorus

please, please, please
don't be cruel
my heart's still true
did I make you mad?
was it something I said?
it's just you I'm thinking of
I love you truly, cross my heart
I want no other love
please don't go
I love you so
my faithful heart
I'm sad and blue
trying to get to you
holding someone new
lay down your arms and surrender to mine
I've got you under my skin
I can't ever win
the tender trap
giddy up a ding dong
giddy up a ding dong
the flame in my heart has died
I'm alone with a broken heart
ying tong ying tong
ying tong ying tong

Stevan

John sticks the black coal shovel into the black coal scuttle. His black hair is shiny. You can look at his hair and see lots and lots of little streaks of shininess. The shininess comes from the yellow light of a glass bulb screwed into a plastic white thing inside a plastic white hat at the end of a twisted brown cord. The twisted brown cord and the plastic white hat and the yellow glass bulb all hang down together from the middle of the lounge ceiling.

And the shininess in his shining black shiny hair comes from hot red coal burning bright.

White and red shininess make two dots in his brown eyes, too.

The lounge is hot.

I love John.

Mum and Dad are out for the night. They went to a party. Aunty Ikey and Uncle Arthur and lots of other adolts are at the party. A party is where you drink and dance and sing. You do it at night. I don't know why. John's holding the coal shovel in his left hand. He's lefthanded. I am too. So's Mum. Dad isn't. Dad does everything with his right hand. All the people in his family do everything with their right hand, he says. A lot of the people in Mum's family are lefthanded. Well that's what she says. And she says lefthanded people are different from righthanded people. She says lefthanded people are queer people. I think Dad thinks that's a silly thing to say. He just laughs when she says about being lefthanded

John digs up a shovelful of coal. He swings around to the fireplace.

He turfs the coal onto the fire.

The fire crackles and hisses and spits. A piece of coal rolls down to the hearth, which is tiles. It's red hot, the piece of coal. John scoops it up with the coal shovel. He turfs it back into the fire. You can see tiny pictures of John in the silver stripes on the fireplace. The silver stripes like silver wings. Silver wings flying over a honey sky. A silver plane flying into a cocoa sun. The silver wings of the silver plane are like little mirrors, that's why. And if you look hard at the silver wings you can see everything. You can see Sissy. She's reading one of the red and gold books. You can see Noel. He's doing a jigsaw. He's bending right down over it. And you can see Alan. He's just mucking round with a footy ball. You can't see the little kids because they're not in the lounge, they're sleeping.

John looks very serious.

'You're in charge,' Mum said to him before her and Dad went out. 'Watch they behave themselves.'

'Alright, Mum.'

John's sitting with me and helping me read one of the red and gold books. We're sitting on the mat. The book's between us. John points at one, two, three, four, five, six coloured pictures on one page. The other page is just black and white pictures and lots and lots of tiny words. We don't look at the page of tiny words. We look at the coloured page. One, two, three of the pictures are white flowers with little bristly yellow things in the middle of the white. And one other picture is an apple. A red apple. And one other picture is a pear. The pear's sort of yellow and sort of red speckly. And one other picture is an I don't know what. A thing that's a bit yellow and a bit sort of greeny.

'What's that?' I ask John.

'The book says it's a quince,' he says.

'Oh. What's a quince? Why's it on this page?'

'I don't know what. I don't know why. Hang on, I'll read about it.'

John starts reading. I wait. I feel good. I feel happy. I love it when John helps me with things. He looks like Dad. I wish Dad was here too. I rock a bit. I keep looking at the coloured page. At the top of the coloured page there's one, two, three, four, five six big black words. I know the first one of the words. It's the word *the*. And at the bottom of the coloured page there's lots and lots of tiny little black words.

'Oh, yes I'm just a pretender,' I start singing, 'pretending I'm doing alright.'

John straightens up.

'A quince is a cousin of apples and pears,' he says.

'A *cousin*?' I say. 'You mean like Wendy's our cousin and

our cousins in the County are our cousins?'

'Yeah, kind of.'

'How can a fruit have cousins?'

'Well you could say relatives if you don't want to say cousins. That's what those words say.'

He's pointing to the top of the coloured page. He's pointing to the six big black words.

'What do they say?'

'The apple and its close relatives, that's what they say.'

We talk about it for a while. John tells me about the little words at the bottom of the page. He says they say that apples and pears and quinces are close relatives. And the little words say they belong to the rose family.

'The *rose* family?'

'Look!' he says.

He turns the page over and we see six coloured pictures on one page and six coloured pictures on another page. And there's more pictures of flowers and more pictures of fruit. And then he turns the page and there's another six coloured pictures. And three of the pictures are of flowers and three of the pictures are of fruit. I know some of the fruit. Plums. Redcurrants. Blackberries. John says the other fruits are peaches and apricots and cherries and grapes and raspberries and strawberries. He reads the little words at the bottom of the pages. He says they say that plums and blackberries and peaches and apricots and cherries and raspberries and strawberries all belong to the rose family.

'What about the redcurrants and the grapes?' I say.

'They don't belong to the rose family.'

'Why are they on these pages?'

'It says something about why but I can't understand what it says.'

'Oh.'

We think for a while about words. We wonder why some are so hard. You know, words.

Words words words words words words words words words word. We're sick of words tonight. So we just look. We sit quiet, looking at the pictures. I like the picture of blackberries best. I love blackberries. The blackberries in the picture aren't only black they've got little blue dots all over them. Which is dots of light. Dots of light like the little dots of light in John's brown eyes.

Beautiful beautiful brown eyes.

Blackberries are sweet and juicy. And they're not only sweet and juicy. They're something else too. They make you feel sort of – sort of floating, or swimming, like floating or swimming in a ditch, a purple ditch, and sort of rich. I don't know the words. I love picking blackberries. Blackberry bushes are prickly. So it's exciting. You have to wriggle in between the prickles. And you get hold of a blackberry. And you give it a wee tug. And if it comes off easy, it's ready. It has to come off really easy. It has to sort of jump off the bush at you. And if it doesn't come off easy, it's not ready. So you don't keep tugging. You leave the blackberry to grow some more till it really is ready. And if you pick enough to fill a billy and take the billy to Mum she'll bake your pickings into a blackberry pie. I love blackberry pie. Mum makes it in a big green pan thing. And when she dishes the pie out to us she pours cream all over the pie.

And it's delicious.

I wish we could go out and pick blackberries tomorrow. We can't go out and pick blackberries tomorrow. This isn't the right time of year to pick blackberries.

'Does everything belong to a family?' I say.

'I don't know,' says John. 'All animals do, and trees do.'

'All animals? And all trees? Why?'

'I don't know.'

I feel sort of excited. I love the idea that everything belongs to a family. If everything belongs to a family – if everything's in a family nothing's alone, nothing's lonely.

'Does moss belong to a family?'

'I think so.'

'Does coal belong to a family?'

'I don't know.'

I feel sorry for coal if it doesn't belong to a family.

John and me sit quiet for a while again, thinking about the pictures. And then we hear someone talking loud. A girl. A girl who sounds sort of fierce and sort of smart. Sissy.

'I'm *thirsty*!' she's saying. 'I'm *really* thirsty so I'm going to the kitchen and drink some *vinegar*!'

Which she knows isn't allowed. Which is why she's saying it.

John looks at her and frowns in a sort of helpless way.

'Stay here in the lounge,' he says.

'Make me!' says Sissy.

'Stay here in the lounge and I'll read you a story,' tries John.

Sissy jumps up. She runs out of the lounge. We hear her banging around in the kitchen. We see her running back into the lounge. She's holding a bottle of brown vinegar. She bends her head back. She holds the bottle up to her lips. She starts gulping it down. It's something all us kids have been doing on the sly. Drinking vinegar. Vinegar tastes good. It makes you feel all sort of fresh and tingly. Mum found out about it a few days ago. She told us off.

'*Never* drink vinegar,' she said. 'If you drink vinegar your blood begins to boil and you start *climbing the walls*!'

She made her eyes go all poppy out when she got to the last bit.

Sissy screamed. I felt sick. We all felt sick. We knew, now. We knew that Mum's not really our mother. She's a witch. Which sort of makes sense that she's not really our mother, that she's keeping us in her house till we're fat enough for her to bake *us* in a pie. And she won't pour cream all over the pie.

She'll pour gravy.

So we stopped drinking vinegar.

Only now Sissy's doing it. And John's panicky. He's lost.

And Alan's holding his footy ball tight. He looks dead. And Noel's put a piece of jigsaw in his mouth. He's chewing it. His eyes are sort of nothing. And I'm frightened. Sissy! Stop drinking the vinegar! Your blood will start to boil! Help! Help!

Nobody's in charge, nobody's looking after anybody.

Come home from the party, Mum.

Come home, Dad.

Chorus

singin' the blues

never thought I'd lose your love

nothin' ain't right

I want to cry all night

you can't be true to two

I almost lost my mind

honey don't

honey don't

I sit and cry

drown in my own tears

love is strange

giddy up a ding dong

giddy up a ding dong

without love there is nothing

love me or I'll lose my mind

please say you want me

please say you care

chains of love

do-wat, a-do-wat, do-wat, a-do-wat

do-wat, a-do-wat, do-wat, a-do-wat

shoobee doobee-wah, do-wat, be-bobbee, bobbee

shoobee doobee-wah, do-wat, be-bobbee, bobbee

shoobee doobee-wah, do-wat, be-bobbee, bobbee

Valerie

I sulk for weeks and weeks, wracking my brain to think of a way out. What can I do? I can't do anything. If I had the money I'd go to see a lawyer in Greymouth. But I don't have the money. If I could find a means of getting out, I'd get out. I've reached a point in my life –

I hate my life, that's that.

I hate him.

And when I say hate. Well, I keep doing my housework. I cook his meals for him. I wash and iron his clothes for him. I don't talk to him. I keep my trap shut. I only cook his meals because I have to cook meals for the whole family. I only wash and iron his clothes because I have to wash and iron clothes for the whole family. But that's it. Of a night, after we've got the kids to bed, we still sit together reading or listening to the radio. And I knit. Or do some darning. But I don't speak a word. I loathe him so much. I sit there wordless. And I sit there thinking.

I think about that first night at the Argonaut. A band playing. Piano and drums and sax. Couples dancing A tall dark young chap in a tweed sports coat. I think about the way I felt those days.

I think about how I feel now.

I look at him, squinting short sighted at his book.

This is what I've ended up with, I think.

This is my *lot*.

YOU HOGGET

Valerie

The silent treatment can't go on forever, so in the end I grudgingly go back to talking to Gil. Not like in the early days, mind you. We don't joke and laugh. We don't cuddle and kiss. We don't – well, we do go back to having sex. Because I like sex. But now it's just having a root and then going to sleep. You wouldn't want to call it making love. And I make him beg me for it, too.

'Come on, dear, give us a love,' he'll say after we've switched off the radio and put out the milk bottles and done our teeth and gone to bed.

'Get away from me, you dirty bugger,' I'll say, snarling.

'Come on, darling. You know I love you.'

'Stop that. I'm tired. Get out of it.'

'Just a quiet little cuddle.'

'Oh all bloody right.'

A big reason why we need to talk is because all of a sudden things blow up in our face.

It happens one afternoon when John and that are at school and I've got the other kids down for their sleeps. I've made myself a brew and sat myself at the kitchen table with my knitting. Stevan's rocking. I'm halfway through a wee cardy. I'm knitting it for Jan. Dark green with a gold fleck. And I'm listening to the radio. Pat Boone singing *Ain't that a Shame*.

And who walks in the door but Gil.

Which whenever he does it, which he does now and then, browns me off. Can't I ever get any time to myself?

He looks worried.

'What are *you* doing home at this hour?' I says.

He looks at me.

'Alright, Val,' he starts to say, and then he stops, and then he starts again. 'Hang on, I'm going to sit next to you.'

So he pulls over a kitchen chair and he sits in it.

'Now, Val,' he says, 'you may want to leave me over this.'

'Oh?' I says. 'What?'

He's looking at me sort of quiet and sad.

'I've been cooking the books at work,' he says, real slow. 'They've found me out and I've just been sacked.'

'You've been – *what*?'

He lets out a big sigh. And he spells it out. One or two old miners, old coots whose backs have had it from long years down the mine, now and again they put their names in the book for a couple of days of light work. The mine paybook. The paysheet. Only the odd day. To keep them in smokes and beer. All he's needed to do, Gil, is put a coot's name in the books for one more day. You know, on the paysheet. One more day than the coot's really worked. Doing it without the coots knowing. And instead of paying the coots – which he hasn't needed to, because they haven't really being doing those extra days – instead of paying them, he's been pocketing the money. Paying himself, like. Not a lot. Ten bob here, ten bob there.

'How much have you flogged all up?' I says.

'Nineteen pound.'

'And what have you been doing with the money?'

'I've been paying for my beer out of it. And now and then a whisky.'

'So you're telling me you're not just a thief but you're drinking a lot more than you've been letting on?'

'Well, yes. Quite a lot more. I'm sorry, darling.'

'All without a word to me, your bloody *wife*, about what you've been doing.'

'I know it was wrong, dear. I'm very sorry.'

Which doesn't really worry me too much, though I'm not going to say that to him. He can stew in his own juice for a while as far as I'm concerned. I know why he didn't say anything to me. He won't have been wanting me to know because he won't have wanted me to get in trouble. You know, through knowing and not telling anybody. The mine boss. Or the cop. Or that. He won't have wanted me to feel bad. He'll have been feeling bad enough himself. He'll have been feeling ashamed. He'll have been feeling guilty.

'And what was that about getting the sack?'

'I'm afraid that's the most serious consequence. The head chap came to see me from down the Grey. He's never liked me anyway. He's Catholic. He left school at fifteen. He resents my being better educated and coming from the sort of family I come from. Holds my class background against me. So, not surprisingly, he was rather enjoying himself. He had a word with his superiors. I'm not to be prosecuted but I'm to pay back the money. I'm to be permanently banned from taking any employment not only in the Mines Department but any other government department.'

'You mean you won't be able to get a job in the public service *anywhere*? Not even if we go back to Canterbury?'

'Not even if we shift to Southland or go to North Auckland.'

'A *fine* bloody kettle of fish.'

'Val, you never undertook to marry a criminal and while I've been reprieved from having to stand up in front of a magistrate I've committed a crime. Theft as a servant. If you want to divorce me over this you'll be more than in the right. I certainly won't stand in your way.'

Which won't solve anything, so what would be the point?

'Get a cup from the cupboard and pour yourself a brew and

pour me another one too and let's talk things over good and proper.'

And, looking sheepish, he does.

And we do.

Stevan

John and me are sitting on the bottom bunk. It's nice sitting with him on the bottom bunk. I can see the sticker saying Vono. The whole house smells of hot biscuits and hot cake because today's Mum's baking day. Lovely rain is falling. Lovely rain is dripping down the window. I feel snug. John's reading me a really interesting comic about Scrooge McDuck.

I love comics about Scrooge McDuck.

Donald Duck is his nephew. Uncle Scrooge, that's what Donald calls him. Donald's got nephews of his own too. Huey, Dewey and Louie are boys like me and they live with Donald and they call him Unca Donald. I think it's hard for them to say *uncle* like it's hard for me to say *in cycle pee dear*. And then there's Daisy Duck. She wears a pink bow on her head, and she's got big fluttering eyelashes and she wears pink high heel shoes. And she's got three nieces called April, May and June. They wear bows on their heads like Daisy. So Daisy and Donald both belong to the Duck family. But she's his girlfriend and he's her boyfriend so that's a bit funny.

It's hard to understand how everyone fits into the Duck family.

Anyway, Scrooge is much more interesting than Donald. And he's much more interesting than Daisy. Scrooge is rich. He's really *really* rich. He's got *umpteen fantasticatillion* dollars! He's got three *cubic acres* of money! I don't know what's three cubic acres and John doesn't know either but we know it's a lot. Scrooge McDuck wears a silk top hat. He wears spats. And he lives in a money bin. A money bin is a great big building filled with money. Scrooge McDuck likes to swim in his money. He likes to dive in it like a porpoise. He likes to burrow through it like a gopher. He likes to toss it up and let it hit him on the head.

Donald Duck calls Scrooge McDuck an old tightwad. Mum says he's probably a Jew. I don't know what's a Jew.

'How did Scrooge get all his money?' I ask John.

'He says he worked hard for it and he saved it all up and he counts every penny.'

'Blackball people work hard,' I say. 'They're not rich, are they?'

'No they're not, but I don't think they count every penny.'

'Aunty Ikey counts every penny but she's not rich.'

'Probably she doesn't save it all up.'

'Oh.'

'If she saved it all up she'd be rich, probably.'

'What about the Griggs? Are they rich because they work hard and save all their money and count every penny?'

John looks up from the comic and has a think.

'Dad says they're not rich really. Dad says they're just comfortable.'

'Aren't we comfortable?'

'I don't think so.'

'Are we poor?'

'I don't know.'

'Are the Griggs just comfortable and not rich because they don't count every penny?'

'They don't count every penny and they don't even count every pound. I think they spend lots and lots of their money. So that'll be why they're not rich.'

I feel sort of worried and unhappy.

'John, why are *some* people rich and *some* people comfortable and *some* people poor?

'I don't know.'

'It's not fair for the poor people.'

'I know. That's why Robin Hood stole from the rich to give to the poor.'

'Why don't poor people steal from the rich to give to themselves?'

'The police would put them in prison,' says John.

'That's not fair either.'

'I know,' he says, and now he looks unhappy.

'Why don't the police put the *rich* people in prison?' I say

'Because that's not the law,' he says.

'Why?'

Valerie

Gil flogging that money from the mine and getting the sack doesn't really worry me. I mean, it's not as though the money was – nineteen quid, for god sake. And it's only from the mine. It isn't as though he's taken anything from any workman or their family. It's just the bloody *mine*. There's nothing to be ashamed of. And, you know, it was worth a try.

I would've done it myself if I'd have had the chance.

We agree that we won't tell the kids. We'll spin them some story. I mean, does it really mean anything that we'll be keeping something like this from the kids? We'll be doing it for their sake. He's their father. The kids look up to him. He's a bit of a hero to John and that. The kids, they need a better life than we had. Me and my sisters. You know, that was a tough life we had. It was a real tough life for us when we were little kids.

Why knock Gil off his pedestal in their eyes? It wouldn't do any good.

So we won't say anything to anybody.

It's bloody well knocked him off his pedestal in my eyes, mind you. Like I says, it's not that he did anything wrong. It's just he was stupid enough to get found out. And lose his job. And get on the public service blacklist for life. And all for nineteen bloody pound. A quid or two for a bit of booze.

So as far as I'm concerned that's him off *his* high bloody horse.

Which is quite good, really. Because it means later on I'll always be able to throw this in his face. You know, when I want something. Or when I want to score a point. Get the upper hand.

Anyway, that's not what we've got to worry about right now. What we've got to worry about right now is how the hell we can pay back the nineteen quid.

And what's he going to do for a job?

And where are we going to live?

When you're living in a house belonging to the Mines Department you can't keep living in it after you've had the sack. We have to get out quicksticks. That's what they've told Gil.

Where will we find a roof for our heads?

He starts asking around and gets offered a job as a tally clerk at Atarau Sawmills. Which is out near Moonlight. The mill owners are a rich family living in Christchurch. A tally clerk is a chap who counts the lengths of timber as they come out of the mill. He counts them and then he adds them all up. Apparently it's real simple. Just writing down numbers on this little blackboard. Gil, if he takes the job, will have his own office too.

Though the money won't be as good as he's been getting.

His salary from the Mines Department has gone up slowly, year by year. So these days he's been getting a few bob over seven pound a week take home pay. The family benefit pays me three pound ten a week. All up, not bad money for an ordinary family. But a bloody stretch with seven kids. I've had to watch every shilling.

'*Less* than you've been getting?' I says. 'When that's been just enough for us to get by?'

'I'm sorry, Val.'

'Well that's what I get for marrying a boozing thief.'

Which is me scoring my first point.

He looks so bad you'd think I'd smacked him one. I nearly feel sorry.

Anyway, we go out with a carload of kids to take a look. We drive along the Moonlight road past the old gold tailings. We drive past the tall straight trees. We catch sight of the lopsided tree with its tuft near the top.

'The *Toothbrush* Tree!' sings out Stevan.

After that bloody tree we go a mile or two further down the road. And then we stop at a bend. A farmhouse burned down there a year or so ago. Gil has an idea that if you climb to the spot where the house was, on top of a wee bit of a hill, you'll get a view down to the Grey. We get out. A smelly swamp. Wild stuff growing. All of us straggle uphill to the spot. One or two of the kids start moaning. I tell them they'll get a clip over the ear if they don't shut up.

'Oh, Mu-u-um.'

And he's wrong, Gil.

'You can't hardly even guess which way to look for the Grey,' I says.

'Could've sworn we'd have a wide sweeping outlook right out across the flats,' says Gil.

'Well who wants to look at the Grey anyway? It's just shingle and water and weeds. It's not as if we don't see it every bloody time we drive to Greymouth.'

So we straggle back down the hill. We get back into the Ford. Gil steps on the starter switch. Off we chug. After a few more miles we get to Moonlight. Gil goes down through the gears. He takes the turn. He goes up through the gears. We come to the mill. It's a group of huge sheds. Gil stops the car. We all get out again. We take a look. The mill's on a muddy hillside. Behind it, long bushy spurs climb right up to the top of the Paparoa Range. Men are slogging away, shoving and heaving logs. One or two of them are whistling. Circular saws are whirring and screaming, slicing into the logs. The work looks hard and dirty.

I reckon what comes out of the mill must not just be sawn timber but a fair few gashed legs and crushed hands.

The tally office turns out to be a wooden hut.

'It leaks in that corner,' says the chap who's handing over the job. 'You've got a power socket, here, to plug in a jug and make yourself a cuppa.'

A row of wooden bungalows belongs to the mill. We park in front of the empty one. We open the doors, pace out the rooms, try the windows. Quite a nice house, actually. The trouble is the woman next door. I can see her at one of her windows, narrowing her eyes, looking us over. She's got a beautiful flower garden. Our kids start climbing up onto the fence between the two houses.

The woman comes bustling out into her yard.

'I won't have that!' she yells. 'Children aren't supposed to be climbing on there!'

Blah blah blah.

I turn to Gil.

'Well that's that,' I says. 'I'll never live next door to someone mean as cat's meat like *that* bloody bag.'

Chorus

rum, tarantulas
carnival, calypso
mangoes, papayas
ça, c'est l'amour
chantez, chantez
une mélodie d'amour
der alte Herr von Lichtenstein
mein Schatz!
ja! ja! ja!

Valerie

Ellen and Eldred come to visit us for a weekend. They drive over the mountain passes in their latest car, a big shiny Customline. The car cruises to a stop in front of our house and we all scurry outside to look. Eldred shakes hands with Gil. Ellen kisses Gil. She kisses me. The kids are running round and hopping up and down. The car's so streamlined it looks like a plane without wings. Out the front the bumper bars and radiator grille are great big wide bands of gleaming chrome. Out the back there's two fins, steel and sharp. Chrome trim swoops from the front along each side to meet up with four chrome strips streaking from the back.

'It's very powerful,' Gil says. 'Whole car weighs well over a ton.'

'Makes ours look like a bomb,' I says.

Ellen smiles at me gently.

'We women don't care about cars, do we, Val?' she says. 'So long as they get us where we want to go.'

As always she looks like she's stepped out of a bandbox. She's wearing the sort of things that women like her wear when they're travelling. Dove grey gloves. A woollen suit, wine coloured. A dove grey pillbox hat with a veil. Wine coloured court shoes. Eldred's in a dark suit and a felt hat. Gil's in a jumper I knitted him myself. I'm in a ratty old cotton dress and my usual sandshoes.

The kids are still running round, goggling at the Customline.

'Why does the car have fins?' says Stevan. 'It isn't a fish.'

'It certainly isn't a fish,' says Ellen, smiling.

'What are they *for*, the fins?' says Stevan.

'To make your grandfather happy.'

'Can we go for a ride, Pop?' says Lynne.

Eldred doesn't say anything. He often seems not to hear kids. Not that it puts off Lynne. I don't think anyone or anything ever put off Lynne.

'Pop!' she says. 'Pop, can we go for a ride in the Customline?'

'Of course you can go for a ride, sweetheart,' says Ellen. 'Tomorrow.'

'After breakfast tomorrow?' says Lynne.

'We'll see,' says Ellen.

'When?'

Eldred cuts her short, in his rumbling sort of way.

'Gilbert, can you point out the house that's on the market?'

'Over there across the street, Dad. The villa with the big bay window.'

'Hmmm.'

And then the whole gang of us go inside our house. The bigger kids carry the overnight bags. Me and Ellen get busy making a brew and buttering scones. Eldred and Gil sit down in the lounge to talk about the villa. The owners have put it up for sale because they're shifting to Canterbury. The asking price is four hundred pound. The two men drink their tea then go over the street. They take a close look at the villa. They come back. Eldred says he thinks it's a good buy. He gives us the money. Well, he gives Gil the money.

Eldred never talks to me about money. I think he thinks women don't have brains enough for anything serious like money.

I wonder if Gil told him about the nineteen quid.

Anyway, the money changes hands. Eldred and Ellen stay a few days. Afterwards, away they go back to Canterbury. The lawyers get busy with the paperwork.

A few weeks later we move into the villa.

The address is 10 Harper Street. It's a cold house. No windows on the sunniest side, so on the odd occasion when rainclouds *do* clear from the sky you're out of luck. The ceilings are ten foot high. A veranda runs halfway across the front. The other half of the front is taken up by the bay window. Three bedrooms are down one side. A huge lounge, a huge kitchen, and a scullery and a bathroom, are down the other side. Cooking is on a coal range. The washhouse is a tarred wooden shed. It's outside in the backyard. A water tank sits on tall posts in front of the washhouse. The coal stack is under the tank. The toilet's outside, too. It's an old long drop. So that's a bit of a backward step. A pit for sewage has been dug at the bottom of the yard and when the can gets full you lug it down the yard and lift a wooden trapdoor and tip the shit and piss into the pit.

'I'm worried one of the kids is going to open that trapdoor,' I says to Gil. 'I'm worried they'll open it and one of them will fall in.'

'I'll fit a padlock,' he says.

'That won't stop them! One of them will fiddle with the padlock and spring it and open the trap door and fall in.'

'They won't, dear.'

'Well if one of them does, they're drowning. I'm blowed if *I'm* going to save anyone by jumping into that pit.'

A picket fence, painted a creamy colour, sits between our yard and the street. A paling fence runs down one side and out the back. A little old cottage sits next to our house, part of the property. It's the original miner's cottage built on the section. An elderly couple, in their eighties, rent it from us. He's an old miner. A few currant bushes straggle along between their cottage and our villa. Redcurrant. Blackcurrant. A cabbage tree grows on the other side of our house. A few scraggy flowers poke their heads up above the yard. Snowdrops and that. The rest of the section is just lawn.

Well, the rank mossy tufts that go by the name of lawn in Blackball.

We do up all the inside of the house, which is a big job. We start by wallpapering. Arthur helps, and Ikey.

We paper the biggest bedroom, the one off the front veranda, which is for the boys. We buy a paper printed with horses and cactus and cowboys. And then we paper the back bedroom, which is for me and Gil. A boring paper striped with pink and grey. And last we paper the middle bedroom, which is for the girls. A long and narrow room, very cold. We buy a paper with dancing ballet ladies on it, to try to make that bleak room look a bit more cheerful.

We all work hard at the papering. The one who works hardest is Arthur. Arthur, when there's work to be done, he'll put his back into anything. And after, when the work's done, he'll kick off his heavy hobnailed work boots and strip off his thick work socks and lie down on the couch and arch his big brown feet and wriggle his big brown toes and call one of the kids.

'Rub my feet for me will you, boysie?' he'll say to John.

'Alright,' John says, because he always does what he's asked by a grownup.

Or maybe Arthur will sing out to Alan.

'Give us a good rubbing, Al.'

We don't bother papering the lounge. The paper already in there is fairly good. I wish we could afford to buy more furniture. The lounge is so big it looks real empty. All we've got in there is the piano and the lounge suite we bought when we were in Brodie Street. The piano's getting more and more wrecked by the kids. They keep climbing over it. They like to make out it's a pirate ship on the Spanish Main. Or a stage coach in the Wild West. And they keep climbing over the lounge suite, too. It's hard to believe that lounge suite was my pride and joy only three or four years ago.

'You'd think swaggers had been camping on it,' I says to Ikey.

Ikey looks at it, cocking her head.

'Camping on it and ripping off bits of upholstery and – and ripping off the upholstery to blow their noses or wipe their bums,' she says.

We turn to each other, grinning.

The next job after papering is painting. Gil quite likes papering but he hates painting. I do too. So while the both of us slave away with paintbrushes, which keep getting all claggy, we both get red and angry. Well, I get angry. Gil doesn't hardly ever get angry. He just gets less chatty, as we work our way along the walls. And then he gets even less chatty.

'Why do these buggers of walls have to be ten bloody feet high?' I says.

'Because they are!' he says.

Which is about as fierce as he ever gets, Gil.

We paint the bathroom, which is tongue-and-groove, fidgety work. You poke the head of your brush into the grooves. Paint starts dripping paint on your arm and your hand. You wipe your hand. You end up with paint on your forehead and on your chin and on your cheek.

And we paint the scullery, which is tongue and groove too.

And last of all we paint the kitchen.

The kitchen is quite a nice room with big sash windows. And it has a great door out to the back steps. A door on a rocking hinge. You just push the door with your open hand. And it opens. And then it *swings* back into place. It's marvellous with the kids. They go through and that door just swings back into place, with a creak and squeak. Next to the door we stand our fridge. The fridge we bought on time payment when we were at Brodie Street. And we've got the battered old wooden dining suite, the suite that we bought a year or two before we come to Blackball.

The sink and bench aren't in the kitchen, they're in the scullery.

We paint the kitchen a dark green. Asparagus green, or so it says on the tins. Cheap. Not the best choice, it turns out.

'Bloody hell,' I says to Ikey. 'Looks more like spew than asparagus.'

Stevan seems to feel the same way. After we slap the paint up of a Saturday he nearly throws up over his dinner on the Sunday.

Sunday dinner is always this big event. I get a forequarter of mutton, usually. Or, if I can afford it, hogget. I slog away all morning. I roast the meat with spuds, parsnips, carrots. I boil up some silverbeet. Or I open a couple of the biggest tins of green peas I can find on the shelves of the shops. I always make a pudding, too. Rice, or bread and butter pudding. Occasionally a jelly. And while I'm toiling over the stove and then dishing up and then eating and then clearing the table, the radio plays the request session. It plays from twelve o'clock to two o'clock every Sunday. The listeners who send in for songs are mostly old crones and old coots. So the session's mostly old songs. Old songs from when I was a kid. Or older songs. Songs from when Mum was a kid. That's why I like to listen. I've got a soft spot for a lot of those old songs, even though what I like best are the new songs.

Anyway, someone nearly always requests the *Nun's Chorus*. You know, that song by Strauss. A song from the waltz days in Vienna.

I hate hearing that song.

That song reminds me of when I was a kid. Mum of a Sunday would sit in the kitchen listening to the *Nun's Chorus*. She'd be singing along. She had a good voice, Mum. We've all got a good voice in our family. Mum hardly ever did sing, though, so – well, it gave you goose bumps the odd occasion when she sung. And that song, when I hear it on the radio, it still makes me think of being back at home with Mum. A kid, being looked after by Mum. Which is stupid, because she never did make me feel looked after, as a kid.

I don't want to be back home really. It's just that I still have this longing for Mum.

So it always makes me feel all morbid, the *Nun's Chorus*.

And this Sunday, the day after we've finished painting the kitchen, that's what's playing on the radio. I'm sitting there listening. I'm feeling like blubbing. And then I look across at Stevan.

He's got his chin down in his chest. He's poking at his peas and meat. He's trying to put a forkful in his mouth but sort of retching and spitting it out.

Which makes me see red.

I work from morning to night for that little shit and he turns up his snotty little nose at what I cook.

He's gone very quiet these days, Stevan. He doesn't rock anymore. He just keeps to himself. He turns the pages of the encyclopaedia. He looks at books that the older kids bring home from school. He plays with wooden blocks. He plays with wooden blocks under the water tank. He lines the blocks up in rows. He says the rows are streets. And a lot of the time he's nowhere to be seen in the house or in the yard. He spends hours just wandering round by himself. You hear about it from people who run across him in this or that shop.

Or down by this or that creek.

And he's always singing. Always singing the hit songs, like I say.

He's a queer kid. I sort of worry about him, when I'm not too busy.

And he's a bloody stub.

John's not a stub. He'll do anything I say. And nor is Alan a stub. If I ask Alan to do something he'll snap to it. The stubbornness set in with Lynne. Stubbornness she shows with cheek and backchat. Stevan's stubbornness is different. He just goes quiet, like I say. He behaves like you're not even there.

He behaves like you're dead.

So, this Sunday he's retching over his peas and mutton. And the kitchen stinks of paint and meat and turps. And I can't stand it anymore.

'You'll sit at the table and you're not getting up till you've eaten every single one of those peas and every shingle shred of that meat!' I yell. 'You'll eat it or you'll get a clip over the ear!'

He doesn't say anything. He just sits there, retching.

'*Eat* it, you ungrateful little sod!' I'm yelling.

He keeps retching and retching.

He doesn't eat it.

Chorus

freight train
freight train
banjo, belle
billy goat
the county jail
hillbilly
the lone prairie
a lost goldmine
a goldmine in the sky
over the mountain, across the sea
a strong west wind is blowing
look homeward, angel
weeping willow
ninety-nine ways

Stevan

The new house is big and empty and echoing. And it's smelly. It smells of tar. I don't know why. And it smells of the horrible paste that Dad and them used for sticking up the new wallpaper. And it smells of horrible *horrible* new paint. And the new paint is ugly. And there's a big long corridor all the way down the middle of the new house and it's dark and scary.

And I don't like the new house.

Why can't we go back and live in Brodie Street?

If we went back to live in Brodie Street it would be good. And it would be good if Molly and Erleen and Jack left their farm near Reefton and shifted back to Brodie Street. And then we'd all be together again. And we'd be happy. And that would be *really* good. Seven years I left the valley. Now I live just for my true love to see, to see. Darling, all the while you belong to me. My loved one dancing the night of the Tennessee waltz. Oh my darling we'll never change partners again. Hand in hand we'll find love's promised land.

Anyway, the new house isn't where I want to live.

But the yard's alright.

It's a really big yard. It's all grass. And there's a little slope halfway between our house and the back fence. It's fun rolling down the slope. Us kids all roll down it a lot. You lie on your back at the top of the slope. And then you roll over once, or twice if you're lucky. And then you're at the bottom. Nifty! And then you run back up to the top. And then you lie on your back again and roll down the slope again, over and over. Which is *nifty* nifty. And there's a cabbage tree in the middle of the backyard. I don't know why you call it a cabbage tree. It hasn't got any cabbages growing on it. The bark looks sort of rough and speckly. And you think it looks grey but then you look closer and you see streaks of brown and tiny blobs of orange. And it's got little bits of fuzz like the wee whiskers you see on a crawly. At the top of the cabbage tree there's some branches poking out all ways. And big clumps of spiky green leaves poke out of the branches.

And when the wind is blowing the spiky green leaves rub against one another and make a lovely sound.

Flicker flicker flicker flicker.

One day the backyard turns into a slaughter yard. A slaughter yard is what you call a yard where you kill things. Dad says so. He won a sheep in a raffle at the pub. He says it's lucky he grew up on a farm because it means he knows how to kill. He doesn't call the sheep a sheep. He calls it the sheep a you hogget.

'Why's it called a you hogget not a sheep?' I ask John.

'Because it's young, it's not an adolt,' John says.

'But why's it a *you* hogget?'

'It just is.'

Dad ties the sheep to the trunk of the cabbage tree. All us kids make friends with the sheep. Wendy comes over to see the sheep.

She comes over with Uncle Arthur. Cock. The you hogget has got big soft eyes and her eyelashes are long like Daisy Duck's. The black bit in the middle of her eyes isn't round like it is in people, it's nearly oblong. And her nose is soft and pink. She's got a few black freckles on her nose, too. She's nervous. Sheep are always nervous.

'What are yous going to do with her?' Arthur asks John.

'Mum's going to roast her,' says John.

I feel sick.

The you hogget sort of understands, I think, because she starts wriggling and squirming. And the knot on the rope tying her to the cabbage tree can't be very strong because all of a sudden she's running away across the yard, and kids are running after her and singing out.

'The sheep's escaping! The sheep's escaping!'

Uncle Arthur runs faster than anybody. He traps the you hogget against a fence. He flings himself on top of her. She tries to buck him off. He wrestles her. She's bucking and shaking and crying.

'Ma, ma, ma.'

Her mama can't help her though. Arthur gets her into a headlock. Dad runs out of the house. He gets hold of the end of the rope. He drags the you hogget back to the cabbage tree. He ties her to the trunk again, and this time he ties a double knot. He says he's going back inside to change his clothes and then he'll be doing the kill. We go back inside too. Mum's in the kitchen cutting us some sandwiches. The sandwiches are luncheon sausage and chutney.

'This is for yous kids. And I'm making yous a jug of raspberry cordial. Yous can pretend it's a picnic. I'm going to Ikey's.'

Mum makes cordial with a packet of sugary stuff that she buys at the shop. You can get all sorts of flavours. You can get raspberry, which is made from red sugary stuff. Or you can get orange. Or you can get lime. Mum rips open the packet and mixes the sugary stuff with water from the scullery tap. I like raspberry cordial. I like lime cordial better though.

'Aren't you going to watch the kill, Mum?' we say.

'Not for quids!' she says.

All us kids take the sandwiches and raspberry cordial outside and we climb up onto the black tar roof of the washhouse and get ready to watch the kill. It's winter now but the day's sunny and when you sit down on the black tar roof it feels nice and warm on your bum. We start eating the sandwiches and drinking the cordial. We have to take turns drinking from a green plastic cup. The you hogget isn't frightened now. She's just standing under the cabbage tree chewing a bit of grass. Dad comes out the back door dressed in old holey brown trousers and an old green bush shirt. I know that old green bush shirt and those old holey brown trousers. They belong to Uncle Arthur.

Cock. Worm. White. Sick. Red.

Dad's holding a great big shiny sharp knife.

The you hogget stops chewing.

'Mama, mama!' she cries.

Dad goes up to her very quiet and gentle and quick as anything he gets her in a headlock, just like Uncle Arthur got her in a headlock. And this time Dad pushes her head back. And he sticks the big sharp knife straight into her throat.

And blood spurts out.

Gobs of red blood are spurting out onto the green grass of the yard. Dad's sort of sawing. Sawing her neck with the big sharp knife.

'What's he *doing*?' says Sissy, who's gone so white she looks a bit like the you hogget.

'Cutting her throat,' says John, who's gone all white too.

'Is it hurting her?' says Sissy.

'No,' says John.

My eyes are shut now. I don't want to look. If I look I'm going to spew up luncheon sausage and raspberry cordial and chutney. I keep my eyes shut tight for ages. When I open them again the you hogget is lying on the grass and she's not moving. Well her feet are sort of twitching. Dad unties the rope from her neck. He ties it around one of her back legs. He throws the other end of the rope up onto a branch of the cabbage tree. He starts heaving. The you hogget must be heavy. He heaves really hard. He heaves and heaves till she's hanging. Dad saws off her head.

The head drops onto the grass.

Blood all over the lawn, it looks like a red crawly pond only it's a crawly pond in the middle of green grass instead of a crawly pond in the middle of black slag.

And then he starts cutting into the you hogget, cutting a line down one side.

'*Now* what's he doing?' says Sissy.

'Skinning,' says John.

We sit on that sticky black tar roof for hours and hours and *hours* while Dad butchers the you hogget. He has to work so hard. He grunts a lot. Skinning the sheep looks like Mum tugging a woollen jersey off one of us kids. And after the sheep's been skinned, Dad stabs into her belly. All her innards come spilling out onto the grass. All sort of sausages and things. All red and bloody and slippery. And there's a horrible smell. It's the smell of a kitchen where a lady's cutting up meat to cook. And another smell too. A smell of poos. And another smell, a sort of soapy smell.

Dad's sawing off the you hogget's feet.

'This is boring,' says Sissy 'Let's go and play.'

So we do. We get down from the washhouse roof and go inside and play cowboys and Indians. We play in the lounge. We climb onto the piano and make it our stage coach. The lounge is a huge *huge* room. All one wall is windows. Windows that sort of poke out like they're nearly another room. You can stand in the middle of the window wall and if you look to one side you see only window and if you look straight ahead you see only window and if you look to the other side you see only window. And outside the window everything is green as green. The front yard's green. And across the street there's no houses, there's a green paddock. And behind the green paddock there's a green hill. And behind the green hill there's green mountains. And it's all different greens. Dark greens and light greens and every green in between.

And now it's starting to rain, a nice soft lovely rain.

Dad comes inside. He's very quiet. Mum comes home when the rain stops.

Next morning it's another cold sunny day. Dad starts tidying out the washhouse because he wants to hang the you hogget there for a few days. He says you have to leave meat hanging. I don't know why. Dad's stacking old things outside the washhouse. Bits of wood, and that. And then he brings out a big board and props it on the wall. The board is a dirty yellow colour and it's thin but it's high and long. It's higher than me standing up next to it. And it's nearly as long as me lying down twice on the grass next to it.

'What's this board for, Dad?' I say.

'It's one side of a packing case. I'll cut it into kindling one day.'

'Can I have it to make a house?'

'Right ho, but we'll want it for kindling eventually.'

'Thanks, Dad.'

The board is so thin and light it's easy to drag across the yard. I don't look at the you hogget. She's still hanging from the cabbage tree. I drag the board to the picket fence in the front yard. I lean it on the fence. And that makes a house! The picket fence is a wall. And the board leaning on the picket fence is another wall and sort of the roof. The grass is the floor. It's a triangle house! And at one end is a doorway and at the other is another doorway.

I feel all safe and cosy.

I go back to the washhouse and get some old sacks. They're pretty smelly. They smell of old spuds. And I borrow Dad's hammer. And I get some tacks. And I put one of the sacks over one of the doorways of my house and tack the sack onto the board. And then I put one of the other sacks over the other doorway of my house and tack it onto the board. Tacking isn't easy because the board is really splintery. And then I put the other sacks down on the grass so my house has carpet.

Nifty.

I take the hammer back to Dad. I go and get an Uncle Scrooge comic. I take the comic to my triangle house and I go inside my triangle house and sit inside my triangle house and look at the comic. Scrooge is having problems because he's got too much money. He's got forty trainloads of cash in his money bin. I know because John read me this story the other day.

I stay inside my triangle house all day, nearly.

Next morning it's really cold. I feel a thrill waking up in the morning to the whippoorwhill's trill. Mum says there's been a heavy frost. Dad goes to work. The big kids go to school. After I eat my porridge I run outside to play in my triangle house. I don't look at the you hogget hanging up inside the washhouse. When I get to my triangle house it doesn't look right. It doesn't feel right. The sack doors are frosty. All white and stiff and glittery with frost. And they smell different. The smell of old spuds is still there, but there's another smell, a sort of icy smell, a smell of something dead.

I lift up one of the sack doors and peek inside.

The inside of my triangle house is really dark. It's really cold. And it smells sort of stuffy. It's sort of unfriendly. I don't want to go inside my triangle house any more.

I drop down the sack door.

I walk slowly back across the grass.

I don't look at the you hogget. Too real is this feeling of make-believe. Too real when I feel what my heart can't conceal. I look up at our scullery window. I can see Mum. She's washing dishes. Steam is curling up around her head. Her cheeks are red and shiny. Her hair is brown and messy. She's looking down at the sink but somehow she's looking somewhere sort of far away. She's singing. I love hearing her sing. I can hear the radio playing. I can hear the baby crying.

I wish we could go back to Brodie Street.

Valerie

After a while I start to get friendly with the lady down the road, Lily Johns. She's about my age, very thin. Dave, her husband, he's a lot older than her. He's a bushman. Lily starts coming over for a brew quite a lot. We talk about babies. Our babies, they're the same age. And we talk about kids. She's got four kids, with the new baby. And of course we talk about our husbands.

I moan to her about Gil.

She moans to me about Dave.

'I might as well be a widow for all the good he does round the house with the kids and that,' she says. 'He's always down the pub playing cards or away at lodge meetings.'

'Well at least he's not drinking when he's at lodge meetings.'

'Isn't he? I don't know.'

'What *do* men do at lodge meetings?'

'One thing I know about lodge meetings is they strut round making out they're important. That's one thing they do at those – those blessed – lodge meetings.'

She never swears, Lily.

'Gil says lodges are mumbo jumbo.'

'Course they are! I reckon he's got a great life, Dave. He's never home. He never gives me a hand. I have to do everything. All he wants, when he comes home, is his meal to be on the table. And no please and no thank you.'

'Can't you talk him into helping out a bit – for a start, helping you with the kids?'

'I'd have more luck asking that pot to help me with the kids,' she says, pointing at a saucepan of mince she's got stewing slow on her range top. 'I'd have more luck asking a skeleton in its coffin down the boneyard!'

'Well can't you at least give it a try asking?'

'No point. He won't do it.'

'Bloody men!'

'Men!'

And then we get back onto talking about our kids.

Chorus

a pair of yellow gloves
a white sports coat
a pink carnation
a million bucks
ain't worth a dime
sha na na na, sha na na na na na, bah-doo
sha na na na, sha na na na na na, bah-doo
at the hop
dynamite
oh boy!
a shiny toy
sock full of candy
yip yip yip yip yip yip yip yip
mum um um um um um
doo wop, do-doo wop
a dollar is a dollar
a dime is a dime
butterfly
honey
let's have a party
moving, grooving

Stevan

The sawmill's brown and red. The sawmill's mossy logs. The sawmill's wood and rust and sawdust. Sap. Bark. Steal tracks running into the sheds. Steal trucks rolling along the tracks. Strong big men unloading logs. Strong big men slithering logs onto big rumbling rollers. Strong big men bending. Strong big men straightening. Floppy felt hats on their heads. Cocks tucked into their trousers. Cigarettes hanging out of the corners of their mouths. It's raining, slow and heavy. Mud's everywhere and it's sloppy with leaves and twigs.

All around the mill sheds you can see green bush on the hills and green bush in the valleys. And right up high, sort of hanging in the sky, the beautiful green high lovely Paparoa Range.

You feel safe when you're under the Paparoa Range.

The sawmill's strange. The sawmill's exciting. The sawmill's cosy and cold and wet and dry.

'The best wood in this bush is red beech,' says Dad.

'Why's it the best, Dad?' I say.

'It's a hardwood, got a very good sheen, a beautiful grain and when you plane it after cutting you can get a nicely smooth surface. The colour's lovely. A builder can use it for flooring. A joiner can use it for doors and windows. A cabinetmaker can use it for decorative work.'

Which mostly I don't know what he means. I don't care, though.

I love being here with Dad.

Atarau Sawmills is a place for men and boys. You can't see any ladies anywhere. And you can't see any girls. Dad brought me with him today because Mum said she's sick of having me under her feet. I don't *want* to be under her big fat bossy bumping stumping feet anyway. Mummy's a mad pie. Dad and me came out here in the back of a lorry with some of the other men who work at the mill. The back of the lorry was dark and smoky. The men were all puffing away on cigarettes. They sang some songs. And they told jokes. I didn't understand the jokes. The jokes were about bosses and the government and ladies and babies.

'Here,' says Dad. 'This is red beech heartwood.'

He holds out a thin slab. A slab that looks like pink cloud. A hard pink cloud with some soft little greenish streaks and a few faint dark smudges like smoke from a twig fire burning under a billy. A beautiful *beautiful* piece of wood. I touch it with my fingertips. I sort of shiver. The slab feels like silk. I know what silk feels like because Nana was wearing a silk scarf one day when we were staying in the County. She let me stroke it.

'Silk from Siam,' she said.

'Thailand, more correctly,' said Pop. 'A country formerly known as Siam.'

Nana didn't say anything to him but I could tell she wasn't happy about him butting in.

'Siamese silk,' she said very quietly.

Dad and me are in his tally shed. He has to go out now and do a tally. He tells me if I like I can stay in the shed. If I do that I can look at the red and gold book and the comics I brought with me. Or he says if I want I can put on my gumboots and my raincoat and help him do the tally. Or I can go exploring.

'I'll go exploring, Dad,' I say.

'Right you are,' he says. 'Watch your step, and don't go too far away, and when it's time for your crib I'll cooee for you.'

'Alright, Dad.'

I go up to the main shed. The main shed is really big. A lot of men are busy. Wheels are spinning. And the main shed's dark. And it's noisy with engines and machines and men shouting and steal trucks banging against one another on the steal tracks and a radio playing hit songs. And it smells of hot oil and hot grease and sap and cigarette smoke. The men are all friendly. They give me a wink. Or they give me a grin and a nod. I love it. Cock. And then I start not to love it. Worm. The men are all so big and strong. And

I'm so small and weak.

And anyway, if I'm in the main shed I won't be able to hear Dad cooeeing me for crib.

So I go out of the main shed.

I go over to a great big stack of sawn timber, which is sort of like lots and lots of wooden steps up to the sky. Well only up to the roof of a shed, not the sky. I start climbing the wooden steps. And I start counting the steps. One and two and three and four and five and six and seven and eight and nine and ten and eleven and – I can't remember what comes next. I stop counting. And soon I'm at the top of the wooden steps.

I love the wooden steps.

Dad still hasn't cooeed for crib, so I go out the back of some other sheds and come to a hill of logs. The logs are rough and thick and hairy. They look like great big hairy legs. The legs of great big hairy men. I start climbing. It's much harder to climb the hill of logs than to climb the wooden steps. The logs are muddy. The logs are slithery. You have to use your hands. You have to climb like a monkey. Or a possum. I wish I had a long twisty twirly tail like a possum or a monkey. The logs smell all sort of dark. You can smell crushed leaves. You can smell wet earth. You can smell sawdust. You can smell coal smoke blowing over from the sheds.

After a long *long* climb I get to the top of the hill of logs.

I love the hill of logs.

I sit there on top for ages and ages. I look down at the mill, all brown and red and busy. I look over the valley, all green and quiet. And then I kneel down and look close at one of the logs. A broken log, mossy. A little twig's sticking out of the log. The twig's really pretty. Its leaves are little and sort of round, but not really round, and they look nibbled on the edges like little bites have been taken out by mice, or birds. They haven't really been bitten, I know. Beech leaves always look nibbled like that. They look like that whether they're red beech leaves or silver beech leaves or black beech leaves or mountain beech leaves. And some of the leaves on the log are bright green like grass in spring. And some of the leaves on the log are dark green like I don't know what but they're dark. And some of the leaves on the log are sort of blushing. The blush is red in some leaves, and in other leaves it's pink. And a few of the leaves are bright red, a lovely bright red.

The red leaves are the leaves that are dying.

And tiny little balls of water sit on top of the leaves. The balls of water are little raindrops. The raindrops are fresh and bright. The brightness is white light from the cloudy rainy sky. It's like the leaves are alive with rainlight.

Only they're dying.

All of them, they're dying.

After looking a long time at the twig I start singing. I'm a whippoorwhill singing on Mockingbird Hill. My home, my sweet home, yes it's Mockingbird Hill. Tra la la, tweedle dee dee dee, yes it's Mockingbird Hill.

'Cooee!' I hear. 'Cooeeeee!'

I look over to the tally shed and see Dad. He's waving. I wave back. He goes inside the shed. I start to climb back down the hill of logs. I feel sad. I don't want to climb back down the hill of logs. I want to stay on the hill of logs always. Yes, it's Mockingbird Hill. I come down to the ground. The rain's not so heavy now. I start walking to the tally shed. My gumboots plop and slop in the mud. I love plopping and slopping. I lift my feet higher every step so my gumboots can plop and slop even more.

I get to the tally shed.

Dad's facing away from the door, sitting on a little wooden stool and bending over a little wooden table. He's unwrapping the crib. I can hear the rustle of the paper. And I can see the back of his neck. I don't like the back of his neck. I feel sick. The back of his neck always makes me feel sick. It's red and wrinkly. One day I asked Mum why it's red and wrinkly. Mum said it's the sun. But the back of Dad's neck isn't the sun. The back of Dad's neck is the back of his neck. I hate the back of his neck. I hate it. It looks like a big cock. A big wormy cock poking itself out of his jersey and going up to his black hair.

I can't stand looking. I look away.

Uncle Arthur. Cock. Worm.

'Mum's cut us cold hogget sandwiches for our crib,' says Dad. 'Cold hogget with mustard.'

I sit down on a little wooden stool next to his little wooden stool. He picks up a sandwich. He hands me the sandwich. I don't know what to do. I don't want to take the sandwich. I don't want to put it in my mouth. I don't want to eat you hogget. And I don't want to eat anything handled by Dad. Dad's hands are sort of like the back of his neck. They're not red and they're not wrinkly, but they make me feel sick. I never like it when Dad handles food or even a plate or a cup if I'm going to use the plate or cup for eating or drinking.

When he touches something it makes it sort of filthy.

I don't know why.

I mean, Dad's not filthy. He's neat. He's tidy. He's always telling us kids to wash ourselves properly and brush our teeth properly and that. He doesn't bring up wind like Mum. He doesn't fart like Mum. He doesn't pick his nose like Mum. But if Mum touches something it doesn't make it filthy and if Dad touches something it *does* make it filthy.

I take the sandwich and pretend that there's nothing wrong.

I bite the sandwich and I want to spew.

I chew the mouthful and swallow it. And I take another bite. And I want to spew. But I don't. I keep chewing. I make myself chew. I make myself not spew. I tell a story. The man who gave me the sandwich isn't Dad. The man's a clean man. I don't know who's a clean man. And when the man makes me a cup of cocoa and hands it to me, I take the cup. I make myself drink. And the man who makes me the cocoa isn't Dad.

And I feel really bad, because why do I feel this way? It's not fair to poor Dad.

Dad's a good Dad.

I sit on the little wooden stool next to his little wooden stool and I make myself eat and I make myself drink and I feel bad and I feel sad and I feel worried and I feel sick and I feel wrong and I feel lonely. I think about the strong big men in the main shed. It's easier to think about all those men in the main shed than the one man by himself in the tally shed. The men in the main shed will still be busy, with cocks tucked in their trousers and cigarettes hanging from their lips. Wheels will still be spinning. The main shed will still smell of hot oil and hot grease and sap and cigarette smoke.

And then I look sideways. I see Dad looking at *me* sideways. He's looking at me with his brown eyes, beautiful beautiful brown eyes. He looks shy. He looks kind. And he looks –

He looks lonely.

Like me.

Chorus

Tammy
cottonwoods
whispering of love
whispering above
in love, in love, in love
breeze off the bayou
store-bought clothes
don't you rock me, Daddy-o
mmm-mm-mm-mm-mm-mm-mmm
mmm-mm-mm-mm-mm-mm-mmm
gotta have something in the bank, Frank
I'm not a juvenile delinquent

whippoorwill, owl, dove
honey from the bee
peaches on a tree
the movie's over
rock-a-billy
rock-a-billy
mortal strife
interest on a loan
meeting with resistance
doop doop doop doop doop
ah ding ding ding, ding ding ding
down down down, down down down
doo doo doo doodle-doop
beefsteak, well done
booze
it's fabulous
a big refrigerator
park the car
factory
phone
reet petite
pay the rent
steaks and chops
spend all my money
whole lotta shakin' goin' on
ooh, ooh, ooh, ooh, ooh
ooh, ooh, ooh, ooh, ooh
moonlight gambler
tight little spot
ain't fakin'
hip cats flipping
sweet chicks sipping
yeah, don't knock the rock

Valerie

All my older kids are doing good at school. John's top of his class. Alan's really good at reading and writing. And so's Lynne. I can't be doing too bad a job as a mother, I think. Well, I hope. And whenever one of my kids heads off down the road for the first day at school it's not just a big day for them it's a big day for me. One of my kids starting school brings back to me how bad and frightened I felt all those years ago when my sisters dragged me off to start at Sydenham School.

And now it's that time for Stevan.

He starts school one morning in spring. A warm drizzly morning. I stand him at the bathroom basin and brush his hair. He was nearly bald for the first year or so after he come out of the womb. When he did start sprouting hair it was tow. He's got a good head these days. Soft and fine, and lots of it. Going the colour of straw. He stands still while I work with the brush. I've dressed him in navy blue shorts and a maroon jersey. He's shy about going to school, I think. He looks up at me with his big green eyes.

Forbes eyes, not Grigg eyes. My eyes.

I see that his mind's full of worry.

'You'll be alright,' I says to him. 'You'll like school.'

I'm not lying, either, because the infant mistress is Frances Driscoll. She's a good teacher. She's kind to little kids. And, like I say, her opinion is that I do a good job with mine.

'Mum, should I hold Stevan's hand on the way?' asks Alan.

'Mum, where's my *Janet and John*?' asks Lynne.

'We better get going, Mum,' says John.

'Now yous kids watch you look after Stevan all the way to school,' I says. 'Watch you take him to his classroom and wait there with him till you see Mrs Driscoll, and then take him over to her, and then when it's playtime I want yous to meet him at his classroom and play with him, and the same thing at lunchbreak.'

'Yes, Mum,' says John.

'Yes, Mum,' says Alan.

Lynne doesn't say anything.

We all walk down the passage to the front door, out onto the veranda and then down a concrete path to the front gate. John opens the gate. A little picket gate. The kids troop through the gateway. John closes the gate. It makes a wee click. John takes Stevan by his left hand. Alan takes him by his right hand. Stevan's looking down at the shingle of the street. The shingle's glistening in the drizzle. I look up at the hillside behind the street.

The hillside's shrubby and green and tussocky.

You stand on the veranda up of a morning. You look up at that hillside. You see the cloud coming over the Paparoa Range.

And you think, *another* wet day.

And you think, too, that the drizzle drifting down the side of the mountains looks a bit like the veil drifting from Ellen's dove grey pillbox hat. The hat she wore when her and Eldred drove over in the new Customline. I feel like crying. I always feel like crying when one of my kids goes down the road to start school. Crying for them. And crying for me. You know, the me who started school way back before having them, before the war, before the factory.

The me who always felt lost at home. The me who always felt lost at school.

Stevan will do alright. He's bright. All my kids are bright. And he's got his bump of knowledge.

'Ta-ta, ta-ta!' I sing out.

'Ta-ta, Mum,' say John and Alan.

Stevan says nothing. He walks slow.

Lynne says nothing. She stumps off on her own, splashing into every puddle.

Well, that's one more off my hands. I turn back to the house and walk up the concrete path to the veranda. Good. Only three kids still tying me down during my working days. A year or from now I'll be standing again at the gate waving goodbye to Noel. A year or so after that, Ross. And then Jan.

All seven off my hands.

And then things will come right. I'll have a bit of time to myself for once.

Only trouble is a fortnight after that drizzly spring morning I miss my period.

Chorus

you and me, brother
you and me, sister
ain't it swell?
juke joint
jukebox pop
jailhouse rock
the stomp, the stroll
swing it, groove it, move it
hear some rock that's really hot
the coolest dance sensation
sweepin' the nation
great balls of fire!
chew my nails
twiddle my thumbs

Stevan

Janet and John are a brother and a sister in a little book at my new school. And in the book they're playing in a yard like our yard in Harper Street. John in the book doesn't look like John in our family. John in our family has got black hair and he's got beautiful beautiful brown eyes. John in the book has yellow hair like me.

Janet in the book has yellow hair too and she looks like Sissy. She's nice, though, not like Sissy.

'Come, John, come,' says Janet. 'Look, John, look.'

'Janet, Janet,' says John. 'See the boats.'

School is alright.

The classrooms are in a long yellow building in a big park with lots of trees all around and it's just down the road from Brodie Street. The classrooms are big and they've got big wide high windows all along one of the walls so you can look out and see the grass and the trees and the birds and the bush on the hills and the sun or the clouds in the sky. At the front of my classroom there's a big long blackboard where my teacher writes with chalk.

The blackboard isn't really black. It's green.

So people should say greenboard.

The greenboard has got a big drawing of Woody Woodpecker on it, drawn all in coloured chalk. Red chalk and green chalk and orange chalk and yellow chalk. Mrs Driscoll, who's my teacher, she drew the Woody Woodpecker. She's good at drawing. She drew him with his beak open. And she drew him with a tube down from his beak to his belly. And she drew him with a sort of circle inside his belly. She drew him to help us learn how to keep our fingernails nice and clean. Mrs Driscoll looks at our fingernails at the start of each day.

'Hands out, children!' she says after she's walked into the classroom and we've all stood up and said good morning.

We hold our hands out.

'Good, Billy,' she says, walking along and looking. 'A bit slipshod, Heather.'

Mrs Driscoll's got a head sort of squashed like a frog but not slimy like a frog. Her face is soft and pink. And her hair is fair and all wavy. And she wears *jewels* in her ears. Red jewels. Or green jewels. So she must be rich. Now she goes over to the greenboard and picks up a white chit which is pinned on the wall. It's pinned on the wall with lots of other white chits.

A chit is a bit of paper.

Mrs Driscoll taught us the word.

The chits are pinned on the wall next to Woody Woodpecker. And there's a name written on each chit. And the name on this chit is Heather. Mrs Driscoll takes the chit and she picks up a little ball of plasticine and she sticks the chit near Woody's open beak. And then she comes back and looks at some more fingernails.

'Good, good,' she says. 'Oh my goodness, Malcolm, did you even *think* about those nails this morning?'

'Sorry, miss,' says Malcolm, sort of shy.

Mrs Driscoll goes over to the greenboard again and picks up a chit that's right next to Woody's open beak. And the name on this chit is Malcolm. Mrs Driscoll moves the chit down into the tube between the open beak and the circle of the belly. She sticks it onto the tube.

If your name gets right down to Woody's belly, it's bad. You have to do a special job that nobody wants to do. Like staying after school and cleaning all the greenboard dusters. And then you start all over again and your name goes right back to the lots of other chits pinned on the wall next to Woody.

Mrs Driscoll looks at some more fingernails.

'Good, good, good,' she says. '*Very* good, Stevan.'

My fingernails are always clean because I'm scared of ending up in Woody's belly.

After she looks at our fingernails we have to go into our groups. One group is called Pixies and one group is called Elves and one group is called Fairies and one group is called Gnomes. I'm a Pixie. And the groups do different things. Playing. And after that we have story time. All us kids sit on mats in a circle on the floor and Mrs Driscoll sits on a wooden chair in the middle and reads from a book. And then there's play lunch. And after that we have drawing time.

And then there's lunch.

If it's raining we have lunch in the shelter shed, which is a big dark shed of green steal where you can eat and play without getting wet. I don't like the shelter shed. It smells funny. It smells of mould and old sandwiches and old socks. If it's not raining we all run around on the grass and play games and that, which is good. And after lunch we go back to the classroom and Mrs Driscoll closes the curtains and we all lie down on our mats and have a sleep. Mrs Driscoll doesn't sleep. She sits at the front of the classroom, at her big wooden desk, and she does her marking.

And after the sleep we do our reading.

'Look, Janet, look,' says John. 'See the aeroplane come down.'

Fly over an ocean in a silver plane, through a jungle wet with rain, and when you come home again, will you belong to me?

I love it when we do our reading. Reading is exciting. And we're not only learning how to read words, we're learning how to write words. And after that we'll learn how to read and write more and more and *more* words. So that's really exciting. Well, reading the little books about Janet and John isn't exciting. They're not interesting, those two kids. The best thing about learning to read is that when I get home after school I can sit down in the lounge with Donald Duck comics and Uncle Scrooge comics and I can read nearly all the words. And I can sit down with the red and gold books and I can read some of the words. The encyclopaedia. I can say that word now. And I can spell it. Well, sort of. I can spell it if I look at the word on the front of one of the red and gold books when I'm writing it.

Today I'm reading stories in the encyclopaedia book called *DIA-GRAP*. I'm reading about Germany.

'A land of great natural charm and beauty,' says the book, 'the birthplace of great writers, artists and musicians, of philosophers and scientists.'

Auf wiedersehen, mein Schatz, ja ja ja, der alte Herr von Lichtenstein, das Bächlein, das Vögelein, in die Welt hinein. I've heard lots of German words in the hit songs. I go and ask John to tell me about charm and philosophers. He knows what charm is but he doesn't know what's philosophers. I go into the kitchen to ask Mum. She's ironing. She hates ironing. Her face is red. Mum's face is always red but when she's ironing it's redder than red, and all sweaty.

'Philosophers are men who talk about the meaning of life,' she says. 'Which is typical of men and anyway it's a waste of time because life doesn't mean anything.'

'Oh,' I say.

'Mind that flex!' snaps Mum.

I'm sort of getting tangled up in the flex. The flex goes into a socket in the wall.

'Sorry, Mum,' I say. 'Do you know the names of the great writers of Germany?'

'I'll great writer *you* if you don't get out of my road!' she says.

'What's for tea, Mum? I ask.

'Pig's tits and treacle,' she says.

Which is what she says when she can't be bothered saying. So I give up on her and go back to the lounge and keep reading.

'German language and literature are somewhat similar in history and content to those of England.'

I have to go and find John and get him to explain six of those words. And then I go and talk it over with Dad after he comes home from the sawmill and goes into the big bedroom to change out of his work clothes and put on his red and blue tartan slippers.

'Dad,' I say. 'Do you know the names of the great writers of Germany?'

'Goethe,' says Dad.

He has to spell it out for me.

'Have you read any books by Goethe, Dad?'

'I can't read German. I can pick my way through books written in French. You'd never know, mind you, that at seventeen years of age I was top of my class in University Entrance French.'

222

'I don't like France.'
'Each to his own, Steve.'
'I like Germany.'
'Right you are.'
I go back to *DIA-GRAP* till it's time for tea. I'm a bit tired of trying to understand the story about Germany. So I just look at the coloured pictures. A picture of under the sea. Fish and seaweed and coral and that. And a big foldout picture of all the different kinds of dogs. And two pictures of ducks. And a war picture of a beach and soldiers and black ships and black smoke and things blowing up. John says it's a battle called Dunkirk. Germany won that battle, he says. Good. And a picture of the sun which is just a huge blue ball with red flames flying out.

John says it's an eclipse. He tells me what's an eclipse.
And then it's tea time.
Curried sausages.
Ew.

Chorus

wake up in the morning
doo doo doo doodle-doop
run away and hide
the well runs dry
the want ads
get a job
crazy stuff
you're so square
whispering bells
doo wop, do-doo wop
life will be nice
like paradise

Valerie

My period doesn't come that week. And it doesn't come the next week. I start to get panicky. I've already got more than enough bloody kids hanging on me like a deadweight. Kids always wanting food. Kids always wanting clothes. Kids always wanting more food and more clothes and –

And I've had it. I'm not having any more kids.

I'm at Ikey's one night. Other women are there, too. We've been playing cards. Now we're all sitting in front of the fire yarning. Coal's burning bright in the grate. A lump of it lets out a hiss. A great big aluminium teapot filled with brew sits steeping on the hearth. A cluster of cups, not a set, motley cups, most of them a bit cracked, sit off to one side of the teapot.

I tell the women I'm pregnant and want to get rid of it.

'Oh, well what you've got to do is get a knitting needle, the way we did in my day,' says an old pruney sort of lady. 'We didn't know nothing about contraception so what we did to get ourselves regular again was pull down our bloomers and squat on our hams and just shove a knitting needle up.'

'Yeah, but that can go wrong, you can bleed bad,' says another old woman. 'And you can get infected and it can kill you.'

'Yeah, but we was desperate,' says the old pruney lady.

Her husband was a miner. He mined in the Grey Valley for years and years and years. She's about seventy. She's had, oh, it sounds like she's had a real tough life, the old pruney lady.

'What sort of knitting needle works best?' says another woman. 'Steel or wood?'

'Doesn't make no odds,' says the pruney lady. 'Watch you use the blunt end!'

All of us laugh.

'What about gin?' asks Ikey.

The old pruney lady gives a gummy grin and says if you want to try gin you'll want a whole bottle to get the baby out. And she says if that doesn't do the trick at least you can say to yourself you'll have a good drunk. I don't like the thought of drinking even a glass of gin never mind a whole bloody bottle. I've never drunk gin. I've had the odd whiff of it when other people have been drinking. And that's been more than enough, even just that whiff has always made me feel sick. Mind you, I like the thought of drinking gin a lot better than I like the thought of sticking a knitting needle up my fanny.

'What are you supposed to do with the gin?' I says.

'You heat it up and you drink it all in one go, and then if you're lucky it'll bring on your pains and the baby will come out.'

'Oh.'

After, I go home and talk it over with Gil. He's not keen. He says we can manage another baby. I say I don't want to manage another baby. I say I've had a gutsful of having a baby and then another baby and then another bloody baby. He says it's against the law. I say I don't give a curse about the bloody law. He says it might make me sick. I say if I go ahead with the pregnancy I'll be bloody sick for bloody months and I'll have a sore bloody back while I've got all the other bloody kids clinging to my bloody skirts. I tell him to go down to his pub tomorrow and buy us a bottle of gin.

'Alright, if it's your wish,' he says.

'My bloody wish is that every bloody man finds out what it's like having to carry round every bloody baby inside his bloody belly, *that's* my bloody wish!'

After work next day he brings home a bottle. A square bottle, clear glass. A label on the bottle shows some joker with a pink face wearing a red and yellow sort of dress, and red stockings. *Beefeater's distilled London dry gin*, says the label. Anyway, we have tea and we do the dishes and we listen to the radio while the big kids do their homework and the little kids play. And then we get the little kids to bed. And then we get the big kids to bed. We've got the fire going. I get a galvanised steel bucket. I pull off my pants and sit on the couch in front of the fire with the bucket between my legs.

'Right,' I says. 'I'm going to go through with this.'

'Are you sure, darling?'

'Go to the kitchen and heat it up.'

So he does, then he brings the hot gin to me in an enamel jug. It's a big jug. The enamel is cream, with a green trim, a bit nicked. Gil pours some of the gin into a cup. He sets the jug down on the hearth to keep it warm. He hands me the cup. I take one smell of it, and –

Urgh!

It's really horrible.

I take a mouthful. Disgusting!

Gulp, gulp – I can't swallow it – but I *have* to swallow it. So I hold my nose and make myself drink the cupful. Gil picks up the jug again. He fills the cup again. I make myself drink that cupful. He picks up the jug, pours me more. And I swallow. I keep swallowing till the square bottle's empty.

And then I'm violently sick. I'm spewing and spewing. I'm spewing into the bucket. I'm splattering gobs of spew onto the floorboards. I'm splattering gobs of spew onto the hearth. Gil looks white. He helps me to bed. I lie in bed, shivering and shaking and spewing. I'm sick all night. Spewing and spewing. Sweating and shivering and shivering and sweating.

Next morning, I get my period.

Chorus

all shook up
who wrote the book of love?
oh, I lie awake in my bed at night
you're treating me mean
my broken heart aches

you make me cry
fools fall in love
fool for your charms
still long for your arms
I've loved you for years
yet you've left me in tears
the skies have gone grey now
I'm deep in the blues
life don't seem worth living
I've lost all I can lose
I'll quit trying
I'm too deep in the blues
love is a melody gone by
I've got no future
I've got no hope
love lingers, don't know why
yeah, just waiting till I die

Stevan

The lounge is cold so I'm sitting right in front of the fire with one of the red and gold books. One of the encyclopaedia books. It's the one called *PAR-SOP*. My bum is on the hearth mat. I'm wearing grey shorts and a blue jersey. I've got bare feet. I've got my feet on the hearth so I can warm my toes. Sissy's sitting next to me. Her bum is on the hearth mat too. She just farted but I don't say anything. If you say something to Sissy when she farts she tells you off and says you're the one who farted, but I never fart, I always hold it in. I don't like farting. I think it's rude. Sissy's wearing a green dress and a brown jersey. She's got one of the encyclopaedia books. It's the one called *A-BON*. Her yellow hair is all messy. Her yellow hair is nearly always messy. She's got her bare feet on the hearth too.

Coal's burning. You can smell it burning. A stinky smell. A black smell. A red smell. Coal is shiny black. Or it's dusty black. And coal is red hot.

Red coal and black coal.

Black. Red. Black.

And stinky smoke goes up the chimney

Sissy's reading a story about Bolivia. The story says that Bolivia is a land of snow and sunshine. And the story says that the history of this republic has been stormy. One day I want to go to Bolivia.

Bolivia's far from the pyramids along the Nile and it's far from the market space in lost Algiers.

I'm looking at a story about the Roman Empire.

The Roman Empire was a long time ago and it started in Italy. And then it got big and strong and after hundreds of years it owned the whole world. That's what they said those days. It was only a little bit of the world, really. Anyway, the emperors lived in palaces and the ordinary people lived in big blocks of flats. And the rich people had slaves. Which wasn't fair for the slaves. And there were stone roads all over the Empire. And there were temples and baths and parks and the people made all sorts of modern things like we use today. They made things out of concrete and they made things out of glass. And they had scissors and keys and saws and jugs and needles and all sort of things. And they had lots of statues of strong handsome men with no clothes on. Which *isn't* like now.

I love the Roman Empire.

Sissy slams her book shut and turfs it onto the hearth mat.

'Give me that one!' she says, and she reaches out to grab my book.

'No you can't have it, I haven't finished with it yet,' I say, pulling it away. 'Go and get one of the other ones.'

Sissy looks at me. I look at her. She's got gooseberry jam on one of her cheeks. I think she must have sneaked into the scullery and scooped out some gooseberry jam with her fingers when Mum wasn't looking. I don't like gooseberry jam because it's too sweet. I like gooseberries when you pick them from the bush and eat them right away. It's not gooseberry season now. And she's not just looking at me, Sissy. She's biting her bottom lip. Which she does when she's going to be a stub.

'Give me that book!' she says.

'No,' I say.

'Give it to me or I'll get the poker and put it in the fire till it's red hot and then I'll burn you with it.'

I don't say anything. I pretend I don't care. Oh, yes I'm just a pretender, pretending I'm doing alright. I need you so much I pretend we'll touch but truly I know I'm lonely. You see, I'm not what you seem to see. No, I'm just a pretender, a pretender pretending I'm doing alright. Sissy picks up the poker. My need is such I pretend too much. She sticks the poker into the hottest coals. I'm lonely but no one can tell. The hottest coals are red hot. I still don't say anything.

Sissy lifts the poker out of the fire. The tip is red hot.

I pretend to keep reading about the Roman Empire. About the plumbing. Which is pipes and taps.

Sissy points the poker at my left foot. I can feel it. It's really hot.

'Give me that book or else,' she says.

'You can read one of the *other* ones,' I say.

She's pointing the red hot tip of the poker closer at my foot. She's not doing it quick. She's doing it very slow. Oh, yes I'm just a pretender, pretending –

Ow!

I turf the book away. I jump up.

Sissy drops the poker. She grabs the book.

I look down at my foot. I can see an angry red spot. It hurts. It hurts a lot. A really sharp hurt. The rest of my foot is white. Only just that one red spot. And it hurts it hurts it hurts it *hurts*. I run out of the lounge. I'm not crying. Crying won't make anything better. Nobody will help me if I cry. Nobody will help me if I tell them Sissy burnt my foot. Dad's still at work. Mum's in the kitchen having a cup of tea with Lily from down the road. Mum will just get aggravated if I tell her about my sore foot. She'll tell me she can't sort out every little fight between us kids. She'll tell me it's something I've got to sort out myself. She'll tell me it's stupid to fight over a book. She'll tell me it's my own fault for stirring up Sissy.

I go into the bedroom where we sleep, us boys. I go over to the steal bunks.

I sit on the bottom bunk.

I look at the oval sticker that says Vono.

I want to die. I want to be dead. Look homeward, angel. I've got no future and I've got no hope. I'd never be blue if you'd only love me half as much as I love you. My love lingers, I don't know why. I'm just waiting till I die. Weeping willow. A million bucks ain't worth a dime. Alone and all shook up. My loved one dancing the night of the Tennessee waltz. Oh my darling we'll never be partners again. I'm not a juvenile delinquent! Who wrote the book of love? Mortal strife. Dark moon. Chew my nails, twiddle my thumbs. I've lost all I can lose. I'll quit trying. I'm too deep in the blues. Wake up in the morning. Off to school. The Golden Rule. Love is melodies gone by, memories of yesterday. It's been so long since you held me tight. You're treating me mean. My broken heart aches. I've played the game but you're to blame for leaving me to grieve all alone.

I'm pushing off when dawn's a-breaking. A love song is a sad song, hi-lili, hi-lili, hi-lo. A love song sings of woe, ask me why I know.

I'm as lonely as can be, lost without your company. Maybe you'll be lonely too, and blue.

No arms can ease this ache within my heart.

I KNOW A STORY

Valerie

Gil only lasts a few months as tally clerk. He sees the wage the yard hands are taking home from their work at the sawmill. He looks at the salary he's taking home. He makes up his mind to stay on at the mill but chuck in the tallying job and sign up as a yard hand. He stops wearing a suit and a white collar to work. He starts wearing an old flannel shirt. And an old threadbare pair of trousers. And a ratty ragged old rugby jersey. He does it not just because the pay's a bit better for a yard hand than it is for a clerk but because of the overtime. He can't get overtime as a tally clerk. There's always plenty of overtime for a yard hand.

He takes on as much overtime as he can get because with all our kids we need the money.

So like I say, instead of dragging me up into the middle class, which is what I thought would happen when I first got together with him, he's dragged himself down into the working class.

He spends his working day heaving wood, hauling wood, dragging wood, weighing wood. His eyes get sore from sawdust. His skin gets red from working outside in the sun and rain and wind. His hands get gouged by the wood and rasped by the steel rims of the railway trucks he handles on the job. After a week or two his hands are a wreck. Broken skin. Bleeding. Scabs on top of scabs. He comes home shickered.

He comes home filthy.
What's the good of all his years at school and varsity?
Nothing.

Chorus

yo no soy marinero
seven wonders of the world
around the world in eighty days
the pub with no beer
stockman, swaggie
Lonesome Town
Jay Bird Street
Nairobi
witch doctor
windmills, tulips
tulips in Amsterdam
Western movies
dead-eye Dick
broken arrow
shoot 'em up
pow!

Stevan

It's a nice warm rainy morning. All us kids in my class are sitting
at our wooden desks doing our reading. The sound of the rain on
the school roof is lovely. The windows are wide open so a whole
lot of sandflies are floating through the room and landing on our
skin and biting. I've been bitten on my ankles and on my neck.
And now a sandfly lights on my wrist. I bend down to take a good
look at it. A sandfly is quite an interesting fly. If you look at it

close you can see that it's got a sort of thin hooked beak. Which is what it sticks into you to get your blood. And when it sticks that beak into you it makes you itchy.

That's alright, though.

A sandfly would die if it didn't suck your blood.

All us kids in the classroom have each got a book, a Janet and John book, and each book has got a number. Book One's the first book you have to learn to read. And then you have to learn to read Book Two. And then you have to learn to read the next book. I'm reading Book Six, which is called *I Know a Story*. Mrs Driscoll is going from desk to desk. If you don't know a word you put up your hand and she comes over and helps you. And she helps you say the words properly.

'We don't pronounce the first part of the word like *fear*,' she says to me when I ask her about the word feasting. 'We pronounce it like the word *feet*.'

'Oh, I get it,' I say. 'Thank you, Mrs Driscoll.'

'Good boy, Stevan,' she says, smiling.

I like Mrs Driscoll a lot but she's always really busy so it's hard to get her to come and help me for more than a minute or two. After she's helped me she's always got to go on to another kid who needs help. Which is a pity. I mean, it's good that she helps *all* us kids but I sort of have the feeling that she likes me a lot. You know, the way I like her a lot. And I sort of have the feeling that she wishes she didn't have to look after everybody in the room and wishes that she could sit down next to me, just the two of us. And she wishes she could read me a story.

And she wishes she could explain the whole story to me. And she wishes she could talk to me about things, about everything. I think she'd like to talk to me about how everything's the way everything is, and –

And *why*. I think she might know.

Somebody must know.

Janet and John books are boring. I hoped the books with the

high numbers wouldn't be as boring at the books with the low numbers but they are. The first story in Book Six is about a pet duckling. Which is boring. And another story is about twins. Which is boring. And another story is about wild ducks. Which is boring. And another story is about the three billy goats gruff, which is alright but I already know it by heart because it's a story Dad likes to tell us when we're out driving on weekends. Dad's good at making the goats talk like goats.

'Ma-ma-ma-ma,' he says, he says it the way the you hogget said it before he cut off her head. 'Ma-ma-ma-ma, please don't eat me, my bigger brother is coming along and he's very meaty.'

Dad's really good when he does the troll talking like a troll.

'I'm a troll, rowly-owl, and I'll eat you for my dinner!'

The story in Book Six says it's only a dwarf under the bridge trying to catch the goats and eat them, which isn't scary. Dad's troll under the bridge *is* scary.

And exciting!

The next story in Book Six is about a boy called Little Peachling. One day a poor man and his wife cut open a peach and inside it they find a tiny baby. Which is silly. A baby's much too big to fit inside a peach. A peach is a cousin of a quince. The poor man and his wife don't have any kids of their own so they keep the baby and they call him Little Peachling. The baby grows up. When he's a big boy he goes out to seek his fortune. Big boys in stories are always going out to seek their fortunes across the Congo, far away across the wide Missouri.

And he's handsome, Little Peachling, but he dresses like a lady.

He wears a pink shirt like a lady. He wears an orange jacket like a lady. He wears blue stockings like a lady. He wears a hat with yellow feathers like a lady. He wears pointy shoes with buckles like a lady. And he's got long hair like a lady.

But he's a boy.

Why?

Little Peachling makes friends with a dog and a bird and a monkey. And then the four of them chase some robbers away from a castle. Little Peachling gets a reward, which means he's not poor anymore, he's rich, and then he sends for the poor old man and the poor old woman and they all live together in the castle and they're rich and happy. You don't hardly know anything about him, though, even by the end of the story. You don't know what he feels. You don't know what he thinks.

He's just a boy, dressed like a lady.

You don't know *why*.

At lunch break the teachers sit in the staffroom with their cups of tea while us kids sit in the shelter shed. The sound of the rain on the roof of the shelter shed is really loud. I love it. And when you look at the rain falling down in front of the shelter shed it looks like a sort of shimmery silvery curtain and behind the curtain it's all green green green green. And lots more sandflies are floating through the shelter shed and landing on our skin and biting. It's good to know the sandflies have got plenty of our blood to drink. And it's good to know my sandwiches today are lettuce and Marmite. And it's good to know I've got a plum.

Mum drove to Greymouth the other day to pay some bills and when she was there she bought a whole box of plums from a fruit shop. She bought them because they were cheap because they were a bit specked but they're still good.

I love plums.

A plum is a cousin of a peach and a quince.

I sit in the shelter shed and I read a comic and I chew my sandwiches and I look forward to my plum. The comic's called *The Golden Helmet*. It's a Donald Duck. It's nifty. Donald's got a job as a guard at a museum in Duckburg. The pay's good and the hours are short but it's boring and he yawns a lot and he doesn't feel like it's a job for a he-man. A he-man is a man who's a real man.

A man like Uncle Arthur.

Big. Strong. Cock.

Worm.

Anyway, a man comes into the museum and asks Donald how to get to the collection of lace and tatting. I don't know what that is, tatting. The man's got long hair like Little Peachling. And he wears a fancy green jacket with black stripes. And he's got long fluttery eyelashes like Daisy Duck.

'Holy cow,' says Donald when he sees the man with the fluttery eyelashes and the long hair.

The man isn't a he-man.

I don't understand what that's about, really. Anyway, the story gets better because Donald and his nephews end up having an adventure looking for old Viking gold in Labrador. Labrador is in Canada, which is a cousin of our country. Canada and Australia and South Africa and Rhodesia and England and Scotland are all cousins of our country. Ireland used to be our cousin, too, but it isn't any more because of the Catholics. *The Golden Helmet's* a good story. It's exciting. A few words I don't know.

After finishing the story I go over to John and ask him to explain to me about the words.

John knows most of them but not crocheted, and not doilies, and not Charlemagne, and some other words. And then the rain stops and we all run out onto the grass and play. And then the rain starts again and it's time to go back into our classrooms. Mrs Driscoll says we're going to do some action songs.

Which is good. I like action songs.

'Boys will do stick games,' she says. 'Girls will do poi.'

The stick games are a bit hard. You have to throw sticks to a boy sitting opposite you. And you have to catch sticks he tosses to you. And you have to click the sticks on the floor. And you have to click the sticks against one another. And you have to do it while you're singing. So there's a lot to keep thinking about. But it's fun. And I like the song. Mrs Driscoll teaches us to sing it in Maori. And she teaches us to sing it in English.

'Alas I will die, oh darling, return to me.'

I like watching the girls swing the poi, too. And I like listening to the girls singing. And after we've all done our action songs we stand up together and sing *Pokarekare Ana*. Which is a really good song. And then we all sit down on our mats on the floor and we do some drawing.

I draw Donald Duck.

I'm getting quite good at drawing him. His beak is the hardest bit. If you start with his beak and do it alright you can draw the rest of him fairly easy. And then you can colour him in, which is fun.

And then I draw Daisy Duck.

And then I draw Scrooge McDuck.

The rain's falling hard when school ends and all us kids go home, splashing through the puddles and looking for frogs.

Mum's lips go sort of tight and white when we get home because our hair's soaking wet and our knees are muddy and our clothes are dripping. She makes us stand in a row in the scullery. She grabs a towel. She rubs our heads dry. She rubs really *hard*. She makes us boys change out of our wet shorts and shirts, and she makes Sissy change out of her wet dress, and she hangs the wet things over the clothes horse in front of the fire in the lounge. And after that we're all allowed a biscuit. You're always allowed a biscuit when you get home from school. Today it's an anzac biscuit. I don't really like anzac biscuits because they're sort of ugly. And they don't taste all that good. An anzac biscuit is just like a blob of dried out porridge.

'What say we play pirates and make the piano the pirate ship,' says Alan after we've eaten up our biscuits.

'Playing pirates is stupid,' says Sissy.

'I better do my homework,' says John.

John's the only one of us who gets homework. Getting homework means you're growing up. John's already nine and the day before I turn six he's going to turn *ten*! I want to go and live with him when he grows up. When he's an adolt he'll be able to live in a single man's hut. Mum and Dad can stay behind with the other kids. Or it would be good if Dad could get a single man's hut next to me and John. We wouldn't have to put up anymore with Mum having her moods and yelling and shouting and clipping us round the ear and whacking us and throwing a paddy.

Dad and John and me living together in two single men's huts without the other kids would be *really* good.

John gets out his homework. Sissy goes to her room with one of the encyclopaedia books, *BOO-DEW*. Alan goes I don't know where. I sit in the lounge and look at the encyclopaedia book *GRAS-LOM*. I start at the back. I always like to start at the back of a book. I think it's because I write with my left hand. Anyway, Mrs Driscoll says to me that you're supposed to start at the front of a book. So when I'm at school I do what she says and start at the front. When I'm at home I start at the back. I look at a great big beautiful foldout picture of a railway locomotive, which is a train engine. The picture's what you call a cutaway. You can see all the insides of the locomotive. It's all tubes and pipes and wheels.

And then I look at a story about lizards. I love lizards. You can find all sorts of geckos in the school playground and in the bush and by the creeks. And you can find all sorts of skinks, too.

After the story about lizards I look at a story about lighthouses. I'd love to be a lighthouse keeper. A lighthouse keeper is someone who lives all alone and looks out at the sea all day and at night makes sure the light is burning. John and Dad and me could be lighthouse keepers together, which would be really nifty.

And then I look at a story about kingfishers, which are quick birds you see by creeks.

And then I look at a story about Jupiter, which is the biggest planet in our solar system and is all stripy, with a big blob in the middle like one of Mum's anzac biscuits. Or like the cocoa sun in the tiles of the fireplace at our old house across the street. I look up from the encyclopaedia book. I think about that house. I think about how till last year we lived in the house across the street. I think about how years and years ago we lived in Brodie Street. I think about how we live now in this house. I think about how we're always leaving houses and never staying. And then I think some more about the cocoa sun in the fireplace tiles, and I think about the silver stripes, and I think about the way the silver stripes look like silver wings, and I think about how the silver wings are a silver plane flying into a cocoa sun.

And I don't know why but thinking about the silver plane flying into the cocoa sun makes me feel sad.

I nearly always feel sad, though, so that's sort of alright.

And then I look at a story about Joan of Arc. One whole page of the encyclopaedia book is a beautiful coloured picture of Joan of Arc. She's got long wavy hair like Little Peachling. And like the man who wanted to see the collection of lace and tatting in the Duckburg museum. She's a knight so she's wearing shiny armour and a white waistcoat with a yellow cross. And she's riding a white horse. The white horse is prancing. Horses are beautiful. I saw lots of horses in the County. White horses and black horses and the horses they call dapple and the horses they call chestnut. And following behind Joan of Arc you can see hundreds and hundreds of soldiers all in shiny armour. And you can see orange flames and purple smoke coming from a battlefield.

People said she was a witch, Joan of Arc. Witches aren't real, though, they're just a story.

I look at stories about Japan and about jaguars and about Iraq and about India and about Icarus who flew too close to the sun, which is just a story, like witches, but it's a good story.

And I look at a story about a man who was called Adolt Hitler.

'There is no stranger story in history,' says the book.

And I look at a map of Guiana.

And then I sit for ages looking at the two best pictures in the book. Which is pictures of two white stone statues. The statues are of strong handsome men wearing no clothes. I love looking at the strong handsome men. One of them is sort of bending over and getting ready to throw a discus, which is sort of like a plate that you throw. His arms and legs are smooth and muscly. He's got a great big cock only you can't see the cock because it's covered in a white clump of putty or something. I look at the white clump quite a lot. It's exciting. The other statue is a god called Hermes. Hermes is smooth and muscly like the discus thrower, and he's got a great big cock like the discus thrower too. Only it's annoying because you can't see *his* cock either because it's covered in another big white clump.

Hermes is standing up straight but sort of easy. He's holding a little baby boy. The little boy is another god called Dionysius. Which is a name I can never remember how to spell. And which is a name I don't know how to say. Gods aren't real, but they're interesting.

Hermes is looking down kindly at the little boy.

I wish I was that little boy.

Chorus

put the clutch down
the freeway
the farmer
the factory
a magic land
chrome, aluminium
manganese
a ton of coal
the chosen few
on bended knees

240

a throne on high
up to paradise
heaven waits
devil eyes
full of lies

Valerie

One day late of the autumn we get a trunk call from Canterbury. Gil's not long home from work. A stormy day. Wild rain drumming on the rooftop like a rock'n'roll band gone amok. I'm in the scullery. I'm getting tea. Corned brisket with onions and cabbage and carrots. I give a bit of a jump when the phone starts ringing. We've only had it for a few weeks. It seems so modern. Well it isn't really, of course. Phones have been around for years and years and years but when I was a kid we could never afford one. Only a few working people had them those days. And now – well, now we've got a chunk of black bakelite screwed onto the tongue-and-groove of one of the kitchen walls. A wee white wheel, a wheel of numbers from nine down to nought, spins on the flank of the black bakelite when you dial the post office, the baker, the dairy.

Gil takes the call.

'Grigg residence,' he says, which is one of his weak jokes.

They get my goat, his bloody jokes.

And then he bursts into tears. Which I've never seen before, ever. Gobs of water flying out of his eyes. Snot streaming out of his nose. It's like his whole head has turned into water and white jelly. And his eyes are wide open while he's blubbing. And he's looking at the wall and at the floor and at the ceiling. And he's looking at me. But it's like I'm not really here. It's like he's looking inside himself and he can't find what he wants to find inside himself, that he's lost.

'I'm coming over,' he's muttering. 'I'm coming over straight away.'

'Who was that?' I says when he lets go of the phone.

He's weeping so much he can't hardly talk. He grabs hold of me. I'm weeping, too. The scullery bench is digging into my back. And the two or three kids who're hanging round in the kitchen have all started howling. Stevan and that. Gil holds me so tight it hurts. I push him away. He bumbles towards the back door. He stumbles down the back steps. He squats on the back lawn.

He holds his head in his hands, sobbing.

The back door rocks quietly on its hinges, creaking and squeaking.

The newspaper

The wife of the Ashburton County chairman was killed when two cars collided head-on on the Main South Road near Rakaia yesterday morning. Another woman and a four-months-old baby were badly shocked. The dead woman was Ellen Jane Grigg, aged 65, who was a passenger in the car of her husband, Mr E. T. Grigg. Mr Grigg was not injured, and the driver of the other car was treated at the hospital as an outpatient. The accident happened about two miles south of Rakaia. Both cars were late English models and were extensively damaged.

Chorus

Flying Fortress
fight for Uncle Sam
a light in the darkness
a bullet through my head
I'm bleeding

Stevan

Nana's dead. Dad was *crying*. Bimbo saw. It's sad. It's very sad.

And it's scary.

Bimbo, where are you going to go-e-o? Bimbo, what are you going to do-e-o?

Bimbo's got a hole in his pants. Nana was soft. Nana was sweet. Bimbo remembers when he saw her on the platform at Rolleston. A lady in a hat. A pretty little old lady. A lady sort of skipping across the platform and holding out her arms and laughing. A lady with brown eyes, beautiful beautiful brown eyes. A lady whose face was all soft with powder. A lady whose mouth was all red with lipstick. A lady kissing Bimbo.

Smack smack.

A lady holding him tight.

They were waltzing together to a dreamy melody. The trill of birds in the treetops. A heart filled with gladness. Tra la la, tweedle dee dee dee. A thrill. And peace and goodwill. Blue moon, blue moon, blue moon. She saw him standing alone without love in his heart, standing with no-one of his own. She knew just what he was there for. She heard him saying a prayer for someone he really could care for. He told a listening star, the way a dreamer will often do, how wondrous she was, how his dream had come true. Hand in hand they'd find love's promised land.

Only she's dead now.

Why?

Valerie

After he gets a grip on himself and stops blubbing and tells me the trunk call was one of his brothers ringing from Trevillick, that there's been a car smash, that his mother's dead, Gil starts phoning the railways, the airfields. He's reeling, but he wants to get over to Canterbury. I'm reeling, too. I'm having vivid flashes. I sort of see Ellen. I see her dressed the way she was when she stepped out of the Customline. Her wine coloured woollen suit. Her dove grey gloves. Her pillbox hat with veil. I know she won't probably have been wearing those things. She's got lots and lots of good clothes. Still, I see her – I see her in that suit, that hat, those gloves. I hear tyres shivering in shingle. I see dust. I see sparks. I hear steel scraping against steel. I hear steel buckling. Chrome radiator grille. Chrome bumper bars. I see the Customline crumpling. I see her head hitting the windscreen. I see the windscreen smashed into jags of glass. I see the glass knifing her face and throat. I taste her blood spurting over the wool, the veil, the leather –

I can't shake it off.

I mean, she wasn't my mother, but –

Gil's beside himself. He can't get over to Canterbury. He can't join his family. He can't get a last look at her body. It's because of the storm. It's one of the worst storms for years. All the airfields are out. A big slip has come down and blocked Otira Gorge. A goods train has been trapped in the tunnel. Railcars and passenger trains have been stopped. A whirlwind has hit near Westport. Cars can't get through the Lewis Pass. Our old Ford would struggle to get over the passes anyway, even if the roads were open, because it's not as roadworthy as it was when we first bought it, the brakes aren't the best. All our neighbours come hurrying round to offer their own cars, but it's no good, the passes have been blocked to anything on wheels.

So we're completely cut off, boxed in on the Coast.

Gil weeps all that first night. He keeps weeping the next day. It's the day they bury her at the cemetery in Ashburton. I don't know why they have to bury her in such a hurry. Must be because she's a smashed up mess. I feel sick thinking about it. Ellen, she was more like a mother than my real mother. The only mother I'll know. Now – now that she's dead, and now – now that Molly's moved to Reefton – and of course Molly and Jack don't hardly ever get time to drive down here to look us up, they're too busy with their new farming life – and we don't hardly ever get the time to drive up there to look them up, what with all our kids and Gil getting worn out by his work at the mill and that – and –

Who's going to keep an eye out for *me*?

I'm crying off and on, though I'm doing my best to hold things together for the sake of the kids.

'Why has she died?' the kids ask.

'It was just an accident,' I says. 'Nobody wanted her to die.'

'Will we have an accident in our car?' they ask. 'Will we die in a car crash too?'

'Don't be morbid. Nobody's having an accident. Nobody's dying, Now get outside and play!'

Me and Gil talk about it every night for weeks. The whole story. The smash was late in the morning. The road was good. It's a main highway. It was a fine day. Eldred was driving at the speed limit. Or at least that's what he says. He was at a place called Overdale. He wanted to pass a slow truck. The road markings on the tarseal there are clear, Gil says. And what do the markings say? No overtaking, that's what they say. Eldred put his foot down on the accelerator and pulled out. He saw another car coming towards him fifty or so yards away. Eldred took his foot off the accelerator and rammed the brake. The Customline started broadsiding. The other car started broadsiding. They slammed into one another on the shingle off to the side of the road. Ellen was still alive but her neck was broken. An artery was cut. She was bleeding deep inside the neck. She died in an ambulance on the way to hospital.

'There's talk of bringing a charge of manslaughter against Dad,' Gil says one night. 'I hope not.'

'Oh?' I says.

'I worry that he'll be feeling guilty.'

'Mmmm,' I says, because I don't want to say what I'm

thinking, which is that his bloody father *should* be feeling guilty for driving so bloody dangerous and killing his wife, so what if he's got all that land and all that money and that he's chairman of the bloody County?

'He'll never forgive himself. Never.'

I bet he will. Men are good at forgiving when it's themselves they're forgiving.

Eldred doesn't get charged with manslaughter. I suppose it's because he's so important. They'd have thrown the book at him if he was just a working joker. I feel snaky about that. But I don't talk about it with Gil. We talk about Ellen. We talk about her a lot. He cries every time he talks about her. He misses her really bad. I try to make him feel a bit better by saying yes she was lovely, yes she was loving, yes she was a good mother and a good grandmother and a good mother-in-law.

After a while it seems like Gil's looking to me for motherly kindness.

As though now she's six foot under I've become Ellen.

I mean, it's not that he goes off sex. We keep rooting. It's just that he sort of looks at me like a boy wanting his mother. It's funny. Him wanting to be looked after as though he's my son. And me feeling like I've lost a mother, too. I don't feel furious with him anymore. You know, the fury I felt that day of the running races around two years ago when he was drinking at the pub. That day when I was standing on the other side of the street with Ikey and all our kids and he looked across and cut me dead.

Well, he's not such a bad chap.

He works hard and does his best to keep us housed and clothed and fed. He's a bit too fond of the booze, it's true. And though I hate it when he's been drinking and comes home silly, well, he needs me. He needs me a lot. He needs me and he knows he needs me. So that's not so bad. That's enough to be getting on with. We're closer now than we've ever been before. We're closer than we were even back in the early days when I was such a fool that I thought I couldn't climb halfway up to his level and that the sun shone out of his bum.

And any time I need to crack the whip all I have to do is say something about the nineteen quid.

After a while we're not talking so much about the smash. We're talking more about whether we need to get out. You know, out of bloody Blackball. We discuss it at nights. We discuss it quite a lot. We try to be sensible. The West Coast has got its good points. Like, you can get a fairly good house without paying too much money. I think that means more to me than anything. Not having to pay the house prices you have to pay in Christchurch. And another good thing about living in Blackball is that it's neighbourly. And you can get out a bit of a night, like I say. You can get out of a night without worrying about your kids.

Blackball's good for those things but then there's things it's not so good for.

'We need to ask ourselves what sort of career the kids will have if we stay on the Coast,' Gil says. 'We need to think about high school for John in another year or two.'

'He could catch the bus and go to high school in Greymouth, couldn't he?'

'We can do better than that. He's got a brain. He needs a good high school. And after high school he needs to go to varsity. He's more than able enough to tackle law or medicine or accountancy.'

'You're saying you want him to do what you wanted to do yourself?'

'I don't want him labouring in a sawmill.'

'The money's alright.'

'Val, we need to shift back to Canterbury.'

I can't really see any of my kids going to varsity or being lawyers or doctors or accountants. But I suppose I can sort of see them sitting at a desk in a high school in Canterbury. Anyway, I want to go back over there for my own sake. I'm getting more and more browned off by Blackball. I hate the shops on Hilton Street.

Poky little dumps. All their stock dusty and out of date. And every time you go inside to buy something there's always these young tarts and old boilers gossiping with one another, tittle tattling, talking scandal about anyone and everyone not there with them in the shop.

And then there's the rain.

'I wouldn't mind better drying weather, which we'll get if we shift back to Canterbury.'

I'm bloody sick of the bloody weather in bloody Blackball. Winter has come on now. You get up of a morning. You look at your heap of dirty washing. You hear the rain thundering down on the iron roof. Or there's been a black frost and when you try to do the washing the taps are frozen and the tank's frozen, with big solid blocks of ice in it. And as the day goes on the frost will wear off. And then black clouds will bank up over the Paparoa Range.

And soon the rain will be teeming down all over again.

You won't see the sun for weeks and weeks.

A lot of people have started leaving Blackball. The mines are going slower and slower every year. The coal's still good coal. And there's still lots of thick seams of it down there in the rocks. Only trouble is times are changing. Young boys whose dads work in the mines aren't following the older men down the shafts anymore when they leave school. They buy a ticket to Christchurch. They get a job on a building site. Or they start standing alongside some assembly line in some factory. Or they head off to the North Island.

'Arthur's worried the mines are going to be closed down,' says Ikey.

'He's a fit strong joker, he'll have no worries getting work even if they do shut them down,' I says.

'Yeah, but where? Not here.'

'Blackball's not exactly the hub of the bloody universe.'

'Blackball's not even the arsehole of the bloody universe, but labouring above ground doesn't pay anywhere near as good as hewing underground.'

And then we start talking about our kids. We talk a lot about our kids. And we talk about getting up the duff. We talk a lot about getting up the duff. The other week I found out I'm pregnant.

My ninth pregnancy!

'Shit, I'm going to have to have it,' I says to Ikey. 'I can't face another bottle of hot gin.'

Chorus

high blood pressure
she smokes in bed
candy on a stick
little blue man
rave on!
fever
my shadow
splish splash
the lights are low
moving and grooving
lightning from the sky
movie star, teenage queen
a cat who's bopping
rock'n'roll band
blue jeans
yakety yak
summertime blues
trying to earn a dollar
lipstick, tight dresses, high heel shoes
wise owl, black crow
rockin' robin
raven

Stevan

Nana waltzed away on the day of the whorl word near Westport. Bimbo's arms now feel so empty as he gazes around the floor. Nana only danced with him for one moment and too soon they had to part. Fly over an ocean in a silver plane, through a jungle wet with rain. No arms will ease the ache within his heart. No lips will stop the tears that start.

A-roll, a-rolling, across the wide Missouri, his lady love she stands awaiting. On the banks he hears her calling.

Now he lives just for his true love to see.

He'll be pushing off when dawn's a-breaking, to cross the wide Missouri where his love she'll stand a-waiting.

Nana flew into a windscreen not up into the sky.

Bimbo knows she's never coming back.

Nana's been buried in a grave.

A false hearted lover will lead you to the grave and the grave will decay you and turn you to dust.

Not one person in a hundred a poor boy can trust.

Bimbo knows it doesn't matter if someone's soft and if someone's kind. Molly. Erleen. Dad. Anybody. Mrs Driscoll. John. Nana. Anybody can go away. Anybody can die. Nobody can help anybody.

Oh, yes I'm just a pretender, pretending I'm doing alright. I need you so much I pretend we'll touch but you see I'm not what you seem to see.

Never place your affection on a green willow tree, for the leaves they will wither and the roots they will die.

A love song sings of woe, ask me why I know.

I'm sitting at a window watching the rain, hi-lili, hi-lili, hi-lo.

Nobody will help Bimbo.

'Now we're entering the County,' says Nana.

Chorus

hula hoop
short shorts
chantilly lace
bailar la bamba
the joint is rocking
spend my money
debt I owe
wallet
he's hip
dirty looks
sixteen candles
purple people eater
rock'n'roll is here to stay
electric guitar
do the twist
the twist
crazy chick
twist
twist
twist

Valerie

The Model A Ford takes us up the valley. We're on our way home from a picnic. Gil's at the steering wheel. He's holding the wheel the *right* way. You know, his hands at ten to two. His eyes are on the road ahead. He doesn't look up. He doesn't look down. He doesn't look sideways. I'm sitting next to him with Jan on my lap. I'm looking up. I'm looking down. I'm looking sideways. I'm looking into the rearview mirror to see what we've left behind. What we've left behind are weedy paddocks and reedy swamps. I look away from the rearview mirror. I look out the front windscreen at the road ahead. Reedy swamps. Weedy paddocks.

'*Why* are we going home so early?' says Lynne. 'It's not *fair*.'

I don't bother to say anything.

It's an afternoon early in spring. The day started out sunny. Which is why we packed the kids in the car for an outing. But clouds come over and now it's blowing a bitter cold southerly. Lynne and Stevan and Noel are in the back seat, with Ross squeezed on Lynne's lap.

'I spy with my little eye,' says Gil, 'something beginning with W.'

'Wire,' says Lynne.

'Telephone wire or fencing wire?' he says.

'Wire,' she says again.

'Well, you're right,' says Gil. 'Your turn now.'

Lynne doesn't say anything. I don't say anything. Gil gives up.

We cross the Grey on the old wooden bridge with railway tracks down the middle. Our rubber wheels go thump, thump, rickety rackety. After the bridge we pass another reedy swamp and a few more weedy paddocks. Gil changes gear and we start climbing the steep tarsealed road to Blackball. Bushes on the side of the road are quivering, dripping. Ferns on the side of the road are nodding, dripping.

I start singing that new song by Debbie Reynolds. The Ames Brothers have done it too. And the Chordettes.

'Tammy, Tammy – '

The kids go sort of loose. They like it when I sing this song.

Noel starts humming along. Lynne too. Stevan's singing under his breath, getting the words wrong.

'I hear the coffin wood whistling above,' he's singing.

Gil goes down on the clutch. The gears grind. The car slogs uphill. The way he *peers* at the road ahead makes me want to grit my teeth. Why does he always have to be so careful when he's driving – so safe, so sensible, so courteous to other drivers, so – so bloody *Gil*! It's aggravating. I mean, even though I'm not feeling fierce with him these days, not since Ellen was killed, now and then I still do get a bit het up about him, about his – his sort of – his sort of *tameness*. As though he's nothing but a little boy. He's like a good, careful, caring boy.

Which is funny because when he's with kids he's always grown up.

He's good to our kids. He's good to neighbourhood kids. They know he won't smack or slap. They know he won't speak any hurtful words. They know he's trustworthy. Which is more than they know about me. And he's still got his good looks. His eyes are as brown as when we first met. And as soft. And his hair's as black and glossy and beautiful as when we first met.

Why, right now, does he make me feel so wild?

The baby shifts itself inside my womb. The doctor says it's now the size of two of my fists. And luckily it doesn't show yet. It doesn't show yet because I'm so bloody fat.

One thing I'm happy about is that before this baby comes out of the womb we'll be back in Canterbury. Nobody here knows. Only one or two. Ikey and Arthur. Lily. I don't want to hear all the gossipy people here going on about me having another baby. I don't want to put up with winks and jokes about Gil needing to tie a knot in it. He's got a job sorted out in Christchurch. We've got a house to go to, too. It's all been jacked up by Bella and Charley. Charley, him being in the motor trade, he knows a lot of people in business. He found the job for Gil. A job as a clerk. And friends of his and Bella's found us the house to rent.

'A breeze off the bayou,' I'm singing. 'Tammy, Tammy – '

So it won't be long before we're shot of the Coast.

Now, when we level off and Gil changes back up a gear, the first thing you see on the town flat is what you always see. The graveyard. Stones stuck on top of holes where the township dumps its dead. Grey granite crosses. Red granite urns. White marble books open on the day of reckoning. The stones look like bones. Bones poking up into a wet grey sky.

Poking up pointlessly.

And, as always, what's noticeable as we wheel past the graveyard and drive up the main road towards the middle of the township, is women's washing. All the washing hanging on the lines is grey. Grey with the coal smoke. Grey like gravestones. Grey like the Grey.

Grit, grime, smuts, soot.

'I've had my whack of bloody Blackball,' I say.

Chorus

stupid cupid
a crying shame
a lovesick fool
it's all in the game
oh yeah
a heart full of lies
it's only make believe
born too late
poor little fool
I don't have anything
pain in my heart
drip drop
oh yeah
the roof is leaking
rain falls on my head
smoke gets in your eyes
driving me insane
you cheated
oh yeah
oh yeah

I cried a tear
I'm so young
we're through
dancing with my shadow
just hanging round
oh, lonesome me
I sit here crying
just a dream
oh yeah
oh yeah
oh yeah
oh yeah

Stevan

Two adolt heads are sticking up over the top of the front seat. Dad's head is one of the adolt heads. Mum's head is the other adolt head. Dad's driving. Mum's singing. Tammy, Tammy. The stuff covering the front seat is called swayed. Dad said that's what it's called. It's dead skin. Dead skin from cows. Or deers. Uncle Arthur goes into the bush with a gun and shoots wild deers. And he shoots wild goats. Cock. Worm. He'll hug you and kiss you. But he'll tell you more lies than crossties on a railway. Or stars in the sky. Adolt Hitler made lampshades out of dead skin. Not dead cows or dead deers or dead goats. He made the lampshades out of dead people's skin. There is no stranger story in history. Swayed is nice and soft and sort of fuzzy. The swayed seats in our car are the colour of honey. And the inside of the car doors and the roof are swayed too. And there's a little saggy swayed pocket on each door, under the window.

Tammy, Tammy –

And the seats are divided into sort of pillows. If you lean your head back against one of the sort of pillows it's cosy. One, two, three – nine sort of pillows on the front seat. And one, two, three – nine sort of pillows on the back seat.

There's nine people in our family. Dad, Mum, John, Alan, Sissy, me, Noel, Ross and Jan.

I hear the coffin wood –

The honey colour of the swayed makes me think of the honey colour of the tiles around the fireplace at our old house in Harper Street. And makes me think about the cocoa sun and the silver wings. A cocoa sun. The world is waiting for the sunrise. Island in the sun. Sunny Italy. A silver plane flying over an ocean, over pyramids on the Nile, over lost Algiers, over jungles wet with rain. A silver plane flying into the sun. A plane diving straight into a cocoa sun. Red sails in the sunset. A barren waste, red as the setting sun.

I wonder if the new people who live in that house look at the tiles the way I used to.

Does my lover feel what I feel when he comes near?

Mum's swaying her head on the swayed while she sings. She sways her head one way. She sways her head the other way. All you can see of her head is a big wavy swirl of dark brown hair. And some brown hairclips. I think the hairclaps are made of steal. Or plastic. And her hair looks a bit waxy. She squirted the waxy stuff out of a tin. A gold tin with a green top. When she sprays the waxy stuff from the gold tin onto her hair it looks like she's trying to kill flies.

You know, with a tin of flyspray.

Anyway, I love looking at her dark brown hair, that big wavy waxy swirl, swaying on the swayed.

I love Mum. I really love Mum. I hate Mum. I really hate Mum. Mum's a mad pie. She's holding Jan in her lap. I wish Mum was holding me in her lap. Jan's alright. Jan's just a baby. It's not Jan's fault that Mum's holding her in her lap. I wish I could climb out of the fuzzy swayed sort of pillows of the back seat and over the fuzzy swayed sort of pillows of the front seat and worm my way onto Mum's lap and press my head against her bosoms which are nicer and softer and cosier even than the swayed sort of pillows and I wish she'd hold me tight and squeeze me and keep singing, singing to me, not to anybody else, only me.

When the night is still, warm and still, I yearn for her charms.

You can't see her eyes right now, but she's got green eyes, Mum. Green is grass and moss and fern and five-finger and flax and crawlies in the crawly pond before they get caught and cooked. And you can't see her cheeks. Mum's cheeks. You can't see her cheeks but they're red. Red is fire and blood and a magpie's eyes and railway carriages and raspberry cordial and crawlies caught by big boys in the deep treacle water of the crawly pond then boiled to death in a billy. Mum's sitting on the swayed and she's rocking from side to side and she's singing. Tammy, Tammy. She's singing and singing. She's tossing her head from side to side. Her head with that waxy wavy swirl of dark brown hair. And she's strong, Mum. And she's weak. And she's happy and she's angry. And she glows and she's dark. And she's scary and she's funny. And she smacks you hard on your bum when she's in a bad mood and she bakes you biscuits and she cooks you cabbage and, and –

And I can't worm onto her lap.

Mum won't let me sit on her lap ever again.

Dad's holding the steering wheel, which is made of grey rubber and black steal. He's holding the rubber bit, which is the rim of the steering wheel. And there's four spokes of black steal coming out of a black steal pipe. And sometimes he reaches out with his left hand and grabs hold of a yellow knob at the end of another black steal pipe. And in front of him there's sort of shiny silver clock things. Only they're not clocks. Dad looks a lot at the clock things.

Wish I knew if he knew what I'm dreaming of. He's alright, Dad. I suppose. Only there's not one man in a hundred a poor boy can trust.

Dad, why do you look at the clock things?

Who are you, Dad?

Dad, I love your black hair. Dad, I wish I could see your big brown eyes. Your beautiful beautiful brown eyes. I wish I couldn't see the back of your neck. Your neck all horrible and red and wrinkly. Your neck like a big cock poking itself out of your jersey. I'm sorry, Dad. I'm sorry the back of your neck makes me feel sick. It's not fair of me to feel sick. You're a good dad. Yes, you're a very good dad. But I wish you didn't kill the you hogget. And I wish you wouldn't go to the pub. You make Mum fierce when you go to the pub. You make her snarl at you. When you come home from the pub you smell all beery, Dad. I don't like you smelling all beery. But I don't think you know you smell all beery. And I feel sorry for you when you come home from the pub and Mum gets fierce with you and snarls at you. You're allowed to go to the pub, aren't you? You're allowed to have a drink.

Your life is hard, Dad.

You have to work and work and work and *work*. It's not fair on you.

And you're sad, Dad. I know you're sad. And you make me feel sad, too. Dad, you don't mean to make me feel sad, but you do. Do you miss your mum, Dad? I miss your mum. I miss my mum. I miss my dad. Tammy, Tammy. I love you, Dad. I'm sorry you're so sad, Dad. Tammy, Tammy, Tammy. Dad, I wish you and me weren't lonely.

We've stopped going uphill. We've come to the town graveyard.

And the grave will decay you and turn you to dust.

TWO AND A JACK IS TWELVE

Valerie

We leave early in the morning. A bleak cold morning, overcast, the ground slippery with black frost. We've got the villa on the market but so far nobody wants to buy. The three oldest boys have gone to school. After school they'll go to Ikey's for tea and then the town taxi will take them to Stillwater. They'll catch the night train to Christchurch. The other four kids and me and Gil are driving over in the Ford. We've had work done on the brakes. I've loaded some hot water bottles in the car to keep off the worst of the cold. I've thrown in some woollen blankets, too. And I've filled a cake tin with hunks of fruit cake. And I've cut dozens and dozens of sandwiches. And I've brewed a pot of tea and poured it into a thermos.

We'll go by easy stages through the Rahu Saddle, pop in to see Molly outside Reefton and then tackle the Lewis Pass.

'I'm planning not to do anything more than second gear on the down slopes,' Gil says.

'Hell's teeth, it'll take us all day,' I says.

'I'm not taking any risks with those brakes.'

A gang of men have loaded the lounge suite and the bunks and the pots and the pans and that into a lorry. A lot of our stuff we're leaving behind in Blackball. The rimu dining suite we brought over with us six years ago is staying. And the rimu bedroom suite we brought over. Those suites were cheap, and they were shoddy, and by this stage they're shot. We leave the piano, too. We never did get around to organising lessons for the kids.

Once we've got the furniture packed, all I can think of is getting out of Blackball.

Gil cranks the starter. The motor kicks in. He spins the steering wheel. He puts his foot down on the clutch. We chug off down Harper Street.

Nobody sees us off, not even Ikey.

'I know I'd howl,' she said yesterday. 'I'd *howl* and *howl*.'

Lily told me she wouldn't come out into the street and wave us away. She said she'd do it from her window. I see her now when we take the turn into Hilton Street. She's holding back her net curtain. She's crying. I'm having a wee weep too. Lily, she's – well, she's as stuck to the spot as a stump. Poor sod. I don't reckon I'll be missing her for long, what with all the work waiting for me once we start trying to set ourselves up again in Canterbury. But she's going to miss me. She's never had any friends up to now, really.

All she's got is that bloody pig of a husband of hers.

Poor old Lily.

'Everybody,' I sing, 'loves a lover.'

I've been singing this song a lot lately. A new hit by Doris Day. The tune's catchy.

Chorus

it's only make believe
the earth and the sky
letters in the sand
sembra un sogno
spinnin' round
oh-oh, oh-oh

oh-oh
the moon
a shining star
ah ya ya ya ya ya
ah ooh ah ooh ah ah
counting the stars above
ahh, ahh, ah, ah, woo
do do do do do
la la la la la la la yah
la la la la la la la ya ya ya yah
the stars that fill the skies
great balls of fire
the little stars
ohhhhhhhh
ohhhhhhhh
see the starlight
every passing day
dark and starry night
the moon up in the sky
mmm-mm-mm-mm-mm-mmm
spinning, spinning, spinning, spinning
spinning like a spinning top
morning, noon and night
the stars flicker in the sky
the twelfth of never
twilight time
a long, long time
la, la, la, la, la, la, laa
starless night
la, la, la, la, la, la
too soon to know
la dee dah, cha, cha, cha
yeah, yeah and a-yeah, yeah

Stevan

'Good, Bobby. Good, Lynnette. Oh dear me, surely to heaven you can do better than *that*, Valmae.'

Mrs Driscoll is checking fingernails. It's my last day in Blackball. I'm excited. I'm excited about going away. John and Alan and me will be going on the night train. I can't wait to get on the night train. I told a glistening star, the way a dreamer will often do. A secret love inside my heart. A secret love that can't wait to be free. Bimbo, where ya gonna go-e-o? I want to cry. I feel sad about going away. I feel bad about going away. I'll be so alone without you. Maybe you'll be lonely too, and blue. I know just how much I'll lose. I'll lose my little darling. I don't want to leave Blackball. Rambling will keep us apart. I love Blackball. I love the West Coast. A love song is a sad song. A love song sings of woe, ask me why I know.

We're going to Canterbury.

Why?

After school we'll have our tea with Aunty Ikey. And after that we'll get the taxi to Stillwater. John and Alan and me will stand on the railway platform under the lights of the night. Other people will stand under the lights too. People from Westport. People from Inangahua. People from Ikamatua. The night will be dark. And then a huge black engine will come pounding through the night. A huge black engine, with smoke pouring from its chimney and sparks flying into the night. And lights. And then all the carriages. Red carriages. One carriage and two carriages and three carriages and four carriages and five carriages and – and inside the carriages, lots and lots of lights, yellow lights, and people looking out of the windows, and the sound of the train, da-dack da-dack da-dack, and steam hissing, and wheels spinning, all oily and greasy and black, and the train going slower, and going slower, and going so slow it'll start to stop.

And steam will still be hissing and hissing.

And doors in the carriages will bang open, and people will be coming and people will be going. And one of the carriages will be for people who go first class. And the other carriages will be for people who go second class. John and Alan and me will stand outside one of the carriages for second class. We'll wait for people to get out. I'll read a white sign on the red wall of the carriage.

'Passengers are warned against standing on the carriage platform, leaning out of the windows, and joining or quitting, the train whilst it is in motion. Strict observance hereof is absolutely necessary'

I'll pretend to be happy. Oh, yes I'm just a pretender, pretending I'm doing alright. People will start going into the carriage. John and Alan and me will climb up. I won't cry. The carriage platform will be steal, painted shiny black. Too real is this feeling of make-believe. Too real when I feel what my heart can't conceal. We'll go inside the carriage. I seem to be what I'm not, you see. The carriage inside will be beautiful. All shiny varnished wood. And red seats. And a curved white roof with a row of all shining yellow lights. And brown nets hanging down for our bags.

And more steal. And brass.

And signs.

'Throwing bottles or other articles off the train to the danger of workmen and others alongside the line is strictly forbidden. To stop train in extreme emergency turn lever down. Penalty for improper use £10.'

And steam will start hissing louder and the stationmaster will blow his whistle and the engine driver will blow his siren and the wheels will start spinning, oily and greasy and black. The West Coast will start to waltz away from me. My arms will feel so empty as I gaze around the floor. And the train will go faster, and faster, and we'll hear the sound of the train on the tracks, da-dack da-dack da-dack.

I'd never be blue if you'd only love me half as much as I've loved you.

And we'll be gone from Stillwater, and then we'll be gone from the Grey Valley, and then –

'Chin up, Stevan,' whispers Mrs Driscoll.

A flash looking lady in a pink cardigan. She gives me a wee pat on my head. A guy is a guy. Comrade Stalin. Cyril Nixon. Pansy Nixon. One of *those*. Dirty sod needs a good belting. Tatting. Not so much lawn as rough pasturage. Vote for the Tories, do you? My *god*! Only bloody *Still*water! You just need to get everything into a routine. A name in a story. Sir Stevan. You know, the usual story. A little boy drowned in a lagoon. Babies don't break easy. They bounce if you drop them. Never heard of anybody being hurt by a magpie. Snoozing, snoring, shitting. Shitting, snoring, snoozing. Boys will be boys. Never ever's a big word. Nobody needs a know-all. Don't slam that door! He's my very own little kiddy. Boys skiting about how good they are at rooting. Mummy's a magpie. Mummy's a magpie. Shut your gob or I'll give you a clip around the bloody ear! Mummy's a *mad*-pie, a *mad*-pie, a *mad*-pie. Shut up! Shut up! Shut up! Shut up! It's a hard life, coalmining. Arithmetic just makes me sick. The figures never act the same, they're always so contrary. I can't hold a tune to save myself. Get outside and play, yous kids! Cut your cheek. Don't *squeeze* me so tight. Ritz assorted biscuits 14 packets. Brass catches are tricky. Bitch and dog vice versa. We mustn't cry. *Never* drink vinegar. If you drink vinegar your blood begins to boil. Three cubic acres of money. I'm worried one of the kids is going to open that trapdoor. Uncle Arthur. He's very fair for a Maori. Rub my feet for me will you? Give us a good rubbing. *Eat* it, you ungrateful little sod! Come, John, come. Look, John, look. Janet, Janet, see the black dog. Pig's tits and treacle. I'll get the poker and put it in the fire till it's red hot and then I'll burn you with it. Vono. Adolt Hitler. No stranger story in history. Nobody's having an accident. Nobody's dying.

I won't sleep till we leave the West Coast. I won't sleep till we go into the tunnel at Otira. After we go into the tunnel I'll try

to sleep again. And I'll try to dream again.
   As if I'll ever sleep again.
   As if I'll ever dream again.
   No arms will ease the ache within this heart. No lips will stop
the tears that start. Once I've gone my dreams will be through.

Chorus

I may never pass this way again
hubba hubba hubba hubba
shooby doo wop ba baa
shooby doo wop ba baa
oo-ee, oo-ee, baby
oo-ee, oo-ee, baby
a moonlit garden
whoa-ooh
ooo-ooo-ooo
the hand of fate
oh wo wo wo oh oh
wo oh oh oh oh oh oh oh
a-rocking and a-reeling
around and around
hula hoop
hula hoop
in a spin
encore
encore
I wonder why
koo-ba, koo-ba, koo-ba, koo-ba
koo-ba, koo-ba, koo-ba, koo-ba
ah-ha-ha-ha, ah-ha-ha-ha
ah-ah-ah-ha, ah-ha-ha-ha
hey-oh, hey-oh

Valerie

The Ford trundles us along Hilton Street. The kids are quiet. Lynne's holding tight onto a book. One of the eight books of the encyclopaedia. Noel's holding a jigsaw puzzle. He does a lot of jigsaws, Noel. As soon as he's finished a puzzle he'll break it up and start doing it all over again. Ross isn't doing anything, just looking out a window. Jan's in the front seat. She's sucking her thumb. She always sucks her thumb. Gil's quiet, holding the steering wheel and working the gears and the accelerator. I'm still singing. One or two people look up and start waving. We pass the shops, the post office, pubs, more shops. We pass rows of wooden cottages. Smoke spews from every chimney into a low dark sky. The ditches alongside the road are icy.

We get to the graveyard.

Gil swings the steering wheel and shifts down two gears. Wet leaves slap against the side of the car as we head down the steep road towards the river flats of the Grey. Ferns are quivering.

Ow! The bloody baby kicks me in the wall of my womb.

'Everybody loves a lover,' I'm singing.

Chorus

over and over
driving me insane
dun dun dun dun dun
dun dun dun dun dun d-d-duh
d-d-dun d-d-dah dah dah
don't know why
d-duh
shooting star
whoa oh, oh, oh uh
ratta ta ta too, ooh ooh

266

whoa oh, oh, oh uh oh uh
ratta ta ta too, ooh ooh
rama lama ding dong
rama lama ding dong
whoa-oh-oh ooh
whoa-oh-oh ooh
just a mystery
bo-bo-bo
all in vain
oh oh oh oh uh
wella wella
woo!
a drag
a drag
uh-uh-uh
uh-uh-oh-oh
ah-mmm, ah-mmm
wella wella wella wella
doo ronde ronde ronde pa pa
doo ronde ronde ronde pa pa
doo ronde ronde ronde pa pa
ba baba ba ba ba ba baba
ba baba ba ba ba ba baba
doo oo oo oo ooo
ouuu huu ouuu
ouuu huu ouuu

Stevan

John and Alan and me are sitting on our red seat. The carriage lights are yellow. John and Alan are playing cribbage. Alan puts down a two. John puts down a jack.

'Two and a jack is twelve,' he says.

Cribbage isn't interesting. I look outside at the night. The night is interesting. The night is black. The night is blue. The night is white. Steal wheels are saying da-dack da-dack da-dack. White signs pop up in the dark. White signs with black words. Station signs. Arnold Valley. Kaimata. Moana. We stop at Moana. A yellow station with a red roof. A few people get off. A few people get on. You can see the lake if you look. Alan doesn't look. He plays a six. John doesn't look. He plays a king. I look. The lake's blue and black and white. And if you put your head hard against the window and hold your hands up to shield your eyes from the yellow carriage lights and the white station lights you can see thousands of stars in the sky.

White stars. Yellow stars.

A red star.

Mars.

And doors slamming, and a whistle, and hissing, and another whistle, and da-dack da-dack da-dack and white signs with black words. Ruru. Te Kinga. Rotomanu. Poerua. Inchbonnie. Jacksons.

We stop at another yellow station under another red roof.

Otira.

I want to cry. Otira's the end. The end of the West Coast. A few people get off. A few people get on. I put my head against the window and hold my hands up to shield my eyes. I can't see stars, only walls. Steep black walls. Walls black with bush. Walls of huge mountains. The only way through the black walls is through a black tunnel. The tunnel to Canterbury.

I don't want to go through the tunnel to Canterbury.

I want to stay on the West Coast.

Away across the Congo sang a happy chimpanzee. That's Molly Muir, going into that shop. A good egg. Take the bloody lot off the bloody capitalists and hand it out good and fair among the working class. It's corker the way it's so *green*! I'd love some fowls. A nice chap. A very nice chap. A bit of a southerly. Rains a *lot* here, doesn't it? Good for growing things. Erleen. Erleen from next door. Just sing out, love. Blackball is a little idyll. Mrs Driscoll. Chin up. Never ever's *two* words! It's the nesting season and it'll be guarding its nest. Off to bye-byes. Teatime! Tea, yous kids! Oh no, Val, I must have good fresh air. He has the bump of knowledge.

Stevan Eldred Grigg, I baptise you in the name of the Father, and of the Son, and of the Holy Spirit.

Seppensola. Seppensola.

Come on, Steve! Let's dance! Tapping down a street with rhythm in my shoes, tapping away my blues, Mrs Tap Toe. The Toothbrush tree! The *Toothbrush* Tree! Beats baking, doesn't it? The first is zero as you see, and then right down the line are one, two, three – Moonlight. Shangri-La. We're making lamingtons. No pain when I do that, young soldier? No grief? Salt of the earth. Little Peachling. Quince. The rose family. Red beech, the best wood. Hardwood. A good sheen. Silk from Siam. A sandfly would die if it didn't suck your blood. We don't pronounce the first part of the word like *fear*.

I'll keep on changing partners till I hold you once more and then, oh, my darling I'll never change partners again.

My lady love she stands awaiting far across the wide Missouri. See the pyramids along the Nile. Watch the sun rise on a tropic isle. Beautiful, beautiful brown eyes. On the banks I hear her calling to me, to me. Now I live just for my true love to see, to see. A-roll, a-rolling, across the wide Missouri. A market space in lost Algiers. You belong to me. A secret love inside my heart. A secret love waiting to be free. I told a glistening star, the way a dreamer will often do. Fly over an ocean in a silver plane, through a jungle wet with rain. The breeze from the bayou keeps murmuring low. Hand in hand we'll find love's promised land. When I want you, all I have to do is dream. When I feel blue, all I have to do is dream.

Steal wheels are saying da-dack da-dack da-dack.

We dive into the black tunnel.

A RUSTY STOVE ON MOCKINGBIRD HILL

Stevan

Once upon a time a long time ago, it was before the whorl word blew that day. You know, the whorl word that blew near Westport. Anyway, we went out driving. And we came to a bend in the road. And we stopped next to a swamp. The swamp was a few miles after the Toothbrush Tree. And it was a few miles before Moonlight. We'd had lovely warm showers all that morning but now the sun was shining. Big beautiful puffy clouds were floating over the Paparoa Range. The clouds were violet and indigo. And the windows of the car were down and you could hear lots of lovely insects humming and lots of lovely birds singing.

'My guess is that if we climb that bit of a hill over there we'll be able to look across the flats and get a good outlook over the Grey,' said Dad.

'So what?' said Mum.

'Well it's where the riverbed's at its widest and I imagine it might be a nice prospect.'

'Oh, alright.'

We got out. Dad opened a farm gate. We went into a paddock. The swamp was in the paddock. The swamp was a beautiful swamp. The water was a beautiful green and brown and even a sort of smoky red in some spots and over the top of the water there were lots of busy dragonflies and bees and beetles darting backwards and forwards and that. And in the middle of the swamp and all around the sides of the swamp you could see lots of lovely clumps of green and orange raupo all sighing and rustling. And lots of lovely clumps of beautiful green and yellow flaxes all nice and spiky and shiny. And lots of beautiful brown and green cabbage trees all whispering to one another, rubbing their leaves together like ladies wiping shredded coconut off their hands after eating chocolate lamingtons.

'Ow!' said Sissy. 'The sandflies are biting!'

Mum was starting to look crabby.

'This is boring,' said Noel.

Dad was walking ahead, quite quick, climbing the little hill. I ran after him, playing the game of stepping into his footsteps. I had to sort of jump, because his steps are bigger than mine, because he's a man and I'm only a boy. Dad and me were the first to get to the little hilltop. The little hilltop was beautiful. The little hilltop was Shangri-La. The little hilltop was Mockingbird Hill. Tra la la, tweedle dee, it gave me a thrill. The little hilltop was all green grass and tussocks and toetoe. Green green grass. Greeny yellow tussocks. Silvery green toetoe.

And an old brick chimney, red and black, stuck up in the middle of the green green grass.

'Was there a house here, Dad?' I said.

'A farmhouse,' said Dad.

The farmhouse must have burned down years and years and *years* ago. And you could see bent old sheets of iron lying around, all lovely and red and rusty. The red rust looked great next to the green grass. And you could see smashed pieces of glass, too, smashed glass lying in the green grass. I looked at one piece of smashed glass and in the glass you could see the violet and indigo clouds drifting over the Paparoa Range. And it was lovely. And I was feeling happy. I was thinking about the people who lived in that farmhouse in the olden days. The mums and the dads and the babies and the kids and how they lived there and ate there and washed dishes there and slept there and talked there and joked there and had fights there and listened to the rain on the roof there and played cards there and read books there and looked up at the orange sun there and drank cups of tea there and rolled down the hill there and now they weren't there, there was nobody.

Mum came up, holding Jan. Jan was whingeing. Mum still looked crabby.

'I was mistaken about the outlook, darling,' said Dad.

Mum squinted up at the sky.

'Don't like the look of those clouds,' she said. 'This place is a dump.'

And they started talking to each other about whether it was a dump or not, so I went exploring. I looked for interesting old things in the grass and the tussocks and the toetoe. I found an old rusty grate. I found an old wooden door, a green door, with the paint all blistering. I found an old rusty fire tong.

And I found a stove.

The stove was a big old cast iron coal range like our one in Harper Street. Only it wasn't standing four square on its little stumpy legs it was lying sort of askew. And it wasn't black and hot and shiny like our coal range it was cold and red and dead and rusty. And the rust was starting to flake off in strips. The strips looked like the cinnamon that you see sometimes in glass jars in shops. Only the rust wasn't cinnamon. The rust wasn't nutmeg. The rust wasn't cocoa. It wasn't what anyone's mother would ever want to use in cooking. And nobody was shovelling coal into the firebox of the rusty red stove. And nobody was stirring a pot on top of the rusty red stove.

The stove was so cold and so red and so dead and so rusty and so beautiful lying on its side in the middle of the long soft wet green grass, like Nana with her snapped neck bleeding on broken glass when the crash smashed the windscreen, it made me want to cry.

A magpie flew overhead and sang its song.

Gloogle-gloogle-gloogle.

I didn't cry. I thought about the soft wet earth. I thought about slugs. I thought about worms. I thought about the red eye of the magpie. I thought about the wide high sky. I thought about rain falling. I thought about rain tapping on rooftops. I thought about rain tapping like laughing people beating time on a tabletop while singing along to songs. I thought about rain gurgling in guttering. I thought about rain spurting down spouting. I thought again about worms. I thought about milk. I thought again and again about rain.

I looked down at the swamp.

The beautiful brown and green and smoky red swamp and the whispering cabbage trees and the lovely clumps of raupo and the lovely clumps of flaxes so nice and spiky and shiny.

And I was happy.

On Mockingbird Hill you're welcome as the sandflies and there's peace and goodwill.

Chorus

it's just a matter of time
never a million years
whoa-ooh-whoa
such a drag
oh yes
oh yes
oh yes
uh-huh
oh yes
uh-huh
oh yes
uh-huh
ooooooh
ooooh-ooooh

whorl word word whorl
once a world of night
now a world of light
the beginning was the word
world of words word of worlds

www.ingramcontent.com/pod-product-compliance
Lightning Source LLC
Chambersburg PA
CBHW031955050726
47590CB00006B/1915